Everything is Interrelated

Christian Trinity and Hindu Advaita
as Experienced by Raimundo Panikkar
and Francis D'sa SJ

Everything is Interrelated
Christian Trinity and Hindu Advaita
as Experienced by Raimundo Panikkar
and Francis D's a SJ

Editor
Kuruvilla Pandikattu SJ

Jnana-Deepa Vidyapeeth
2019

Everything is Interrelated: *Christianity Trinity and Hindu Advaita as Experienced by Raimundo Panikkar and Francis D'sa SJ*-Jointly published by the Rev. Dr. Ashish Amos of the Indian Society for Promoting Christian Knowledge (ISPCK), Post Box 1585, Kashmere Gate, Delhi-110006 and Jnana-Deepa Vidyapeeth, Ramwadi, Nagar Road, Pune-411014.

© JDV, 2019

Online order: http://ispck.org.in/book.php

Also available on amazon.in

"Published with the help of the Institute of Missiology – Germany"

ISBN: 978-93-88945-12-7

Laser typeset by

ISPCK, Post Box 1585, 1654, Madarsa Road, Kashmere Gate, Delhi-110006 • *Tel:* 23866323

e-mail: ashish@ispck.org.in • ella@ispck.org.in
website: www.ispck.org.in

Creative and Constructive Scholar of Cosmotheandric Vision and Promoter of Dialogue Between Indian and Western Traditions

Born 1936 Gokak Falls, Belgaum District, Karnataka, India.

1953 entered the Society of Jesus

1964 M.A. Philosophy, University of Poona, Pune. Gold medalist plus Radhakrishna Prize for Philosophy

1964-68 Theology, University of Austria, Innsbruck.

1969-73 Ph.D. University of Vienna (Indology)

1973 Joined JDV Staff, first in the Faculty of Philosophy and then in Theology.

2001 Retired as Professor of Systematic Theology and Indian Religions.

Since 1975 Regular Guest Professor in Innsbruck till 1990. Guestprofessorships at the Universities of Fribourg (Schweiz), Frankfurt (Theologie Interkulturell), Salzburg, etc.

From 2003 to 2008 Endowment Professor for Missionswissenschaft und Dialog der Religionen at the University of Würzburg, Germany.

2007 Honorary Doctorate in Theology from the University of Frankfurt/M, Germany.

2016 Honorary Doctorate in Theology from the University of Tubingen, Germany.

Scholarly Publications in English and German on Christianity and Hinduism.

Also, Sanskrit Word-Index series on the early Upanishads, the Bhagavadgita, and Shankara's Commentaries on them.

Contents

Part - I
Panikkar's Cosmotheandric Experience

Part - II
Unfolding of Cosmotheandric Experience

Contents

Part - III
Cosmotheandric Experience:
Journeying Beyond

Appendices

Foreword

Rev Richard De Smet SJ and Rev Jean de Marneffe SJ were two important thinkers that JDV has produced over the course of years. Richard had deep love for Indian Philosophy. He had the admirable capacity to make it more palpable and visible. He would make it very presentable and attractive to the students. His thinking was far beyond the capacity of the ordinary students. Therefore, he would make it as simple as possible for the students to grasp. He had a deep scholarly mind and was always familiar with the nuances of the thinking of the time. So, he was well accepted as an authority on Indian philosophy, at the university circles.

So he had a combination of both scholarly attitude and an affable nature, that made him a beloved of the students. At the same time, he was very acceptable to the public or the scholarly world. His own thinking was evolving with regards to Indian philosophy and religious thought.

But I think his capacity for making these things attractive to the students was admired as a teacher.

De Marneffe remained mostly with the Western philosophical thinking. Especially the metaphysical roots of the philosophical traditions of the West. So he was immersed in the thoughts of the west, that he wanted to transport to India, not in terms of just delivering them to the students. Through these deep thoughts, he wanted to open up an avenue for dialogue between the west and the East. So what DeSmet achieved in relations to Indian philosophy, I think, de Marneffe achieved in terms of Western philosophy. making it available, readable and visible to the Indian audience and students.

De Marneffe had a special love for the students but was rather difficult for him to translate those concepts into more intelligible ways to the students in the classes. Because of his teaching, we developed a kind of love for philosophical thoughts. To seek, read and deepen our awareness much more, as we progressed in our studies.

De Marneffe had a very personal approach to people, in spite of his philosophical standing in the Western system. So he was deeply personal and at the same time thoroughly Western in his philosophical questions.

I had a privilege of knowing them personally since they accompanied me, when I was a student of JDV. Further, I am happy that I too belong to the same Jesuit Province, Calcutta.

These were the two giants who made Jnana-Deepa Vidyapeeth (JDV) known to the Indian intelligentsia, especially of the philosophical world. Therefore, we owe much to them and we think that their memory will continue in the minds of the students in the future. We hope that they will delve deep into their thinking and contributions.

They both have also contributed to the Indian Philosophical Encyclopaedia. In fact, they have contributed not only in terms of articles and publications, but also developing the spirit behind it, which was to make the Encyclopedia available to the student and the intellectual world of India.

So as we honour their memories, let us dedicate ourselves to serious study and reflection and analysis so that we become both well-versed in our knowledge system as well as we be persons committed to learning and teaching in JDV, taking it to new heights. They were pioneer philosophers who were in ongoing dialogue between Eastern and Western traditions.

Following their footsteps, I am happy that Faculty of Philosophy, Jnana-Deepa Vidyapeeth, is bringing out this volume on Cosmotheandric vision, which furthers the encounter between Hindu and Christian visions of reality. I am confident that the readers will find this volume challenging, evocative and promoting peace and harmony in the world. I recommend this book to all seekers of truth and followers of wisdom!

George Pattery SJ
Vice-Chancellor
Jnana-Deepa Vidyapeeth,
Pune

Introduction

Cosmotheandric vision is seeing the whole reality (humans, world and God) as intimately connected. They may be distinct and yet linked or bonded together. Against the anthropocentric vision, where human beings feel superior to the world, this vision provides an experience of deep inter-relatedness among human beings, the rest of the world and the Divine.

First proposed by the Indian-Spanish thinker Raimundo Panikkar (1918-2010), this vision has been popularised in India by his friend and follower, Francis X. D'Sa SJ (1936-). Two quotes from Panikkar will make things clear. "The cosmotheandric intuition is the totally integrated vision of the seamless fabric of the entire reality... the undivided consciousness of the totality" (Panikkar, The Cosmotheandric Experience).

"There are not three realities: God, Man, and the World; but neither is there one, whether God, Man or World. Reality is cosmotheandric. It is our way of looking that makes reality appear to us at times under one aspect, at times under another. God, Man, and World are, so to speak, in an intimate and constitutive collaboration to construct Reality, to make history advance, to continue creation (Panikkar, The Trinity and the Religious Experience of man, London and New York 1975).

The cosmotheandric intuition expresses the all embracing indissoluble union, that constitutes all of Reality: the triple dimension of reality as a whole: cosmic-divine-human. The cosmotheandric intuition is the undivided awareness of the totality." What Panikkar proposes is to live so open to this triple dimension of reality, open to others, to the world, and to God that we might achieve harmonious communion with the all: the cosmotheandric reconciliation. It is a matter of an experience more mystical and ineffable than philosophic in the traditional sense, but it breaks the customary philosophico-theological molds (http://www.raimon-panikkar.org/english/gloss-cosmotheandric.html).

Since 2005, Philosophy Faculty, Jnana-Deepa Vidyapeeth, Pune, has been organising a Lecture Series in honour of two eminent philosophers, Richard De Smet and Jean de Marneffe. The Lecture of 2017 was given by a panel of eminent philosophers/thinkers on "Cosmotheandric Vision of Raimundo Panikkar," with Rt Rev Dr Francis D'Sa SJ as the keynote speaker. It was held on Friday-Saturday, Dec 8-9, 2017. Eleven scholars, including two foreigners, presented papers to an audience of about 240 young seekers!

In simpler language a cosmotheandric vision is one where we feel ourselves intimately and totally related (or connected) to the cosmos, fellow human beings and the divine (both as depth and height). Here the crass anthropocentrism vanishes so that we can embrace the whole of reality, which are distinct and still related.

Such a vision (or experience) does make a difference in our day to day life, since "the most practical thing is a good theory!" The theory that provides the cosmotheandric vision can alter the way we live in the world, we look at the world and behave among ourselves. That will transform ourselves and the world. That would provide a solution for the ecological crises we face and provide us with a viable lifestyle which is harmonious, peaceful and sustainable

The keynote address by Prof D'Sa SJ, Professor (Emeritus, Jnana-Deepa Vidyapeeth) gives a perspective to this vision, where the entire reality may be experienced as a Christic adventure. This adventure presupposes a progressive understanding of time, which unfolds itself in history and through human beings. This is followed by three articles that deal with the time-consciousness from the cosmotheandric vision. The first one by J.M.X. Gnanadhas Joseph, Research Scholar, Jnana-Deepa Vidyapeeth, elaborates the three-fold structure of our experience of time. The next one by Parciush Marak, Research Scholar, Jnana-Deepa Vidyapeeth, takes up the transhistorical consciousness of Panikkar. The last article in this section by Arun Philip Simon, Research Scholar, Jnana-Deepa Vidyapeeth, relates time to sacrifice in the context of modernity. It may be noted that Prof D'Sa has been personally mentoring these three research scholars in exploring the rich and experiential insight of cosmotheandric vision.

The next three articles elaborate the cosmotheandric experience of Panikkar. Prof Kuruvilla Pandikattu SJ, Jnana-Deepa Vidyapeeth, Pune, takes up the all-inclusive and all-embracing aspect of this insight, which may be traced to the advaitic understanding of reality. While Dr Isaac Parackal OIC, Jnana-Deepa Vidyapeeth, Pune, looks at the integrating dimension of this vision, Prof EP Mathew, Loyola College, Chennai, explores the ecological (or better ecosophical) dimension of this experience.

The third part is the application of this profound experience to various dimensions of life. Prof Sebastian Velassery, Jawaharlal Nehru University, New Delhi, related it to phenomenology and lived experience. Prof Johnson Puthenpurackal, Vijnananilayam College, Eluru applies it to the human violence and the possibility of peace. Dr George Joseph, Arul Anandar College (Autonomous) Karumathur, puts this vision to a critique of and by modernity. Donald R. Frohlich, University of St. Thomas, Houston TX and Carlos Miguel Gómez, Universidad del Rosario, Bogotá, invite us to rediscover the sacred in nature. The final article by Prof Jose Nandhikara, CMI, Vidya Kshetram (DVK), Bangalore, explores the Theanthropocosmic Vision inspired by the analytic philosopher Ludwig Wittgenstein.

Through these papers we hope to show that the experience of cosmotheanric vision can be founded on the Christian vision of Trinity and the Hindu vision of Advaita, as indicated by both Panikkar and D'Sa. This this insight becomes a meeting point for the two traditions of Hinduism and Christianity.

We have included a concise response by participating research scholars to each of the major articles, which makes the conversation going. Further, we have included an appendix regarding the details of the conference and the persons of De Smet and de Marneffe.

We are glad to dedicate this volume to Prof. Dr.Dr.h.c. (multi) Francis X. D'Sa SJ, who has tirelessly promoted cosmotheandric vision and dialogue between Hinduism and

Christianity. It may be noted that he has been awarded two honorary doctorates and has significantly contributed both to the Philosophy and Theology Faculties of Jnana-Deepa Vidyapeeth, Pune. We want to rejoice with him as he has been honoured with the second honorary doctorate by University of Tubingen, Germany in 2016.

We also want to acknowledge the dedicated service that Dr Cyril Desbruslais SJ, Guest of Honour of the Conference, has rendered to Jnana-Deepa Vidyapeeth. He has been an inspiring teacher and effective communicator to thousands of students, who have passed through the corridors of JDV for more than 40 years.

I am grateful to the staff and students of Jnana-Deepa Vidyapeeth, who have made this conference a success. Their cooperation and synergy have been astounding. Especially I recall the support given by Prof Selva Rathinam, the President, Rev Vincent Crasta and Jose Thayil, the former and present Registrars, Rev Alex G, the Treasurer. I also remember Prof George Pattery SJ, the Vice-Chancellor, JDV for presiding over the Conference.

We hope that these papers will help us to appreciate the intimate connection in reality, to develop a sustainable and harmonious mode of living and foster to dialogue between religions in today's world.

The Editor
November 28, 2018

Part - I
Panikkar's Cosmotheandric Experience

The Significance of the Cosmotheandric Experience: 'The Entire Destiny of Reality is a Christic Adventure'

Francis X. D'sa SJ

Abstract

Raimon Panikkar's Cosmotheandric insight not a simple, straightforward formula that claims to solve all our problems whether human, divine or cosmic is real. This fundamental Insight into the mystery of Reality offers neither a solution nor an interpretation, much less an explanation of Reality. It is a real metaphor, which cannot be expressed in other words. It reveals the reality where everything is related to everything but without monistic identity and dualistic separation. Here Christophany becomes a radical revelation is without geographical or historical limits; neither is it restricted by culture and religion.

Keywords

Cosmotheandric experience, Christophany, Christic adventure, Time consciousness, Tempiternity, Yagna (sacrifice), Metaphor.

1. The Metaphor of the Cosmotheandric Insight

The temptation to reduce Raimon Panikkar's Cosmotheandric Insight to a simple, straightforward *formula* that claims to solve all our problems whether human, divine or cosmic is real.[1] Apart from making a caricature of it, it will miss the point altogether. The Cosmotheandric Insight into the *mystery of Reality* offers neither a solution nor an interpretation, much less an explanation of Reality. It is a real *metaphor*, not a figure of speech. A genuine metaphor is really true but not literally, i.e., it cannot be expressed in other words.[2] On the other hand, a figure of speech is ornamental language that can be dispensed with. A real metaphor belongs to the highest levels of language; it is revelatory language!

2.   The Emerging Mythos

Panikkar officially concludes his *opus magnum, The Rhythm of Being. The Gifford Lectures,* with the following sentences:

> Summing up: a new *mythos* may be emerging. Signs are everywhere. I have already given many names to fragments of this dawning: cosmotheandric insight, sacred secularity, cosmology, ontonomy, radical trinity, interindependence,[3] radical relativity, and so on. I may also use a consecrated name: *advaita*, which is the equivalent of the radical Trinity. Everything is related to everything but without monistic identity and dualistic separation. I have tried to spell it out throughout these pages.[4]

There are a number of things worth highlighting here, especially if one is not too familiar with Panikkar's language. He introduces us to the *emerging mythos*, a new awareness on a world-scale, with the help of eight metaphors from diverse traditions beginning with the cosmotheandric insight and ending with his favourite *advaita*, on which is strung another equivalent (radical Trinity), followed by a pithy sentence on the essence of *advaita*. These are important signs of the emerging *mythos. Mythos,* the source from which metaphors emerge, is the overarching horizon through which the consciousness of a culture operates in human beings. These metaphors are neither synonyms nor equivalents. Panikkar calls them homeomorphic (or functional) equivalents.[5] A metaphor owes its inexhaustible richness to the fact that it is grounded in its *mythos*.[5] This is the fountainhead of all cultural life and growth.

3.   Homeomorphic Equivalents

Of these metaphors, the cosmotheandric insight with its Trinitarian content has evidently been inspired by the Christian Traditions, as is ontonomy by the scientific paradigm, *advaita* by the Vedanta Traditions, radical relativity by the *pratītyasamutpada* of the Buddhist Traditions, etc.

Our task here is to bring out the significance of the cosmotheandric insight. The expression comprises *cosmos*, *theos* and *aner*, i.e. Cosmos, God and Man or, the Cosmic, the Divine and the Human or even as matter, freedom, and consciousness.[6] As of now we did not have in English (!) one word, one adjective, expressing the Cosmic, the Divine and the Human dimensions as cosmotheandric does! It draws attention to the organic unity of the three Dimensions of Reality, highlighting the ontological unity of *all* Reality.

The other metaphors, like for instance, *sarvam sarvātmakam*, have their unique significance in their respective cosmovisions. They are homeomorphic equivalents. That means the *significance* that, for instance the metaphor cosmotheandric insight has in the Christian cosmovision is similar to the significance that, for instance, the metaphor *sarvam sarvātmakam* has in the Kashmiri Shaiva Systems. However, this does not equate the cosmotheandric insight with *sarvam sarvātmakam* or vice versa.

Returning to the trinitarian content, the original Father-Son-Spirit, is widened and re-interpreted by Panikkar as cosmotheandric. He calls the reinterpreted version *radical*

Trinity.[7] But both relate to the *triple dynamic* that operates in Reality. The linguistic expression like always is a child of its time and highlights the concerns of its time.

4.   Jesus's Reinterpretation of Judaic Theism

At least after his foundational experience Jesus boldly reinterpreted Judaic theism in the language of a very intimate kind of personalistic Theism summarized in the vocative "abba-Father." The Early Church in its formative years expanded this invocation into another invocation, the Trinitarian Father-Son-Spirit. The inspiration for this can be traced back obviously to the separate use of all these three nouns in the Gospels, especially of St. John.

The Father, as the Early Councils had insightfully grasped, was *fons et origo*, the source and origin, of all that was, is and will be. In a secular age like ours what makes sense is, one, Man is a totally dependent being, a being that is dependent in every way! Two, Man is a communitarian being, not an island.

Early Christianity expressed this relationship between Father and Son simply as the Son. This is a recognition of the fact that the human being cannot become a human being without a sense of belonging and without an experience of tenderness. Without a true sense of belonging as expressed in mutual tender relationships, human beings ultimately turn out to inhuman who solve their problems not through dialogue but violence. The normal human mode of relating is listening and loving.

Thirdly, the Early Church conscious of the depth of the tender love that obtains between Father and Son saw that this beginningless process derives from and is kept in being and refreshed as it were by the Spirit (of the Father and of the Son!). The Spirit that we are speaking of is the Spirit of togetherness where I and YOU meet in a WE.

In our search for meaning, meaning in life, an area where we all meet in spite of our cultural and religious differences, we realize that our traditions need updating, so that, one, their significance does not disappear through irrelevance and, two, that their growth through dialogue with our neighbouring traditions and cultures ensures that the indispensable task of bridge-building for mutual understanding and peace is attended to.

5.   Sacred Secularity

As I write this I hear the news that the Karnataka Journalist Gauri Lankesh was shot dead in Bengaluru last night (6th September). Gauri Lankesh was an ardent secularist and saw the future of India in a pluralistic society, themes which are symbolic of Panikkar's treatment of the Secular having worth of its own. This highpoint he named *sacred secularity*. It is connected with the view of the World as Sacrament. The opposite of the sacred is not the secular but the profane. The emerging myth, Panikkar had discovered, wears secular clothing and has taken on special significance which goes beyond what the eye has not seen, the ear has not heard, etc. (1 Cor. 2:9).

When committed citizens like Narendra Dabholkar, Govind Pansare, M. M. Kalburgi and Gauri Lankesh fearlessly proclaim "secular" values like freedom of expression in a pluralistic society and lay down their lives for it they were witnessing to something that gave meaning to their lives. All this in my interpretation is the *leit-motif* of Panikkar's sacred secularity and the emerging myth. What we have recounted till now is just the unfolding.

Panikkar has been the sole exception among theologians to uphold the sacredness of secularity. He alone, as far as I am aware, has taken the phenomenon of the Secular seriously.[8] European theologians from their historical experience of secularization in the nineteenth century tend to reduce everything secular to secularism and rail against it. But Panikkar speaks discerningly: "One of the mature traits of our rightly criticized epoch is the acute awareness of what I call *sacred secularity*. This world (*saeculum*) is sacred and our secular moves have transcendent repercussions."[9]

These are some of Panikkar's original contributions. The more I read them the more I see how there is a unifying thread throughout. What lends significance to (most of) his writings, *is cosmotheandrism leading to his Christophany* – all this on the background of his critique of the traditional understanding of time and history. This is the highpoint of the significance of the cosmotheandric experience! But before that we have to consider Panikkar's threefold structure of time-consciousness.

6.   Panikkar's Threefold Structure of Human Time-Consciousness

This will be a great help for us to find a way of going about the cosmotheandric path.

Popularly we understand time as past, present and future. In his treatment Panikkar ignores this and treads the phenomenological path and speaks of the threefold structure of human time-consciousness where he surprises us with the themes nonhistorical consciousness, historical consciousness and transhistorical consciousness.[10]

Panikkar admits that there is the difficulty of choosing a neutral terminology in these headings. The expression historical is very loaded. For practical reasons however he settles on the labels nonhistorical, historical and transhistorical – these are primarily mentalities than descriptions that can be exact and precise.

Because it is almost impossible to summarize Panikkar's thoughts, I have selected phrases and sentences which best evoke what he is suggesting and pointing at in the pages dealing with the threefold structure of time-consciousness.

Nonhistorical Consciousness

By nonhistorical consciousness Panikkar means a prehistorical way of thinking that is dominated more by space (94) than time which here is natural, not cultural. The seasons of the Earth measure time, not the exploits of Man. Time is a rhythm of nature...and is anthropocosmic... (95) The world of pre-historical Man, his environment is the theocosmic, the divinized universe (95), the divine permeates the cosmos (96). Nonhistorical consciousness could also be called the *pre-scriptural mentality*...It entrusts everything to memory. The presence of the past is in the living of it (97). For pre-historical Man food is dynamic communion with the entire universe, food is sharing in the cosmic metabolism, it is the symbol of life, the intercourse with all that there is, the greatest bond among humans and equally the greatest signs of fellowship. (98)

Historical Consciousness

Historical time is understood as the thrust towards the *future*. (100) "People and peoples are set whirling into motion, their movement accelerates not because they want to overcome space or be victorious over it, as nomadic tribes or pre-historical Man might do, but because they want to conquer *time*, as well as to demonstrate their excellence and superiority over others (a superhuman role). Wars are waged to make the victors great and their children powerful. Man works under the mirage of an historical future to be achieved: a great empire to be built, a better future to be conquered, an education for the children, to make ends meet, etc. The entire modern economic system is based on *credit*, i.e., the mortgage of the future."[11]

Modern science means the ability to foresee the future... The paramount question here is to know *how* things will happen in space and time – because then you can *control* them. (104) Space and time become the paradigms of reality. Something is real for us when we can locate it on the grid of spatio-temporal Cartesian coordinates. From here we immediately deduce that something is real when it is a fact, and, when the "fact" belongs to the past, it has to be an historical fact. Jesus is considered to be real if he is an historical figure – whereas Kṛṣṇa, for the nonhistorical hindu mentality, would lose his reality if he were to be described as only an historical personality. (104)

The world of historical Man is the anthropocosmos, the human world, the universe of Man. He is not dependent on the seasons, and as little as possible on the climate. Historical consciousness has overcome the fear of Nature. The meaning of life is not to be found in the cosmic cycle but in the human one... (105)

If the discovery of the Script could be said to have been the decisive break between pre-historical and historical consciousness, the corresponding event here – which opens up the post-historical period – is the discovery or invention of the internal self-destructive power of the atom. So powerful is its nature that it has ceased to be what it was purported to be *akṣaram*, indestructible. It has ceased to be atomos, indivisible, ultimately simple and, in a certain sense, everlasting. The splitting of the *atomos* has also exploded historical consciousness. (106)

In-between Panikkar discusses the Crisis of History (108-119) which comes to the conclusion: "the historical imperative has failed." (118) "History has become not a dream but a nightmare. Man, said to be a historical being, discovers that he cannot make history." (119) ...the meaning of life does not lie in the future or in shaping society or transforming Nature, but in life itself, lived in its present and actual depth." (119)

Historical consciousness is busy discharging the past into the future; the present is just the intersection of the two. (124)

Transhistorical Consciousness

We need now not a reform but a radically different alternative, that "will have to begin with the *status quo* and try to convert it into a *fluxus quo* conducive to a New Heaven and a New Earth" ... In any event, such an alternative demand is nothing short of a *radical change in consciousness* [my highlighting]. (121)

Panikkar's analysis discovers the reason for his:

In western parlance, the passage from a monotheistic worldview to a trinitarian vision.

In eastern words, the overcoming of dualism by *advaita*, the transition from a two-storey model of the universe to a non-dualistic conception of reality. (121)

In philosophical language, it boils down to finding the middle path between the Scylla of dualism and the Charybdis of monism.

In a more contemporary way of speaking, we could say that it amounts to experiencing the sacredness of the secular. I mean by secularity the conviction of the irreducible character of time, i.e., the sense that Being and time are inextricably connected. Time is experienced as constitutive dimension of Being; there is no atemporal Being. *Sacred secularity* is an expression meaning that this very secularity is inserted in a reality that is not exhausted by its temporality. Being is temporal, but is also "more" and "other" than this…

If we take pluralism not as political strategy but as a word representing the ultimate structure of reality, we shall have to overcome the assumption of a single human pattern of intelligibility. (121)

Nonhistorical consciousness sees life mainly in the interplay between the past and present; the future has hardly any weight… (124)

Transhistorical consciousness attempts to integrate past and future into the present; past and future are seen as mere abstractions. (124)

They [contemplatives] live the present in all its in-tensity and in this tension discover the in-tentionality and in-tegrity of life, the tempiternal, ineffable core which is full in every authentic moment…The future of *today* is not tomorrow; it is in trespassing the inauthenticity of the day in order to reach the to-day in which paradise abides. The meaning of life is not tomorrow, but today. (124-125)

Pre-historical Man has fate. He is part and parcel of the universe. Historical Man steers destiny. He predestines where he stands. He arranges his own life. Transhistorical Man lives his lot. He is involved in the total adventure of reality by participating in the portion "allotted" to him or by willingly shaping the part that he is. (128)

The pre-historical mentality does not have to justify Man's existence to itself or to others. The human being lives like any other living being. Historical consciousness has to justify, i.e., to prove the value of Man's existence by his *doing*, i.e., by creating his own world with its values. Modern Man is worker. Transhistorical Man has lost both the pre-historical naiveté and the historical optimism/pessimism. He feels the urge to be what he is supposed to be by occupying his proper place in the universe. (128).

The world of transhistorical Man, his environment, is the cosmotheandric universe. The renewed interest in astrology, for instance, is due not merely to the desire to know what will happen…but to the increasing awareness that personal destiny is linked both with the fate of society and with the adventure of the entire cosmos. (128)

The destiny of Man is not just an historical existence. It is linked with the life of the Earth (ecological interlude) and with the entire fate of reality, the divine not excluded…Love is the supreme principle, the linking force which brings everything together…life has to make sense even when all the idols – progress, civilization, peace, prosperity, paradise – fail. (128-129)

In sum, transhistorical consciousness is not worried about the future because time is not experienced as linear or as an accumulation and enrichment of moments past, but as the symbol of something which does not exist without Man but cannot be identified with him, either. It is neither the City of God nor the City of Man that transhistorical Man is about to build. He or she would rather concentrate on building or bringing to completion the microcosm that is Man, both individually and collectively mirroring and transforming the macrocosm altogether. (130-131)

In the last paragraph of the chapter on Transhistorical Consciousness (120-133) Panikkar attempts to sketch [his experience of] transhistorical consciousness. I have quoted it fully. In case you do not have the opportunity to read the book, at least you will have this paragraph to read and meditate on - repeatedly.

Sharing in the unfolding of Life, assisting at the cosmic display of all the forces of the universe, witnessing the deployment of time, playing with the dynamic factors of life, enjoying the mysteries of knowing and no less the mystery of living, waking not haunted by the doings of the day ahead, but gifted with the being bestowed in the present, not wanting oneself to succeed at the price of others' defeat, or wanting to "distinguish" oneself by doing something 'extra'-ordinary, as if the ordinary were not enough, just walking in the divine Presence, as the ancients used to say, being conscious of the systole and diastole of the world, feeling the assimilation and disassimilation of the cosmos on both the macro- and the micro-cosmic scales, lending sensitivity to the stars and atoms, being the mirror of the universe and reflecting it without distorting it, suffering as well in one's own flesh the disorders of the world, being oneself in the laboratory where the antibodies or medicines are created, not being unaware of the forces of evil or the trends of history, but not allowing oneself to be suffocated by them either, each of us overpowering these demons in our own personal lives, understanding the songs of the birds, the sounds of the wood and even all the human noises as part of the vitality of reality expanding, living, breathing in and out, not just to go somewhere else (and never arrive) but just to be, to live, to exist on all the planes of existence at the same time the tempiternal explosion of the adventure of Be-ing...*this is transhistorical existence.*

7.   Christology and Christophany

Whatever we have discussed up to now gets its significance in the world of Christophany, a world that is altogether different from that of Christology.

Christology focuses on doctrinal development and history; and is limited by culture. Building on that Christophany strikes a distinctive path, that of very a personal encounter with the Risen Christ.[12]

Christology begins in time and builds on history but still cannot reach Christophany unless one realizes first that though it is *in* time it is not *of* time in much the same way that though tempiternity is *in* time it is not *of* time. To understand this and its implications we have had to go through the three modes of time-consciousness and discover that the treasure in the field of time is really transhistorical time, that is, timelessness which Panikkar calls tempiternity.

After this, I introduce Panikkar's *creatio continua* and *incarnatio continua* and indicate how these tempiternal currents have temporal effects within the cosmotheandric process. We can understand here the role both of the Secular and of the Divine in our lives. There are spontaneous Christophanic activities that are confirmations of such a process. With this we come to our concrete tasks (like daily work) where the grip of time *on us* makes our lives miserable, unless of course we learn from the ancient Indians to overcome this grip of time with the help of Sacrifice (Yajña). That this is not a mere fantasy exercize we learn from the diverse Christophanic signs that accompany the effort.

Christology is a study of the doctrines about the Christ that have developed in the course of the history of the Church in certain cultural regions of the West. More importantly Christology concentrates on working out what Panikkar calls the *identification* of Jesus,[13] whereas Christophany, Panikkar's neologism for the *experience* of the Triune Mystery revealed in Jesus, has to do with the *identity* of the Christ. Christology concerns itself with the *what* of Christ but Christophany with his *who*.[14] It is this Mystery that *opens believers* up to the revelation of the Divine, the Human and the Cosmic in their own traditions and cultures as well as in other traditions and cultures. However other religious traditions may have their own names for such an enterprise.

To begin with tempiternity, we need to get in touch with *our own experience of time*. We cannot experience the past. What we do experience is the *past that is operative in the present,* which is *the past-present*. Similarly, we cannot experience the future![15] What we experience is *the future that is operative in the present, the future-present*. That is to say: *Our authentic experience of the present consists of bits and pieces of a continuum that comprises the past-present and the future-present*. What we call the present is in fact the integrated awareness of the past-present and the future-present. What we casually call the past and the future are illusions that have been built up over the years.[16]

Not Time *and* Eternity but Tempiternity

But from our cosmotheandric conviction we need to realize that there is something important that is missing in our thematic awareness. Earlier we stated, time is always experienced as time-consciousness! It is this time-consciousness that we have to retrieve and thematize! In this experience, there is a depth that Panikkar has called tempiternity, a compound of *tempus* and *eternitas*, of time and timelessness. This timelessness does not come after time, after our death, as it were. We have to realize this depth, we have to become masters of time – a lesson we can learn from our traditions.

Creatio Continua and *Incarnatio Continua* in the Cosmotheandric Scheme

Panikkar's critique of the traditional understanding of time shows that we actually experience time - at least partially - as a continuum. The creation-incarnation and the time-continuum of our experience are two different time-models which like oil and water cannot go together. In the creation model creation is a once and for all event in the past – looking forward to its fulfilment in the future (in eschatology).[17] This does not fit in with the continuum model.

What have *creatio continua* and *incarnatio continua* to do with cosmotheandrism? All three represent the same reality but from three different perspectives. Cosmotheandrism speaks of the three dimensions of Reality. *Creatio continua* is the perichoretic process of these three dimensions. *Incarnatio continua* focuses on the specific activity of the divine dimension.

When Panikkar discusses *creatio continua* he implies a continuous process; its freshness at every moment liberates us from a fixed and rigid universe. The universe is part of an on-going triune creative process, not a mere unidimensional - historical and temporal - project. It participates unceasingly in the *creatio continua*. This is an important aspect of the *perichoresis* of the three dimensions of Reality.

After that Panikkar introduces *incarnatio continua* that liberates us from living in a merely historical and temporal universe because he makes us conscious of our divine dignity that is beyond time and history.[18] Whereas *creatio continua* is, so to say, the larger vision, *incarnatio continua* is the small print. If the *incarnatio continua* appears to centre on Man the *creatio continua* is seen to focus on all three dimensions.

Panikkar states repeatedly in his Writings that Man is more than Man.[19] But this knowing is notional knowledge, not real knowledge. Real understanding would impact us very differently and would change us, our life-style, our values and our world-order in important ways.[20] Our everyday life is full of mechanical and inauthentic acts and drudgery. There is hardly any awareness that every act of ours is unique and unrepeatable, that any one of them could be the last. This is the reason for the superficiality and lack of seriousness in our acts. We do not live in the present. We are either lost in the past or in the future but we are not fully alive in the present. The tempiternal element that every act contains escapes us. The uncertainty of death does not impact our life; the newness of *creatio continua* does not excite us and the freshness of *incarnatio continua* does not astonish us.[21] Living intensely in the present, aware of its *tempiternal core*, could change all this.

History, however one may understand it, is not the measure of Man. Man is more than history, more than time, though time is connected with something that gives worth to Man. Temporality is characteristic of all modes of consciousness.

We do not experience history the way time-consciousness impacts us.

Tempiternity is both the dwelling place and the work-place, as it were, of Christophany. In Christophany the *totus Christus* is both present and at work. Christophany escapes us because being in the grip of time we are blind to the tempiternal aspect looking for Godot.

Sacrifice (Yajña) saved Man from the Grip of Time[22]

For the ancients sacrifice, the ultimate texture of reality,[23] saved Man from the grip of time. Sacrifice was for the ancient Indians the navel of the earth, the centre of Reality. As the Śatapatha-brāhmana says, "All this, whatever exists, is made to share in sacrifice." III, 6, 2, 26.

To make it short, Panikkar applies secularity as the ritual of modernity to *work for the welfare of all.* Such work *as the homeomorphic equivalent of sacrifice* is redemptive! Persons working for others keep the wheels of life moving in this world and thus become masters, not slaves, of time.

Alas, modern work methods too are becoming increasingly degrading, and enslaving. We are no more masters of time. We need to retrieve the tempiternal moment in our simple but profound human experiences that occur in time but are not bound by time. Human beings are uniquely related to all other beings. Here ontonomy functions on the microscale and cosmotheandrism on the macroscale. Where beings function optimally, then it is a sure sign that Christophany has come into its own!

Panikkar's (brief) cross-cultural analysis of time is a rough indicator of the local temporal (and consequently cultural) conditions. The task of the Pundits is to work out the respective homeomorphic "Krishnaphanies," "Allahphanies," "Shaktiphanies," etc.! The hope is that in this way the other cultures and religions will complement the mosaic initiated by Christophany.

From the Christian perspective Christophany reveals itself specifically but diversely in the different cultures of our world. It emerges from an experience of the "Abba, Father," an experience that gives birth to a new awareness, as it did in the case of Jesus. This point of departure is *sine qua non*. From here Jesus exclaimed the Mystery as "Abba, Father" and proclaimed the christophanic role of the poor in spirit, of those who mourn, of the meek who will inherit the earth, of those who hunger and thirst for righteousness, of the merciful, of the pure in heart who will see God, of the peacemakers, of those who are persecuted for righteousness' sake, etc.

Christophanic Activities

Those involved in Christophanic activities like enlightening fellow citizens about the dangers of unhindered technocratic innovations, others like promoting harmony and understanding among racial or ethnic groups, educating citizens about the social, economic, political and environmental consequences of sectarian, short-term and short-sighted policies, can discover that such commitment is their real success and not the outcome in the first place. *Communitarian processes like these contain meaningful moments of real tempiternal joy and fulfilment.* Waiting for a future supposed to usher in a definitive peace or a classless society or a resolution of all conflicts once and for all will ultimately be fruitless. Such promises tend to remain elusive if not empty.

Some Christophanic Signs

Calling on the name of Christ does not imply that one has the mind of Christ. Empty words have nothing to do with self-emptying. His life on earth, bereft of privileges was from beginning to end one of self-emptying: joining those wanting their sins to be washed publicly in the Jordan of common humanity, eating with so-called sinners, associating with pagans, and finally being condemned to die among criminals on the cross he departs - with no bitterness but with promise of a place in paradise to the thief on his right who asks to be remembered when he is in his Kingdom. In his ministry, he was particular about highlighting in public the faith of those who were considered outsiders like the centurion, the syrophoenician woman and a woman of compromising reputation who anointed his feet in public. He praised those whose faith had cooperated in their healing or even those whose sins had been forgiven. He did not condemn the woman caught in adultery (who was about to be stoned) but he did question her accusers whether anyone among them was without sin. And consciously he chose the company of sinners because, he said, he had come to heal the sick and not the healthy.

These were some of the christophanic signs that led people to believe that God was fully present in Jesus in whatever he did and whatever he taught. He did not ask his hearers to wait for the end of the world for the arrival of the Kingdom of God - because tempiternity was tangible whenever and wherever he healed the sick and spoke of God as his Father and of all people as God's children.

What he believed in was the truth that sets one free; what he proclaimed was the truth that can be experienced by the heart of a lover, can dispel the doubts of the wavering and strengthen the believer. It is the truth that *makes sense* only to those who live on hope, are sensitive to the world of love and open up to the wonder of faith.

The all-important task *now*, Panikkar says, is to concentrate on building or bringing to completion the microcosm that is Man, both individually and collectively: mirroring and transforming the macrocosm altogether.[24] True, Christophany has not yet been fully manifested[25] though it is operative at least partially everywhere and at every moment of time, in every tradition, culture and religion.

This, of course, is a Christian formulation and that's why it isn't and cannot be complete. The other religions and traditions will have to contribute to complete and complement this picture by witnessing to their experience and their hope. Maybe their witness will come up with a different name for the Ultimate Mystery they experience. The name of Christ could be something homeomorphic to the name they confess.

Once we begin to grasp the meaning and significance of interreligious and intercultural dialogue, cultural disarmament, the quest and education for peace, and environmental harmony and responsibility, etc. Cosmotheandrism will bring us the realization that our lives are not to be narrowly understood either as *our* life or merely as *human lives* but also and in a true sense *cosmic* and *divine* as well. Christophany opens up new horizons on all sides.

It is then that we shall realize the criminality of waste. Objects will gradually cease to be merely objects. There will be bodies, animated, interdependent bodies which we once took to be objects. Moreover, Christophany will deepen awareness of life's inter-in-dependence and interconnectedness. Our natural and social relations will become more obvious and more meaningful; and in that measure our moral obligations will be the more enlightened and more significant.

Conclusion

Christophany's revelation is without geographical or historical limits; neither is it restricted by culture and religion. However, its reception is another matter. It is marked by all the limitations of the one who receives it. But those who have eyes to see and ears to hear will gradually assimilate the mind that was in Christ Jesus, a mind that witnesses to the insistent inspiration of the on-going creative process. The Spirit of the *incarnatio continua* too is incessantly at work in all beings to activate and foster the ontonomic drive in them so that awareness spreads and deepens that the Christ in the hungry, the thirsty, the strangers, the naked, the sick, and in the prisons, has to be cared for if he is to be discovered and his grace experienced. In any authentic Christic vision meaning in life is expressed in and through such performative acts.

Other traditions have their specific visions too. When we engage with them in sharing our visions we shall all mutually broaden, deepen, diversify and even correct the understanding-and-formulations of our respective "Christophanies."[26] Homeomorphic transformations will occur in the traditions that take part in such a sharing.

Endnotes

[1] The sentence is part of a larger context. Panikkar, *The Rhythm of Being, The Gifford Lectures* (Maryknoll, New York: Orbis Books, 2010), 260: "The universe is Father, Christ, and Holy Spirit, as I tried to formulate it over half a century ago, taking Christ, the *Christus totus* of Augustine, to its eschatological culmination in connection with I Cor XV, 28. In this sense the Christian complement to Genesis I,1 ("In the Beginning

God created heaven and earth") should be John I,3 ("all has come to be through me" – the Logos, inseparable from the incarnated Logos). This leads me to a follow-up of the *creatio continua* by an *incarnatio continua*, of which Christ is the head following the Christian Scripture. This is not the direct concern of this study, but it may be an hermeneutical key to it. *The entire destiny of reality is a Christic adventure* [My highlighting of the last sentence]."

[2] Francis X. D'Sa, Re-Searching the Divine. The World of Symbol and the Language of Metaphor, in: Job Kozhamthadam (Ed.), *Interrelations and Interpretation*. Philosophical Reflections on Science, Religion and Hermeneutics in Honour of Richard De Smet, S.J. and Jean de Marneffe, S.J. (New Delhi: Intercultural Publications, 1997), 141-173.

[3] R. Panikkar, *The Rhythm of Being*, 404.

[4] R. Panikkar, *The Rhythm of Being*, 404.

[5] Panikkar, *Myth, Faith and Hermeneutics. Cross-Cultural Studies* (New York/ Ramsey/Toronto: Paulist Press, 1979), especially the Introduction.

[6] Panikkar, *The Cosmotheandric Experience*. Emerging Religious Consciousness (Maryknoll: Orbis, New York, 1993; Indian Ed. Motilal Banarsidass: Delhi, 1998), 121.

[7] Panikkar, *The Rhythm of Being*, 250: "The radical Trinity I am advocating will not blur the distinction between Creator and creation – to use these names – but would, as it were, extend the privilege of the divine Trinity to the whole of reality. Reality is not only 'trinitarian' it is the true and ultimate Trinity."

[8] Panikkar, *Worship and Secular Man* (Maryknoll: Orbis, New York, 1975).

[9] Panikkar, *The Rhythm of Being*, 350.

[10] Panikkar, *The Cosmotheandric Experience*. Emerging Religious Consciousness (Maryknoll: Orbis, New York, 1993; Indian Ed. Motilal Banarsidass: Delhi, 1998) Part Two, The End of History, 79ff.

[11] Panikkar, *The Cosmotheandric Experience*, Historical Consciousness, 104ff.

[12] See my forthcoming contribution, Time, History and Christophany, in: Peter C. Phan & Young-chan Ro (Eds.), *Raimon Panikkar: A Companion to his Life and Thought* (James Clark: Cambridge). To appear shortly.

[13] Panikkar, *Christophany*. The Fullness of Man (Maryknoll: New York, 2004: Indian Ed.). The Identity of Christ is not the same as his Identification, 153-155.

[14] See footnote 3.

[15] Panikkar, The Mirage of the Future, in: *The Teilhard Review*, Nr.2, Vol. VIII (1973).

[16] Panikkar, *The Cosmotheandric Experience*, Historical Consciousness, 104ff: "People and peoples are set whirling into motion, their movement accelerates not because they want to overcome space or be victorious over it, as nomadic tribes or pre-historical Man might do, but because they want to conquer *time*, as well as to demonstrate their excellence and superiority over others (a superhuman role). Wars are waged to make the victors great and their children powerful. Man works under the mirage of an historical future to be achieved: a great empire to be built, a better future to be conquered, an education for the children, to make ends meet, etc. The entire modern economic system is based on *credit*, i.e., the mortgage of the future."

[17] Part of this eschatology was the world-judgment without clarifying whether the end of time was in time or outside of time).

[18] Panikkar, *Christophany*, 128. My italics.

[19] Panikkar, *Christophany*, 129.

[20] Panikkar, *Christophany*, 130.

[21] Panikkar, *Christophany*, 131.

[22] Panikkar, Time and Sacrifice. The Sacrifice of Time and the Ritual of Modernity, in: J.T. Fraser (Eds.), *The Study of Time*, New York, Springer, 1978. See also Panikkar, *Worship and Secular Man*, (Maryknoll: Orbis, New York, 1975); Time and History in the Tradition of India, Kāla and Karma, in L. Garde etc.(Eds.), *Cultures and Time*, UNESCO, 1976; The Mirage of the Future, in: *The Teilhard Review*, Nr.2, Vol. VIII (1973); Towards a Typology of Time and Temporality in the ancient Indian Tradition, *Philosophy East and West*, Nr.2, Vol XXIV (April 1974); Man as a Ritual Being, *Indian Theological Studies* (1979).

[23] Panikkar, *The Vedic Experience*. Mantramañjarī. An Anthology of the Vedas for Modern Man and Contemporary Celebration (Pondicherry: All India Books, 1977), 346-431. A highly original interpretation of Yajña.

[24] Panikkar, *The Cosmotheandric Experience*, 137.

[25] Panikkar, *The Cosmotheandric Experience*, 115.

[26] See "Dialogue and Proclamation". Reflections and Orientations on Interreligious Dialogue and the Proclamation of the Gospel of Jesus

Christ. Pontifical Council for Inter-Religious Dialogue. Rome, 1991. Among the four kinds of dialogue this Roman document speaks of is the Dialogue of Spiritual Sharing.

Response

We have been for some time, listening to the relevance of a great visionary's still greater vision – the Cosmotheandric vision propounded by Raimon Panikkar. This insight has always been one of my favourites. And the task now entrusted to me is to respond to the paper presented.

I was thinking, why is it that this so-called Cosmotheandric vision has come to gain a world-wide recognition with implications across different fields of knowledge, be it philosophical, theological, political, social or cultural.... This is simply because of the attempt Panikkar made to inter-twine the three different horizons - Theos, Anthropos and Cosmos. And none of them would any more be, at least in theory, independent of the other. The world is meaningless without humans, and the humans cannot exist without the world. God cannot be known and experienced without the humans and the world. In other words, there is an existential, ontological connection between the world, God and the Humans.

If that is the case, any disturbance that any one of them experiences, will certainly disturb all three of them. Thus we have a philosophical reason for Jesus crying at the tomb of Lazarus.......

A God who sheds tears at the cries of humans..........

A nature that grieves at the fall of humans.........

And in turn, a human that sheds tears at the cries a fellow human, or another that grieves at the fall of the nature around.

This is the vision that Cosmotheandrism envisages.

And now I would like to raise two questions for clarification; the first to myself and the other to the speaker.

We have been, from the morning, listening to the Cosmotheandric vision; and what happens often is that the vision remains forever a vision. Will I be willing to set out to experience that vision - a

Comotheandric experience? Or will I be able to make this vision part of my consciousness - a Cosmotheandric consciousness?

This is the question to myself and my own life will have answer it.

And now the question to the speaker.

The world today is after development. And we very well know that almost all the development strategies we now have are not really sustainable. In this context, is it not possible for us to formulate a Cosmotheandric strategy for sustainable development?

And with this question to the speaker, I remain. **-Rijo Devasia CST**

The Threefold Structure
of Human Time-Consciousness
According to Raimon Panikkar

J. M. X. Gnanadhas Joseph

Abstract

In a normal sense history means the collection of the events in a chronological order which is sometimes biased, subjective and one-sided. But Panikkar speaks of three forms of consciousness i.e. pre-historical, historical and post-historical and three moments of human time-consciousness i.e. non-historical, historical and trans-historical. These are not chronologically related but *kairologically* related and they are intertwined and coexisting though we find the qualitative differences. These three are not talking about the primitive person or person in the present and future but the historical man one who has latent forms of non-historical and trans-historical time-consciousness. So they depict the mentality of a human person. Panikkar humbly accepts that the language is so limited to explain what he really meant by using the normal terminologies like pre, post, historical, non, and trans.

Keywords

Historical man, Time-consciousness, Historical-consciousness, Non-historical consciousness, Trans-hisotiral consciousness.

Introduction

Raimundo Panikkar is a man of contradiction to those who are floating along the current. But for the swimmers against the current he is the lighthouse, a visionary. His vision is "*Cosmotheandric*," a triadic relationship of reality for which he in his book *The Cosmotheandric Experience: Emerging Religious Consciousness* explains the path to attain. In this paper I would like to highlight explain what he meant by history, space, time, period, anthropology, yardstick, language both written and oral to substantiate his vision which occure in Part Two of the above mentioned work: *The End of History*.

In a normal sense history means the collection of the events in a chronological order which is sometimes biased, subjective and one-sided. But Panikkar speaks of three forms of consciousness i.e. pre-historical, historical and post-historical and three moments of human time-consciousness i.e. non-historical, historical and trans-historical. These are not chronologically related but *kairologically* related and they are intertwined and coexisting though we find the qualitative differences. These three are not talking about the primitive person or person in the present and future but the historical man one who has latent forms of non-historical and trans-historical time-consciousness. So they depict the mentality of a human person. Panikkar humbly accepts that the language is so limited to explain what he really meant by using the normal terminologies like pre, post, historical, non, and trans.

By the next terminology "Period" he meant "ways around or recurring ways of being human" but not in the mass media sense. Though he had other forms like past-directed, future-oriented and present-centered he preferred non-historical, historical and trans-historical.

Approaching Time-Consciousness

Time always has a past, present and future but Panikkar's concept of time is totally different. The now is the past-present and present-future. The ability to detect the three modes of human time-consciousness Panikkar proposes us to have an awareness of the transcultural character of time.[1]

Consciousness defines person (man) who is a speaking animal, precisely having self-consciousness and has something to speak of his/her own self. In order to communicate its subjective intentions it needs words. Panikkar calls it a speaking consciousness, *sabda brahman*. The minimum conviction, what we need as Panikkar says, is "that we are historical beings living in history as our proper world, as the proper environment."[2] "The fulfillment of human life is no longer seen exclusively, or even mainly, in the historical unfolding but also in transtemporal experiences (not *atemporal* but *tempiternal*)."[3] He explains the inadequacy of the physical sciences and philosophical anthropology studying man as subject as well as object of study. He proposes transcultural or cross-cultural approach in order to get an adequate knowledge.

The historians, the biologists, the sociologist, use different yardsticks and scales but Panikkar proposes the astrological scale which is based on the Earth's rhythm and human language as true yardstick.

Non-historical Consciousness

Here Panikkar makes difference between the non-historical consciousness which is latently present in the modern cosmopolitan dweller and the prehistoric man. After the invention and spread of writing the prehistoric man lost his memory which includes the personal involvement in life and put on the reminders in the form of writings which is stored, frozen and fossilized in the archives, clay, stone, leaves, or artificial materials. Prehistoric man lived in space not in place and time is *cosmic* or *anthropocosmic*. His concern was birth, puberty, marriage, death, eating, playing, dreaming and etc. His world is *theocosmic*. He saw the world is full of gods and everything is divinized. The divine permeates the cosmos. The supreme principle is Harmony. The prehistoric man believed the nature which always marched with the rhythms of the cosmos not the structures like state, church, scriptures, empire, kingdom and collective enterprises. He had no idea that the state or any institution will uplift or enhance the value of the individuals. Panikkar calls this as pre-scriptural mentality and the non-historical consciousness.

Everyone on the present age or the historical man has this non-historical consciousness which has to be triggered or kindled. It is an invitation to live with memory not with reminders. The focus is not how I am going to live but how I lived (tradition) and how I am living. No fear of death because in birth man overcomes death. Prehistoric man considers food as the symbol of life, sign of fellowship which causes a dynamic communion or intercourse with the entire universe and the fellow human. So he spent 90% of income for food. On the contrary historical man spends 10% of income for food and 90% for weapons, electronic gadgets since his vital needs lie there. On the one hand Main value of Non-historical man is Joy, on the other hand Hope becomes the basic value for historical man. Still in some of the cultures this non-historical consciousness is prevalent even today.

Historical Consciousness

There is a movement from village to city, agriculture to civilization, from sun time to clock time or cosmic time to human time. Here the thrust is future and future only. It is a struggle for freedom from bondage and fight against nature, fate, Earth for the better future where man can live the life in fullness. So called civilized man is the non-natural man who has no harmony with nature. He could not find fullness in each temporality but believes in the future eternity by transcending temporality. He wants to transcend time and space. After conquering earth, he wants to conquer moon and further the entire space. As immanence is the main category of non-historical consciousness so the transcendence becomes the main category of historical consciousness. Historical consciousness interprets immanence as a sort of negative transcendence or synonymous with identity whereas non-historical consciousness treats immanence as neither negative nor identity (or) neither one nor two as mystics of historical world experience.

Conclusion

Panikkar compares historical consciousness with non historical consciousness using two examples one in the Indian tradition and another from Bible, dowry and story of Esau and Jacob respectively. Here we take only the last one.

The fight between primitive and modernity is strong today. In order to pull down non-technological culture and break down autochthonous rhythms and introduce modern technology the technocrats first introduced foreign time-consciousness against the village time which has its seasons and its past and future. In the story of Esau and Jacob, Esau is depicted as non-historical consciousness and Jacob as historical consciousness. Esau is the symbol of eating and Jacob symbolizes the Semitic civilization, the kingdom, church, heaven, paradise, justice, liberation, Promised Land. Jesus also in a way irritated the sons of Jacob and had the non-historical mind stating that not to worry about tomorrow. The trust was shifted from person to money or savings by insisting on investments, banks and products. The elders are taught to believe in money rather than grandchildren. Man started to work for historical future which is like mirage trying to conquer time and claim superiority or dominance over others. Modern Science tries to conquer even the nature so that it has control over nature, for example, by predicting eclipse correctly. Here knowing is to control not to love. The world of historical man, his environment is the *anthropocosmos*. He wants to overcome day and night, seasons and tides, cold and heat at last whole universe. Nature has been tamed and subjugated. Here justice is the supreme principle. There is no place for ghosts in historical man.

Panikkar says that the Historical life is a display of man's possibilities before his fellow humans. He holds, "Historical man stands alone in the world theater – without Gods or other beings, living or inanimate."[4] As the break through from pre-historical to historical is the invention of script so the break through from historical to post-historical is the invention of the internal self-destructive power of atom. The splitting of the *atomos* has also exploded historical consciousness.

Endnotes

[1] See the article by Arun Simon Philip, included in this volume.

[2] Raimundo Panikkar, *The Cosmotheandric Experience*. Emerging Religious Consciousness (Maryknoll: Orbis, New York, 1993; Indian Ed. Motilal Banarsidass: Delhi, 1998), 85.

[3] Panikkar, *The Cosmotheandric Experience*. Emerging Religious Consciousness, 85.

[4] Panikkar, *The Cosmotheandric Experience*. Emerging Religious Consciousness, 106.

Transhistorical Consciousness in Panikkar's Thought

Parciush Marak SJ

Abstract

Panikkar treads the phenomenological path and speaks of the threefold structure of human time-consciousness: nonhistorical consciousness, historical consciousness and transhistorical consciousness. According to him these three times are experienced simultaneously. This paper is concerned mainly with transhistorical consciousness. Panikkar observes that modern science and technology are fast changing the fabric of our human society. However, 'development' has remained empty and meaningless to the masses. He concludes that "the historical imperative has failed." He proposes an alternative which demands a radical change in consciousness. Transhistorical Man must assume theanthropocosmic vision. Finally, the paper reflects on Panikkar's idea of transhistorical existence to which all are invited to.

Keywords

Transhistorical, crisis of history, Sacred secularity, tempiternity, cosmotheandrism, Transhistorical Man, theanthropocosmic.

Transhistorical consciousness is the third mode of human time-consciousness, according to Raimon Panikkar. It is concerned with a lifestyle that is not exclusively historical. It is a consciousness which reaches the fullness of time, since the three times are simultaneously experienced – the past and the future are lived in terms of the present. It is a response to and a way out of *the crisis of history,* that we confront today.

The Crisis of History

Science and technology are penetrating everywhere, and the paneconomic ideology has become the only system of "communication." The myth of progress has practically collapsed. There is really no issue of "development" for the famished masses. Modern technology *cannot* bring solution to this.

There is equally dis-enchantment among the rich. The rich could justify their comforts by persuading themselves that "in due time" the masses would also enjoy them. Now we can no longer believe it. It is ingrained in the System that the rich get richer and the poor poorer.[1]

Panikkar comes to the conclusion: "the historical imperative has failed."[2] History has become not a dream but a nightmare. Man, said to be a historical being, discovers that he cannot make history. This is what Panikkar calls the crisis of history.

Beyond the World of History

Today there are the world movements for peace, ecology, etc. They are symptoms of the crisis of historical civilization and attempts to find a way out. Without a transhistorical dimension, even these movements would be co-opted into the System.

We need now a radically different alternative that will have to begin with the *status quo* and try to convert it into a *fluxus quo* conducive to "a New Heaven and a New Earth." Such an alternative demands nothing short of a *radical change in consciousness.*[3]

This means:

In western parlance, the passage from a monotheistic worldview to a Trinitarian vision. In eastern words, the overcoming of dualism by *advaita*, the transition from a two-storey model of the universe to a non-dualistic conception of reality.[4] In philosophical language, it boils down to finding the middle path between the Scylla of dualism and the Charybdis of monism.

In a more contemporary way, we could say that it amounts to experiencing the sacredness of the secular. Panikkar means by secularity the conviction of the irreducible character of time, i.e., the sense that Being and time are inextricably connected. Time is experienced as constitutive dimension of Being. *Sacred secularity* is an expression meaning that this very secularity is inserted in a reality that is not exhausted by its temporality. Being is temporal, but is also "more" and "other" than this.

Panikkar uses the word "tempiternity" to express this unity. He calls *cosmotheandrism* the experience of the equally irreducible character of the divine, the human and the cosmic, so that reality – being one – cannot be reduced to a single principle.[5]

The historical Man must separate himself from the System in order to live as Man. This does not necessarily mean flight into the mountains or mere escapism from history. It certainly does mean a pilgrimage to the "high places" of the human spirit and the human Earth. This also means helping fellow beings on their way to this new conscientization, which Panikkar calls Realization.

Realization

Here are some of the traits of Realization:

> Transhistorical consciousness attempts to integrate past and future into the present; past and future are seen as mere abstractions. "...the meaning of life does not lie in the future or in the past, but in life itself, lived in its present and actual depth."[6] This is the experience of contemplatives. They [contemplatives] live the present in all its in-tensity and in this tension discover the in-tentionality and in-tegrity of life, the tempiternal. The future of *today* is not tomorrow. The meaning of life is not tomorrow, but today. "The outcome of the transhistorical consciousness is an integrated vision of reality."[7]

Transhistorical Man assumes a more or less conscious *theanthropocosmic* vision of the universe: he finds himself, within a cosmotheandric *reality* in which all the forces of the universe – from electromagnetic to divine, from angelic to human – are intertwined.[8] Everything is interrelated and linked; all must play their own roles.

Transhistorical Man lives his lot. He is involved in the total adventure of reality by participating in the portion "allotted" to him. Transhistorical Man has lost both the pre-historical naiveté and the historical optimism/pessimism. He feels the urge to be what he is supposed to be by occupying his proper place in the universe. The world of transhistorical Man is the cosmotheandric universe. He is increasingly aware that personal destiny is linked both with the fate of society and with the adventure of the entire cosmos.

In sum, transhistorical consciousness is not worried about the future because time is not experienced as linear or as an accumulation and enrichment of moments past, but as the symbol of something which does not exist without Man but cannot be identified with him, either. It is neither the City of God nor the City of Man that transhistorical Man is about to build. He or she would rather concentrate on building or bringing to completion the microcosm that is Man, both individually and collectively mirroring and transforming the macrocosm altogether.[9]

Conclusion

Panikkar takes into account the crisis of history and he attempts to find a way out of this. He proposes a different alternative which demands a *radical change in consciousness*. Transhistorical Man must assume *theanthropocosmic* vision. This will enable him to be what he is supposed to be by occupying his proper place in the universe. Transhitorical man is envisaged by Panikkar as: waking not haunted by the doings of the day ahead, not wanting to succeed at the price of others' defeat, not wanting to "distinguish" oneself by doing something 'extra'-ordinary, being the mirror of the universe and reflecting it without distorting it, aware of the forces of evil or the trends of history, but not suffocated by them, overpowering demons in his own life, and understanding the songs of the birds.[10] Panikkar, thus, invites us to *transhistorical consciousness* and *transhistorical existence*.

Endnotes

[1] Raimon Panikkar, *The Cosmotheandric Experience: Emerging Religious Consciousness*, ed. Scott Eastham (Maryknoll, N.Y.: Orbis Books, ©1993), 110.

[2] Ibid., 118.

[3] Panikkar, *The Cosmotheandric Experience*, 121.

[4] Ibid., 121.

[5] Ibid., 121.

[6] Ibid., 119.

[7] *ACPI Special Series*, Vol. 2, Puthenpurackal, Johnson OFM Cap (Ed) *Raimon Panikkar, Being Beyond Borders: a Commemorative Volume* (Bangalore, India: Asian Trading Corporation, 2012), 174.

[8] Ibid., 127.

[9] Panikkar, *The Cosmotheandric Experience*, 130-131.

[10] Ibid., 120-133.

Time and Sacrifice

Arun Philip Simon SJ

Abstract

Religious sacrifices are a human attempt to overcome the human limitation in overcoming time. Panikkar sees the interpretation of the non-temporal as trans-temporal (not merely after-life) by the secular mindset as closer to the genuine religious insight. We don't overcome time, but it is redeemed by revealing the tempiternal core. This makes the modern work the heir of traditional sacrifices leading to the welfare and salvation of the world.

Keywords

Time, Sacrifice, tempiternal, Panikkar, work.

Introduction

This short write up on the intimate relationship between time and sacrifice is a short summary based on a paper "Time and Sacrifice – the sacrifice of Time and the Ritual of Modernity,"[1] presented by Raimundo Panikkar for an international Conference on 'The Study of Time' in Alpbach, Austria.

According to Panikkar, human being experiences three important limitations in his being, which are in knowledge, space and time.[2] When human beings are more or less able to accept the limitation in knowledge and in spatial dimension, the limitation in time is painful and humiliating. As temporal beings, we are surrounded by birth and death. From time immemorial, different types of sacrifices were the means to cope up with the human desire to go beyond the limitations of time. The human history reveals similar tension between one and many, being and becoming, change and continuity and so on. Panikkar proposes a complementary approach, rather than a dialectical approach, to deal with these dichotomies.[3]

The human history reveals different approaches by human beings to deal with the tension between time and eternity.[4] One approach was to overcome it either by denying it or by transforming it. Other one was to accept the human condition as noble and beautiful or have an attitude of despair and absurdity.

Sacrifice

Rituals are the actions by which humans try to reach the inaccessible[5] (examples being liturgical dress, embrace of peace, saying a prayer along with medicine). Sacrifice are the rituals which help the human beings to transcend the factual human situation and reach what s/he wants – health, riches, a prosperous family, heaven, wisdom, joy, divinity. Though sacrifices vary in different traditions, they are expressions of the same human desires. The sacrifice is extremely important in Vedic and Christian traditions.[6] According to Vedas, it is the highest action by which human collaborates with God and the world to sustain the entire universe. The world came into being through sacrifice and humans attain immortality through the same. By re-enacting Christ's sacrifice in liturgy, Christians are entering into a relationship with the act which has redeemed the world. It forgives the past sins and the future grace is granted. Sacrifices in different traditions connects us to the recesses of the past and to the reservoirs of the future, to the beginning of the world and has eschatological significance.

The ritual of sacrifice happens in time; time is born out of sacrifice and it dies in the sacrifice to reveal the tempiternal[7] core of the time[8]. According to him, the traditional religions understand non-temporal as after-life or liberation forgetting the Kingdom of God or Brahman within. Panikkar sees the interpretation of the non-temporal as trans-temporal by the secular mindset as closer to the genuine religious insight.

Secular Work

Work is a way in which humans repay the debts to the past and the society and justify one's existence.[9] The Pauline saying that 'one who doesn't work shouldn't eat' is a latent feature of many cultures. Thus, work is sacred and demands a sacred consecration. But this work is the task of free citizens and not of slaves. The work of different citizens allows the nations to prosper, and citizens to reach a well-deserved paradise. Doctors, lawyers, engineers, officials, labourers, politicians and farmers could be seen as the priests of this modern religiousness.

Secular Sacrifice of Modern Man (Woman)

A Christian or a Vedic sacrifice may not be performed by the modern secularized man (woman), but they are doing sacrifice in a difference sense for the welfare and salvation of the world[10]. Panikkar considers modern work as the heir to traditional sacrifice because of various factors like sacred work time, rules and regulations of the work and the fruit called the welfare of the world[11]. The work done by doctors, farmers, honest officials, intellectuals are some of the examples. Thus, Panikkar senses the extreme significance of karma-marga in the modern secularized world (he is not denouncing the other two forms – *bhakti* and *jnana*). He is neither endorsing all the modern work as karma-marga nor being dismissal of the exploitation associated with the modern work, but is trying to capture the connecting link between the traditional sacrifice and modern work. Panikkar hopes for a mutual fecundation of the past and the present, traditional understanding of sacrifice and modern work in an authentic encounter to produce an appropriate fruit as the time ripens.[12]

The forgetfulness of inter-dependence between various dimensions of the reality has led to a crisis in modernity; but going back is not a viable option. The modernity could be represented by a clock and it represents the human desire to have mastery over time. Time is coextensive with being, but not exhausted by it. Liberation resulting from genuine secular sacrifice is not a movement from temporal to intemporal, but from inauthentic time (which is boring, repetitive and enslaving) to authentic time and life.[13] In otherwords, it doesn't save us from time, but saves the time itself, i.e. time is redeemed, sublimated to reveal the tempiternal core. For Panikkar, time without tempiternity is corpse. Tempiternity is not to be confused with time, but inseparable from time and stays in the very heart of time.[14] This understanding (not rational knowledge) helps us to understand the transcendent dimension of all the work and to unravel the full potential of the work. At such a level, human work becomes an authentic heir of the traditional sacrifice and an authentic expression of the human desire to have mastery over time.

Considering the different types of sacrifices, Panikkar would put down three main features of sacrifice[15] as 1) it should be an act (including involvement, commitment, praxis, work); 2) It should be adequate for our times. 3) It should be re-enactment of something primordial, fundamentally human (not absolute newness/uncritical past), but a renewal.

Conclusion

Traditional sacrifice was the human ritual to transcend the temporal limitation and to enter the plane of Gods. Panikkar identifies the secular work as the modern heir of traditional sacrifices. When we are able to relish (and teach others to relish) those tempiternal moments of the work (sacred or secular), it becomes a genuine sacrifice; it leads to the salvation of the world. The work becomes prayer.

Endnotes

[1] Panikkar, Raimon. "Time and Sacrifice – the Sacrifice of Time and the Ritual of Modernity," in Proceedings of the Third Conference of the International Society for the Study of Time, ed. J.T. Fraser, N. Lawrence and D.Park (Osterr College, Alpback, July, 1978), 683-725.

[2] Ibid., 687.

[3] Ibid., 686.

[4] Ibid., 688-690.

[5] Ibid., 691.

[6] Ibid., 695-696.

[7] While *temporality* comprises present, past and future, *tempiternity* represents "the crystallization of this very moment without ulterior distensions". It is neither eternity nor temporality. "*Reality is not exhausted in temporality*: it is not temporal now and then eternal later, but rather tempiternal" *(Culto y secularizacion)*. The future does not really exist; genuine hope, which is incorrectly called "of the future" must try to discover in each moment that fullness that we seek: it is possible to find the future in the present. "Time is the other face of what has come to be called eternity, so time and eternity form what could be called *tempiternity*. Eternity does not come *after* time – nor does it exist *before*. Man's life on earth is not simply *a pilgrimage toward God, reincarnation, or nothingness,* but rather constitutes a *rhythm* in which every moment is inhabited by its other eternal face" *(The Cosmotheandric Experience)*. And so, "If you are trying to live your life in fullness, you will have to live it today without

waiting for tomorrow", he writes after a long and perilous pilgrimage. "One must be ready to abandon history and to say goodbye to time"; it is about coming to discover that "each step is the fulfilment of the journey, of the *yatra*" *(Pellegrinaggio al Kailasa,* Sotto il Monte 2006). http://www.raimon-panikkar.org/english/gloss-tempiternity.html

[8] Panikkar, Time and Sacrifice, 697.

[9] Ibid., 706.

[10] Ibid., 705.

[11] Ibid., 707.

[12] Ibid., 710.

[13] Ibid., 708-709.

[14] Ibid., 711.

[15] Ibid., 713.

Part - II
Unfolding of Cosmotheandric Experience

All-Inclusive and All-Embracing: Holistic and Advaitic Vision of Panikkar

Kuruvilla Pandikattu SJ

Abstract

Panikkar's integrated understanding of reality, which includes the cosmic, the human and the divine. I believe that the rediscovery of the significance of cosmic and human may be indirectly traced to his intimate encounter with Hinduism and the secular world, whose differences and diversity he respected. His cosmoetheandric vision, the fullness towards which all religious search points to challenges us to make dialogue as a necessary way of life. It urges us to respect the sacred secularity and to move from the religions of the Book to Word and Wisdom. It invites us to listen attentively to fellow-human beings, to the world and to the Divine, all of which form necessary part of being human today!

Keywords

Cosmotheandric vision, Panikkar, Sacred secularity, Dialogue, All-inclusive life.

Raimundo Panikkar is one of the most important philosopher-theologians who have contributed to dialogue between religions. In this paper, we shall focus on Panikkar's integrated understanding of reality, which includes the cosmic, the human and the divine. I believe that the rediscovery of the significance of cosmic and human may be indirectly traced to his intimate encounter with Hinduism and the secular world, whose differences and diversity he respected.

1.   Cosmotheandric Vision

The cosmotheandric intuition, proposed by Panikkar, is the
integrated vision of the *seamless fabric of the entire reality,* the
undivided consciousness of the totality, where the differences
between them are affirmed and transcended. In his own words:
"There are not three realities: God, Man and the World; but
neither is there one, whether God, Man or World. Reality is
cosmotheandric. It is our way of looking that makes reality
appear to us at times under one aspect, at times under another.
God, Man and World are, so to speak, in an intimate and
constitutive collaboration to construct Reality, to make history
advance, to continue creation."[1]

The cosmotheandric intuition expresses the all-embracing
indissoluble union that constitutes all of reality—the triple
dimension of reality as a whole: cosmic-divine-human.
The *cosmotheandric* intuition is the undivided awareness of the
totality. What Panikkar proposes that we live as open to the triple
dimension of reality – to others, to the world, and to God – so
that we might achieve harmonious communion with the all, that
is, the *cosmotheandric reconciliation.* It is a matter of an experience
more mystical and ineffable than philosophic in the traditional
sense, but it breaks the customary philosophico-theological
moulds. Going beyond such moulds, cosmotheandric dimension
is another way of expressing the *radical trinitarian* conception of
reality, on which Panikkar has spent so much of his research.
The *triadic* structure and the *trinitarian* conception in Panikkar
are not merely in his thinking but also in his methodology.

Thus Cosmotheandrism, the goal and fullness of all religion,
is an indispensable concept for understanding Panikkarian
thinking. The cosmotheandric intuition, the cosmotheandric
mystery, or more precisely although less euphonically,

the theoanthropocosmic reality, reveals that it is relationship that unites the Divine, human and cosmic reality.[2] From such a vision, "The Divine, the human and the earthly (cosmos) are the three irreducible dimensions which constitute the real."[3] So "the cosmotheandric intuition is not a tripartite division of beings, but an insight into the threefold core of all that is insofar as it is."[4]

Understanding this vision requires the advaitic perspective of non-dualism and of *radical relativity* and a *new innocence* that overcomes the fragmented vision of reality that we humans have, in order to achieve that understanding and unitary experience of the reality in which we are immersed.

This *new innocence* "has been freed from the longing for perfection, which necessarily implies being better than the rest... It is pure aspiration... [It is situated in] the realm of pure grace."[5] The aspiration to *harmony* is established in reality when we are in accord" and presupposes good humor, sweetness, serenity and peace, which are manifestations of the structure of reality. It is not the ingenuous dream of wanting to recover paradise, but rather "the healing, in modern Western culture, of the wound the Enlightenment inflicted by separating epistemology from ontology, by making knowledge the hunt for the object by the subject. Thus, no part of the dichotomy between the object, the objective thing disconnected from man and the subject, subjective mind, falls outside the 'concupiscence of objective knowledge'; rather the new innocence envelopes knowledge and the knower in the same act because it knows that the one is not given without the other, without the relationship.[6]

In fact such an experience is the basic experience of Christianity, claims Panikkar. Therefore, he writes emphatically: "If the Christian message means something, it is this experience of the cosmotheandric reality of all being, of which Jesus Christ, true God and true Man, is the paradigm. In Christ Matter is not on its own, nor is Man on one side and God on the other; none of these intrinsically united dimensions surpass the others, so that it does not make sense to affirm that Christ is more divine than human, more worldly than heavenly, or vice versa. The veil of separation has been torn, and the integration of reality begins with the redemption of man."[7]

Panikkar develops his cosmotheandric vision of reality with reference to three major religious traditions to which he 'belongs': the Christian Trinity; the Vedanta Hindu *advaita*; the Buddhist *pratītyasamutpāda*. He claims, nonetheless, that the threefold pattern—traditionally theos-anthropos-cosmos— are invariants of all religions and cultures. He describes the cosmotheandric principle as an "intuition of the threefold structure of all reality, the triadic oneness existing on all levels of consciousness and reality." In Christian terms, ultimate reality, the Trinity, is one but also three; in Hindu terms the ultimate unity of all things is literally neither one nor two (*advaita*); in Buddhist terms everything is radically related to everything else (*pratītyasamutpāda*).

The cosmotheandric principle could be stated by affirming that the Divine, the human and the earthly–however we may prefer to call them–are the three irreducible dimensions which constitute the real, i.e., any reality inasmuch as it is real... What this intuition emphasizes is that the three dimensions of reality are neither three modes of a monolithic undifferentiated reality, nor are they three elements of a pluralistic system. There is rather one, though intrinsically threefold, relation which expresses the ultimate constitution of reality. Everything that exists, any real being, presents this triune constitution expressed in three dimensions. We are not only saying that everything is directly or indirectly related to everything else (the radical relativity or pratītyasamutpāda of the Buddhist tradition), but also stressing that this relationship is not only constitutive of the whole, but that it flashes forth, ever new and vital, in every spark of the real.[8]

Panikkar's formulation of reality as cosmotheandric contests the general assumption that reality is identical to Being. He asserts that there is also Non-Being, the abyss, silence and mystery, that is part of reality. Nor can consciousness be totally identified with reality: there is also matter and spirit. As Panikkar expresses it: "reality is not mind alone, or *cit*, or consciousness, or spirit. Reality is also *sat* and *ānanda*, also matter and freedom, joy and being."[9] In fact, this is for Panikkar the fundamental religious experience: "Being or reality transcends thinking. It can expand, jump, surprise itself. Freedom is the divine aspect of being. Being speaks to us; this is a fundamental religious experience consecrated by many a tradition."[10]

Three assumptions lay behind Panikkar's cosmotheandric vision. The first is that reality is ultimately harmonious. It is neither a monolithic unity nor sheer diversity and multiplicity. Secondly, reality is radically relational and interdependent so that every reality is constitutively connected to all other realities. There is an organic unity and dynamic process where every 'part' of the whole 'participates' in or 'mirrors' the whole. This corresponds to the ancient notion that every reality is a microcosm of the macro-universe. A contemporary version would be the *Gaia* principle. Thirdly, reality is symbolic, both pointing to and participating in something beyond itself. We do not have a God separate from the world, a world that is purely material, nor humans that are reducible to their own thought-processes or cultural expressions. While it is important to recognise the 'symbolic difference' between the Divine and the world, as between one religion and another, according to Panikkar, all cultures, religions and peoples are relationally and symbolically entwined with each other, with the world in which we live, and with an ultimate divine reality.[11]

The Divine dimension of reality is not an 'object' of human knowledge, but the depth-dimension to everything that is. The mistake of western thought was to begin with identifying God as the Supreme Being (monotheism) which resulted in God being turned into a human projection (atheism). Panikkar moves beyond God-talk to speak of the divine mystery now identified in non-theistic terms as infinitude, freedom and nothingness. This essentially trinitarian inspiration takes as its cue the notion that "the Trinity is not the privilege of the Godhead, but the character of the entire reality."[12] As he states, he wants "to liberate the Divine from the burden of being God."[13]

Here Panikkar's concern is not to overthrow the central insights and experiences of the theistic traditions but to acknowledge that "true religiousness is not bound to theisms, not even in the West."[14] He is especially sensitive to the modern secular critique of traditional religions in their generation of various forms of alienation, pathology and disbelief. The suggestion is that we need to replace the monotheistic attitude with a new paradigm or a new *kosmology* precisely in order to 'rescue' the divine from an increasingly isolated, alienated and irrelevant existence. Sardonically expressed, the divine is not a "*Deus ex machina* with whom we maintain formal relations." Rather, the mystery of the divine is the mystery of the inexhaustibility inherent in all things, "at once infinitely transcendent, utterly immanent, totally irreducible, absolutely ineffable."[15]

Of course, this Divine dimension is discernable within the depth of the human person. Humanity is not a closed system and, despite whatever forms of manipulation and control are exercised, the aspect of (divine) freedom remains. Nor is the world without its own dimension of mystery since it too is a living organism with endless possibility as the astrophysicists and neurolinguistics, among others, are showing us today. Moreover, the earth has its own truth and wisdom even if this has largely been ignored in recent centuries by too many cultures and religions.

Such a vision impels us to be dialogical and to experience the sacred in the secular. So the following two subsections deal with these insights.

1.1. Dialogue as Way of Life

Science today has discovered interdisciplinary as core to its success. Unlike in the past what brings progress are not 'geniuses in isolation, but scholars in collaboration.' Thus co-authoring, collaborative strategy has become part of the scientific research paradigm.

May be inspired from this fact and also based on his own experiences, Panikkar has been an ardent advocate of inter-religious and intra-religious dialogue.[16] In fact he sees dialogue essentially as part of life and so we can easily affirm that dialogue is a way of life.[17]

One of the chief aims of dialogue is peace among people, better yet, harmony. Panikkar would therefore plead for both visible and invisible harmony.[18] So, for him dialogue has become imperative and today it has become essential part of being human and being religious. "Thus, encounter and *dialogue* between these *ways of life* become imperative. Here one should carefully distinguish the merely dialectical, in which a crypto-missionary will to power may still be operating, from the truly dialogical dialogue, in which each partner remains open to the possibility of being converted by the other."[19]

Thus Panikkar has dedicated his whole life to furthering respectful religious *dialogue* between the world religions. That is why *New York Times* praised Panikkar quoting Joseph Prabhu, a professor of philosophy at California State University, Los Angeles, "He [Panikkar] was one of the pioneers in opening up Christianity to other religions and learning from them. … We can see the new waves of Christianity moving toward the non-European world in the 21st century, and he prepared the ground for an authentic dialogue between Christianity and other faiths, and beyond that for the cross-cultural conversation which marks our globalized world."[20]

1.2. Sacred Secularity

Related to cosmotheandric vision and dialogue is the intimate relationship between the sacred and the secular. The world of matter, energy, space and time is, for better or worse, our home. These realities are ultimate and irreducible. There is no thought, prayer or action that is not radically cosmic in its foundations, expressions and effects. The earth is sacred, as many a tradition proclaims. More than this, there is no sacredness without the secularity of the world (literally *saeculum*). Panikkar speaks of 'sacred secularity' as the particular way in which the divine and conscious dimensions of reality are rooted in the world and its cosmic processes.

Panikkar insists that there is something more than pure materiality even in a simple stone.[21] Through its existence in space and time, the stone is connected to the entire universe with which it shares its destiny. Notions of inert matter, amorphous space and neutral time are superseded with reference to the ancient wisdom of *anima mundi*: the universe is a living organism constitutive of the Whole.[22] Moreover, science itself is on the way to recovering something of this lost insight through its recognition of the indeterminacy of matter, the open-endedness of space, and the indefinability of time. In Panikkar's terms, there are "no disembodied souls or disincarnated gods, just as there is no matter, no energy, no spatio-temporal world without divine and conscious dimensions."[23] Every concrete reality is cosmotheandric, that is, a symbol of the 'whole.' It is not only God who reveals; the earth has its own revelations.

Matter, space, time and energy are then co-extensive with both human consciousness and the divine mystery.[24] There is something unknowable, unthinkable, uncanny or inexhaustible which belongs to the world as world. This means that the final unknowability of things is not only an epistemological problem (due to the limits of the intellect) but also an ontological fact (integral to the very structure of beings). Other traditions will call this dimension nothingness, emptiness or even Non-being insofar as it is that which enables beings to be, to grow, to change, and even to cease to exist.

2.   Integrating and All-Inclusive Life

Based on a holistic or advaitic vision we have studied in the previous section, Panikkar attempts to lead a life that is wholly integrative, dialogical and all inclusive. In this process science and the material world are important. In order to appreciate Panikkar's attempt, we begin by seeing Panikkar' deeper vision of human being. Then we study his attempt to overcome the tribal vision of Christian existence, leading to existence that is collective and connected.

2.1. Deeper Vision of Human Being

Regarding the mystery that is inherent in life, Panikkar affirms radically: "The mystery of life existence, human nature, God, is certainly not understood by those who understand, if or their understanding of the mystery is reduced to their capacity to understand, and it is thus incomplete."[25] Similar to this ineffability of God is our understanding of ourselves. So Panikkar seeks a deeper, refined, nuanced vision of human beings as necessarily related to the Divine and the world.

The human dimension carries within itself the capacity to know, to be aware of and to be conscious of others and of oneself. This consciousness is the human dimension of reality and it is not reducible to humanity: "Consciousness permeates every being. Everything that is, is *cit*." In other words, consciousness relates not only to humans who know but to everything else that is actually or potentially known—including a far galaxy on the other side of the universe. In this sense, "the waters of human consciousness wash all the shores of the real." From the other perspective, the human person is never reducible to consciousness. It is evidently the case that humans participate in the evolving cosmos of which they are a part. They also participate in the divine mystery of freedom.

Continuing this experience, Panikkar presents human experience as a threefold reality: aesthetic, intellectual and mystical. He critiques technocratic culture for reducing human life to two levels (the sensible and the rational), forgetting, if not despising, the 'third' realm (the mystical). The 'third' realm is not a rarified psychological state, but a 'further' depth-dimension within all human awareness. This 'mystical' dimension comes to the fore as a moment of realization that a certain experience is unique, ineffable, non-repeatable.

Panikkar's intention is to show that genuine human experience involves the triad of senses, intellect and mystical awareness in correlation with matter, thought and freedom. Each act en-acts the cosmotheandric mystery. In his own words: "We cannot sense, think, experience, without matter, logos, and spirit. Thought and mystical awareness are not possible without matter, indeed, without the body. All our thoughts, words, states of consciousness and the like are also material, or have a material basis. But our intellect as well would not have life, initiative, freedom and indefinite scope (all metaphors) without the spirit lurking as it were, behind or above, and matter hiding underneath."[26]

This cosmotheandric insight stresses human identity with the worldly character and temporal nature of the cosmos; it also manifests a human openness towards the infinite mystery that *ipso facto* transcends human thought. The basis of such affirmations is human experience itself which somehow refuses to sever itself from the totality of Being: we experience ourselves to be something 'more' than mere pawns of nature in the evolution of matter, passing egos in the flow of time, or temporary insertions in the expansion of space. This too has been the fundamental insight of every religious tradition, urging us to cross borders and overcome our limited, tribal way of looking at life or God.

2.2   From the Book to the Word

In crossing borders, Panikkar does not hesitate to acknowledge one's own faults. Panikkar asserts: "I believe in the incarnation, and I think that after the misadventures of the past 2,000 years Christianity should stop being the religion of the Book and become the religion of the Word—a word that Christians should hear from a Christ who lives, as Paul says, yesterday, today and always. Then their faith can become more of a personal experience. To present the faith to men and women today doesn't mean trying to introduce a little Thomism here, a little Judaism there, and so forth, but to reach them at their deepest existential, humble and mystical level."[27]

Thus for Panikkar, "the Christian truth is not the monopoly of a sect, a treatise imposed by a kind of colonization, but an eruption that has existed since the dawn of time, which St. Paul defined very well as 'a mystery that has existed since the beginning,' and of which we Christians know only a very small part."[28]

In this context we can understand that Panikkar, "the apostle of inter-faith dialogue and inter-cultural understanding,"[29] *who was* conversant in a dozen or so languages and fluent in at least six languages, traveling tirelessly around the world, lecturing, writing, preaching, and conducting retreats. His famous Easter service in his Santa Barbara days was typical of him and would attract visitors from all corners of the globe. Well before dawn they would climb up the mountain near his home in Montecito, meditate quietly in the darkness once they reached the top, and then salute the sun as it arose over the horizon. Panikkar would bless the elements – air, earth, water and fire – and all the surrounding forms of life – plant, animal, and human – and then celebrate Mass and the Eucharist. It was a profound "cosmotheandric" celebration with the human, cosmic, and divine dimensions of life being affirmed, reverenced, and brought into a deep harmony. The celebration after the formal service at Panikkar's home resembled in some respects the feast of Pentecost as described in the New Testament, where peoples of many tongues engaged in animated conversation. At the center of these celebrations was the sparking personality who combines "the quiet dignity of a sage, the profundity of a scholar, the depth of a contemplative, and the warmth and charm of a friend."[30]

In his later works, Panikkar tried to recast Christianity as a nontriumphal faith and to combat what he called "tribal Christology." Christianity, he argued, was not intended to be an invasion force bent on conquering other gods and, in the colonial period, other peoples. So Panikkar told *The Christian Century* in 2000: "The whole history of Christianity is one of enrichment and renewal brought about by elements that came from outside itself," then he added, "If the church wishes to live, it should not be afraid of assimilating elements that come from other religious traditions, whose existence it can today no longer ignore."[31]

3.   Conclusion

"To be religious today is to be inter-religious." This popular sayings finds its best practical and philosophical exponent in the person of Panikkar. His cosmoetheandric vision, the fullness towards which all religious search points to challenges us to make dialogue as a necessary way of life. It urges us to respect the sacred secularity and to move from the religions of the Book to Word and Wisdom. It invites us to listen attentively to fellow-human beings, to the world and to the Divine, all of which form necessary part of being human today!

Endnotes

[1] Panikkar, *The Trinity and the Religious Experience of Man* (London and New York 1975).

[2] His lectures, on the concept he called "the cosmotheandric experience," or the interplay between the Divine, the human and the cosmic, were published in revised form in 2009 as "The Rhythm of Being."

[3] Raimundo Panikkar, "The New Innocence," *Cross Currents*, Vol. XXVII. No. 1 (Spring, 1977), 12.

[4] Raimundo Panikkar, "The New Innocence," *Cross Currents*, Vol. XXVII. No.1 (Spring 1977), 12.

[5] Raimundo Panikkar, *La nueva inocencia*, Estella Verbo Divino, 1993.

[6] Raimundo Panikkar, *La nueva inocencia*, Estella Verbo Divino, 1993. See http://www.raimon-panikkar.org/english/gloss-cosmotheandric.html.

[7] *Culto y secularización. Apuntes para una antropología litúrgica*, Madrid 1979.

[8] Panikkar, *The Trinity and the Religious Experience of Man* (London: Darton, Longman & Todd, 1973) 74.

[9] Panikkar, "Religious Pluralism: The Metaphysical Challenge" in *Religious Pluralism*, collective work (South Bend, Indiana: University of Notre Dame Press, 1984), 112.

[10] Ibid., 114.

[11] See Panikkar's early scientific studies and our discussion of these in Chapter Two. The cosmological thrust of those studies seems confirmed in more recent writings such as: Paul Davies, *God and the New Physics* (London: Penguin Books, 1984); idem, *The Mind of God: Science and the Search for Ultimate Meaning* (London: Penguin Books, 1992); Stephen Hawking, *A Brief History of Time* (Toronto: Bantam Books, 1988). Stephen Happel's rhetorical reading argues that Hawking's metaphors lead toward a deconstruction of time, whereas Davies' metaphoricizes narrativity. Happel, "Metaphors and Time Asymmetry: Cosmology in Physics and Christian Meanings" (Private Manuscript, Catholic University of America, 1991). In my reading, Panikkar's 'metaphors' of *temporality and tempiternity* are more closely aligned to Davies' narrative and teleological understanding of time. See Gerard Hall, "Multi-Faith Dialogue in Conversation with Raimon Panikkar," *Australian Association for the Study of Religions* Annual Conference July 2003, See http://dlibrary.acu.edu.au/staffhome/gehall/hall_panikkar. htm, accessed March 3, 2013.

[12] "The Rhythm of Being," Panikkar's Gifford Lectures, private manuscript, ch 5. Quoted in Gerard Hall, "Multi-Faith Dialogue in Conversation with RaimonPanikkar", Australian Association for the Study of Religions Annual Conference July 2003, http://dlibrary.acu.edu.au/staffhome/gehall/hall_panikkar.htm, accessed March 3, 2013.

[13] "The Rhythm of Being," Panikkar's Gifford Lectures, private manuscript, ch 7. Quoted in Gerard Hall, "Multi-Faith Dialogue in Conversation with RaimonPanikkar", Australian Association for the Study of Religions Annual Conference July 2003, http://dlibrary.acu.edu.au/staffhome/gehall/hall_panikkar.htm, accessed March 3, 2013.

[14] "The Rhythm of Being," Panikkar's Gifford Lectures, private manuscript, ch 7.

[15] Gerard Hall, "Multi-Faith Dialogue in Conversation with Raimon Panikkar", Australian Association for the Study of Religions Annual Conference July 2003, http://dlibrary.acu.edu.au/staffhome/gehall/hall_panikkar.htm, accessed March 3, 2013.

[16] Panikkar understands the intra-religious dialogue as a re-examination of one's own spiritual tradition Raimundo Panikkar, *The Intrareligious Dialogue* (New York: Paulist Press, 1978) or *Le dialogue intrareligieux* (Paris: Aubier, 1985).

[17] Day-to-day-life with others makes us sensitive to the demands of our increasingly multicultural and interreligious societies. At the same time no one can ignore the fanaticism, the violence, and the murderous intent of the contemporary world. The situation is desperate, given the cultural and religious diversity we encounter in today's context. That is why Pope Benedict XVI, addressing the ambassador of Guinea, said, "In spite of difficulties the Catholic Church is determined to continue its efforts to encourage comprehension and respect between the believers of different religious traditions ... In union with all people of good will, believers contribute to building up a society free from every kind of moral and social squalor, so that each one can live in dignity and solidarity" (See Sr. Bruno-Marie Colin, OSB "Nuns and Interreligious Dialogue Reflections Drawn from Personal Experience," Monastic Interreligious Dialogue http://monasticdialog.com/a.php?id=735, accessed January 3, 2012).

[18] Panikkar, *Invisible Harmony: Essays on Contemplation and Responsibility* edited by Harry James Cargas (Augsburg Fortress Publishers, June 1995).

[19] Panikkar *The Intrareligious Dialogue*, 117.

[20] William Grimes "Raimon Panikkar, Catholic Theologian, Is Dead at 91" *The New York Times*, September 4, 2010. http://www.nytimes.com/2010/09/05/us/05panikkar.html, accessed February 23, 2011.

[21] For this section, including the footnotes, I am indebted to Gerard Hall, "Multi-Faith Dialogue in Conversation with RaimonPanikkar", Australian Association for the Study of Religions Annual Conference July 2003, http://dlibrary.acu.edu.au/staffhome/gehall/hall_panikkar.htm, accessed March 3, 2013.

[22] *The Rhythm of Being: Panikkar's Gifford Lectures*, chaps. 6.

[23] *The Cosmotheandric Experience* (Maryknoll, NY: Orbis Books, 1993), 79.

[24] Ibid.

[25] Raimon Panikkar, *The Trinity and the Religious Experience of Man* (New York: Orbis Books, 1973), 48.

[26] Panikkar, "The Radical Trinity" In *The Rhythm of Being*, chap 5.

[27] Raimon Panikkar "Eruption of Truth: An Interview with Raimon Panikkar" *The Christian Century*, (August 16-23, 2000), 834-36 http://www.religion-online.org/showarticle.asp?title=2015.

[28] Ibid.

[29] Scott Maniquet, "Raimon Panikkar, 'theologian, mystic, priest and poet' dies" *Holy Post*, (Sept 2, 2010), http://life.nationalpost.com/2010/09/02/raimon-panikkar-%E2%80%98theologian-mystic-priest-and-poet%E2%80%99-dies/ accessed January 23, 2012.

[30] Ibid.

[31] He adds further, "Prudence, however, is a value that should be maintained; I certainly understand the voice of Catholic authority when it is raised against widespread superficiality." Raimon Panikkar "Eruption of Truth: An Interview with Raimon Panikkar" *The Christian Century*, (August 16-23, 2000), 834-36.

Response

The concept of cosmotheandric vision is approached differently throughout the paper as cosmotheandric reconciliation, radical Trinitarian, triadic, Radical relativity, the new innocence. It is true that the cosmotheandric vision can be best understood in terms of Christian understating of trinity, Hindu understanding of ultimate unity of reality (advaita) and in Buddhist understanding of *pratītyasamutpāda*.

According to Panikkar's cosmotheandric vision, Reality is ultimately harmonious, radically relational and interdependent and symbolic. It implies that all cultures, religions and peoples are relationally and symbolically entwined with each other.

Thus, Trinity is not the privilege of the Godhead, but the character of the entire reality. For, he wants to liberate the Divine from the burden of being God. In other words, it is to rescue God/divine from an increasingly isolated, alienated and irrelevant existence. Panikkar as an ardent advocate of inter-religious and intra-religious dialogue proposed that such dialogue is an imperative and is the need of the hour.

Some pertinent issues which could be raised in this context are:

We live as open to the triple dimension of reality— if so, what predominantly compels or fails us in the understanding of cosmotheandric vision of Panikkar?

Panikkar proposed that dialogue as an imperative. I see that we speak about the preservation of the uniqueness of our culture, tradition, language and religion. If we involve in dialogue (or on the process of dialogue) as Panikkar, don't you see the possibility of missing our own uniqueness by the dominance of one over the other? - **Emmanuel Satheesh MSFS**

Cosmotheandric Vision:
A Call to Integration

Isaac Parackal OIC

Abstract

The Cosmothendric vision of Panikkar articulates the holistic character of reality which is three dimensional-Divine, human and cosmic. These three dimensions are the irreducible constitutive dimensions of reality. *It* is a call for integration. *Panikkar's vision attempts to overcome the absolute instrumentalization of the world, fragmentation of the human and the meaninglessness of the Divine.* It provides a unified and integrated perception of reality. Further, the vision Panikkar is an authentic expression of life in which from electromagnetic to Divine and from the angelic to human are interrelated and intertwined. He looks at life positively and for him life means the incorporation of the Divine in the human and its impregnation of all the structures of the material world. Therefore, a spirituality based on the Cosmotheandric vision would be a deeper awareness of the sacredness of creation that would lead us to live an authentic life of harmony, communion and love.

Keywords

Comotheandric Vision, Tempiternity, Fusion of Horizons, Time and Timefullness, Integrtation, Inter-relatedness, Perichoresis.

Splendid thoughts come from splendid minds. Every era is honoured with great thinkers but a few of them only could make an influence in the society. However, the contemporary era has been blessed by a number of splendid minds and Raimon Panikkar was one among them. He was a great visionary and thinker whose ideas have made deep impact on the thinking pattern of the society. The Cosmotheandric vision of Panikkar cuts across the barriers of time and distance, cast and creed, science and religion, sacred and secular. Any view that compartmentalizes reality, whether philosophical, theological or scientific, cannot explain reality meaningfully. However, in the Cosmotheandric vision of Panikkar, the uniqueness of each dimension of reality, namely Divine, human and cosmic is properly upheld and meaningfully explained. One dimension is not exalted at the cost of the other,nor reduced to the other. Panikkar has well-articulated the relation between these dimensions of reality and the 'mystery aspect' of their interrelation without confusion. The beauty of the Cosmotheandric vision lies in its affirming the uniqueness and the indispensability of the Divine, the human and the cosmic. This triadic notion constitutes reality and makes it real. That means, one dimension cannot be parted from reality without annihilating reality itself. Reality is neither *one* nor *many* but *polarity*. In this holistic vision, all the three dimensions of reality–Divine, human and cosmic–areequally important, and in that way, every being is Trinitarian. The nature of reality is polar and each pole is constitutive of the 'whole.' This intuition results from a mystical experience in which knower, known and knowledge meet.[1] In this article, we look at the relevance of Cosmotheandric vision, seen in terms of its authenticity and integration.

1. Global and Holistic Perspective

Panikkar's Cosmotheandric vision opens up new horizons of wholeness and inter-mingling. Humans can no longer live in splendid isolation without having contact and communication with one another. To live in geographical boxes, closeted in the neat compartments, segregated into economical capsules, cultural areas, racial ghettoes, separated by the citadels of cast-superiority have become the things of the past.[2] One example may support this: over a century ago, only a very few percent of people moved more than a hundred miles from their birthplaces. The modern technologies have made travel easier, and in a matter of hours we can travel across the seas in and around the world. This has made possible not only the intermingling of peoples, but also the coming together of cultures and values.[3] A good number of contemporary western youth is irresistibly attracted to oriental spiritualities while oriental youth is also fascinated by the western life-style and culture. The African drums are invading western music and western technology invades Africa and Asia.[4]

Panikkar analyses the present day situation with factual evidences. In his writings, the contemporary situation is very well pictured. Panikkar strongly believes that "the time for one-way traffic in the meeting of cultures and religions is, at least theoretically over."[5] For him, each culture has a proper place in the globe and has something to offer for the other. In this way, Panikkar's vision accommodates everything globally and interconnects everything with the thread of non-dualism (*advaita*). Panikkar's vision stands as something that overcomes not only the dichotomies spawned by compartmentalisation (including the body-soul split) but also the estrangement of human and nature and the dualism of God and the world. The Divine, the human and the cosmos become less and less real because of human blindness to see the unity in the mere apparent diversity. This fragmentation of seeing and knowing becomes the fragmentation of reality itself. For example, the myth of space and time: the myth of space with its threefold division of 'God above,' 'human in between' and 'underworld below' needs to be re-interpreted. The myth of time with its stringent division of 'past, present, future' stands in need of new hermeneutics. In this situation, Panikkar's vision provides a unified and integrated perception of reality. Underneath the diversity of common experience, Panikkar discovers a rhythm of harmonious oneness which weaves together the inner vitality of life and reality. Panikkar realizes the beauty of this interrelatedness that brings everything to a concordance.

2.   Vision of Originality

Panikkar's Cosmotheandric vision stands as a vision of life, which results from his urge to encompass, become, and to live reality to the fullest.[6] We can trace this interest to get immersed totally in life, right from his early years. His concern was always to have communion with reality and to have a grip of it, not only with the intellect but also with the whole person. This can be seen in his way of treating the ultimate questions of reality with the total participation of his person rather than explaining in a merely theoretical way.[7] We can see that the Cosmotheandric vision is the crystallisation of his thinking.[8]

The total involvement of his person is manifested in his writings and ideas. He does not want to separate his 'personal life' and 'professional occupation.' He confesses that he has chosen both the paths of a specialized academic and an a-cosmic monk because he sensed the attractive and appealing power of both. For him, a professor is not a businessperson but a 'confessor' who makes a confession about his own life. Moreover, in his opinion, a monk is not a loner of *monachos*, but one struggling to be unified within. Therefore, he views his vocation as a struggle to make a synthesis that is all embracing and wholesome. In this regard, his vision is the reflection of his personal life itself, which originates from his own struggle to understand reality. So, his writings are his 'confessions' concerning his internal struggle for unity and synthesis, and the accomplishment of his vocation as a professor and a monk.[9]

His life can be seen as the fulfilment of his words: "In order to be authentic, the experiment must be also an experience; it must originate in the deepest corners of 'one's personal' being."[10] He himself acknowledges the excruciating tensions he has gone through and the 'existential risk,' he has taken to

articulate his vision that does justice to reality.[11] He did not want
to lose or mislay anything that exists, in this long and tedious
process. He mentions that he has passed through different
stages and ultimately reaches the stage of a monk who carries
with himself the heaviest burden in the existential venture.

The originality and authenticity of his vision can be well
traced from his own words. He has the personal conviction
that his ideas are not mere secretion of the brain but the
condensation of his life lived and the experiences suffered.[12] The
integrity of Panikkar is more evident as he himself witnesses,
"everything somewhat is autobiographical. I am using in my
writing only words whose meaning I myself have grasped."[13]
He acknowledges that his writing is a meditation and medicine
to him. It allows him to ponder and contemplate deeply the
mystery of reality. He even conceives it as an incarnation
process.[14] Here, we see a sage in Panikkar, who, meditating
on the cells of organism discovers a network of dynamic
interrelatedness, which consolidates and weaves together the
inner vitality of reality.

The originality of his vision is very well expressed in his
idea of re-visioning of reality. In this re-visioning, he urges
to have an 'anthropological turn' or a 'cultural mutation.' This
involves a change in human perception of reality. In other
words, a complete change of heart (a radical *metanoia*) amounts
to a 'mutation' in human self-understanding. This radical re-
vision certainly calls for a new understanding of space and
time. Panikkar's Cosmotheandric vision stands on the re-built
pillars of space and time. Just as there can stand no building
without pillars, so too there exists no reality without these two
dimensions of space and time. In this respect, he appears as
an architect and a poet, for "the architect senses the space of

his time, while the poet rhymes the times of his space."[15] As an architect and a poet he seems to sense and discover (or re-cover) the rhythm of reality in his vision.

3.   Fusion of Horizons

The Cosmotheandric vision opens up new horizons of understanding that extends to all levels of life. It touches every core of reality and enhances a basic confidence in reality. Dynamic with playfulness and filled with insights his vision covers a breath-taking range—encompassing many disciplines, the entire globe, and the sweep of history. His writings have subsumed natural science, philosophy, theology, history of religions, hermeneutics and many other allied disciplines. Panikkar is at once a philosopher, a scientist, a theologian, and a mystic. However, even with these terms we cannot capture the heart of his vision, which is a revelation to all those who look at reality with their coloured eyeglasses of partial worldviews.

The crisis we face today is threefold, the ecological predicament, the humanistic crisis and the theological dilemma. The one-sided anthropocentric worldview, which is controlled and carried by reason, made us forget the interconnectedness of reality. We fail to make a synthesis among the different spheres of life because of our lack of patience empowered by reason, and overconfidence that originates from the sensory knowledge. What is at stake then is a satisfactory and sufficient account of reality, an integrated understanding of the Divine, the world and the human. We see this division in all areas of life, the body-soul split, the sacred secular bifurcation, the God-world–human separation, the past-present-future partition, science-faith severance, worship-work segregation etc. In this situation, Panikkar's vision urges us to make a complete transformation, which removes the dichotomy and fragmentation and helps us view reality as an 'integrated whole' that accommodates the human, the cosmic and the Divine. Panikkar's vision attempts to overcome the absolute instrumentalization of the world, fragmentation of the human and the meaninglessness of the Divine. His vision seems to stretch beyond the rational and tends towards the intuitive realm that gives us the mystical orientation and insight. His words are evocative in the realm of the spirit.

4.   Synthesis of East and West

Being a child of two cultures (an Indian father and a Spanish mother), Panikkar had the privilege to go through both traditions of East and West and compare them in the light of his own life experiences. This life experience helped him understand the goodness of both traditions and synthesise them without losing their uniqueness.

Panikkar's Cosmotheandric vision can be seen as a synthesis of East and West. In his writings, he combines the ideas of the eastern and the western traditions. For example, he makes use of the non-dualistic idea of *advaita* tradition of India throughout his vision. Also, he vividly uses the Buddhist notion of reality especially when he speaks of radical relativity etc. We can see many ideas of the western tradition in his writings that range from Pre-Socratics to postmodern thinkers.[16] It is somehow evident that he is most especially influenced by the philosophy of life and existentialism.[17] Panikkar views East and West as two centres of thought, which cannot be seen as geographical locations but as anthropological categories. Interestingly, he states, "Each one of us has an 'East' and a 'West,' an Orient and an Occident."[18] He considers them as symbols, which are not the exclusive possession of some groups or religious families.

5.   Vision of Accommodative Character

Panikkar's attempt to fuse the eastern and the western ideas indicates the accommodative character of his vision which surpasses the 'either/or' question of reality. He presents a balanced view without extremes, and blends the basic dimensions of reality in an appealing manner. He explains the need for harmonious blending of the ideas because his vision itself is a vision of relation. For him, being is essentially a relation. The very structure of reality reveals a relation.[19] The very feeling of our limitedness and insufficiency makes us tend towards others and be in relation.

Panikkar understands the different worldviews as creative and he believes that the different ideas can be accommodated and transformed into creative polarities. As his methodology would make it clear, no worldview can claim monopoly because, by its very definition, it is only one particular perspective of the world. No worldview can provide us the real picture of the world. No single outlook can become the norm that evaluates the other views. All are valid and complementary.[20] According to Panikkar, this is what the Trinitarian dynamics is all about; it is where everything contains in everything else; each person represents the community and each tradition corrects, complements and challenges the other.[21]

The accommodative attitude of Panikkar's vision is inspiring. For him, unity implies diversity, and harmony of reality implies the presence of dialectically opposite polarities. The world order itself is maintained only by one dimension pulling in one direction and the other in the opposite. This is the 'discordant concord' of different voices of human traditions. If all the discordant voices are reduced into one voice, the beauty will be lost.[22] Therefore, his pluralistic vision allows for polar and tensible co-existence between different human attitudes, cultures and traditions. This is what is meant by creative polarity.[23]

Another motivating element in Panikkar's thinking is that he adapts himself to diverse worldviews. He is willing to admit that his thinking is no more than one opinion among many.[24] He acknowledges that his opinions, beliefs, philosophy or religion are as limited, vulnerable, debatable and subjected to critique as any other is.[25] He also admits that his vision is not at all a well-articulated or finished vision once and for all.[26] We can provisionally call it the 'unifying myth' that is not yet spelled out; it is not yet logos.[27] It is only a starting point.[28] It is still an emerging vision which represents the emerging religious consciousness of our time.[29] This shows the intellectual humility of Panikkar to acknowledge the limitedness and inadequacy of his vision.[30] Writing to this writer, he says, "You deal with inescapable problems today. I have learnt much from your pages. You are perceptive enough to speak of my inconsistencies and you avoid saying contradictions. Your criticism is enlightening."[31]

6. Integral Eco-Vision

Modern human being endowed with reason and assisted by a limited anthropocentric vision of reality has instrumentalized nature for one's own purposes. Guided by the goddess of reason and the objective thinking of science human being has the belief that the mastery over nature leads to the height of success. One's adoration and admiration have gone after the progressive thinking of science. This exploitative mentality is considered as the progressive thinking of the modern world. Human being has looked down upon anything that has to do with the 'mystery.' The mystery aspect of reality is perceived as something that is against the spirit of science. Human being's scientific and technological pride feels threatened and offended at the thought of anything beyond one's control. 'Mystery' has given way to 'mastery.' Dazzled and overwhelmed by the astounding accomplishments of science modern human being thinks that the most efficacious approach to know reality is the experiment. However, through experiment one can never know earth's wisdom just as by experiment alone, one will never discover the mystery aspect of the human body and its real life. This experimenting attitude results not only in the disrespect of the Divine and the human but also the exploitation of nature. In this context, we can situate the integrated 'eco-vision' of Panikkar.

Panikkar analyses very beautifully the estrangement of humans from nature while he deals with historical consciousness.[32] In this moment of historical consciousness human being seems to be in dialectical opposition to nature and being a civilized human being one considers oneself as a non-natural being. One's home is no longer the earth but the ideal world. Historical human being tames and subjugates nature. Nature is demythicized; there is no mystery about it. The sacred thread of collegiality that has woven the artistry of nature becomes broken and scattered into pieces.[33] Human beings have not simply taken their sustenance from the earth, but they have further exploited and violated her.[34] The way, Panikkar puts forward this idea of further exploitation is remarkable: "But the cosmotheandric circle is broken if we convert *agriculture* which is a sort of love-making with the Earth, into *agri-business*, which amounts to the violation of Nature, significantly called world 'resources,' for the profit of the exploiter."[35] The 'maximum' has replaced the 'optimum.' The denuded forests, the polluted atmosphere and the stained seas are the best example of this exploitation.

The Cosmotheandric vision has an inspirational analysis of nature. He elevates nature to the level of a person. For him, the earth is our mother. She is our very self.[36] To destroy our relationship with nature is to destroy our very selves. In this sense, human survival is inextricably linked with the survival of nature. The elevation of nature from objective level to a personal realm further implies the need of experience to understand the earth rather than to experiment. In this experiential level, we allow nature to penetrate us. Here, we are not only 'seeing' but 'hearing' too. That means, this process of experience is both active and passive at the same time. By allowing the earth to speak, we discover her wisdom.

Panikkar flavours his ecological vision further with the traditional idea of *anima mundi*. By this concept, Panikkar states that life is not the privilege of humans alone but human person shares in the life of the universe.[37] In other words, human being as a microcosm is sharing the life of the earth, which is the macrocosm. He makes a remarkable comparison in order to show the dignity of the earth. He makes use of the ideas from the Indian philosophy and the western traditions.[38] In this comparative analysis, we can see the mind of a hermit who gives obvious preferentiality to the philosophy of nature and eschews the modern scientific approach. This view seems to be very similar to the Hermetic philosophy of nature.[39] It shows also the traits of Jaina philosophy.[40]

Another notable thing in Panikkar's ecological vision is his use of 'ecosophy' instead of ecology. Panikkar justifies this shift because '*ecosophy*' adopts a dialogical attitude towards the earth seeing it as 'Thou.' He is of the opinion that mere ecology is not adequate to convey the meaningfulness of our view regarding nature. Further, Panikkar opines that we have to hold a dialogue with the earth. This idea of dialogue runs parallel with his fundamental view that human task is to participate in reality and its cosmic rhythms.[41] This participation also implies the cultivation of friendship with her. Besides the reason Panikkar has presented above, there are three other reasons for this shift. Firstly, he avoids the terms, which have too much affinity with reason or modern scientific thinking; the term 'ecology' is pregnant with rational connotations. Secondly, he prefers to coin his own terms instead of using the traditional ones in order to picture reality more effectively.[42] The name he has given to his vision itself stands as an evidence to this. Thirdly, he understands the new vision about the earth as the new wisdom. This is precisely the new innocence, about which he speaks repeatedly.[43] Thus he avoids the traditional term 'ecology' and replaces it with 'ecosophy' in order to convey this new vision or wisdom.[44]

7. New Understanding of Matter and World

In Panikkar's writings, we see a positive appreciation and admiration of matter and the world. For him, every being stands in the world and shares its secularity. Our everyday experience discloses that there is nothing that enters human consciousness without at once entering in relation with the world.[45] This implies that we cannot even think of God and human beings who may fail to partake in secularity. If there is nothing, it amounts to absolute nothingness. The final foundation for the belief for the existence of something is that the world exists.

The way in which he shows the significance of matter and the world is interesting. He elevates matter to a higher realm by saying that "every material thing that is, is God's, or more precisely, God's thing, God's own World."[46] Likewise, he explains human relationship with the world too. Human beings cannot survive without the cosmos. Moreover, our needs are dependent on the cosmos.[47] To become human, one has to be cosmic. However, there is no question of 'has to' because human being *is* always cosmic and has no existence other than in the world.

The idea of the world as a symbol is another notable contribution of Panikkar. In his vision, the world is the symbol of the Divine. His idea of *symbol* is noteworthy: symbol has a revelatory function and it reveals the symbolized reality in a symbolic way. The relation between the symbol and the symbolized is ontological.[48] The symbolised exists in and through the symbol.[49] Reality is not exhausted in the symbol, but there is no reality out of or independent from the symbol. Here, he brings forward the example of human body: my body is a symbol of my person. 'I' exist in my body and my person reveals itself through my body. However, my body does not exhaust my whole personality. I am more than my body. Nevertheless, without my body, my personality cannot exist.[50] In this way, he gives a very positive value to the world and matter and raises them to the symbol, which symbolizes the Divine. Therefore, the world and matter are indispensable in the understanding of reality.[51]

Moreover, this view contributes to a better understanding of the *sacramentality* of the world. Panikkar seems to be bold enough to affirm, "The *saeculum* (world) is not in jest or passing, provisional, unreal or a shadow or what we would like to call it in order to attenuate the impact of an unjust and violent status quo."[52] Here, we see the voice of a prophet who is very much concerned about the contemporary situation of the society. He urges us to take the world seriously. By this, he asserts that the material world is real and insuperable though not exclusive or complete. The real cannot be disassociated from the bodily and it cannot exist without matter, though it does not consist of matter only.[53] Life is not only about the material world. Life means the incorporation of the Divine in the human and its impregnation of all the structures of the material world.[54] The world is no longer that which is fleeting but it is the very clothing of the permanent, the eternal and the immutable.[55] This is precisely what we mean by *sacramentality* of the world.

8.   Innovative Anthropology

Panikkar's vision holds human beings in high esteem. For him, "To be Man is not just to be a small piece of intelligent matter crawling in the universe, or a great individual walking on earth. Man is a conscious agent in the very destiny of the universe."[56] Therefore, it is very clear that human beings have a great role to play in the universe. Human dignity lies in one's being commissioned to bring the universe to perfection.[57] For Panikkar, human being is the microcosm that mirrors and transforms the macrocosm, the world.[58] They influence mutually.

Panikkar's anthropology provides us with a new insight that extends to the realm of the cosmic and the Divine dimensions. Panikkar even uses the notion of humans as a reflection, an image of the whole reality.[59] Does it mean only a passive reflection? No, it is an active partaking. "Man participates in the cosmic rhythm not only as a 'spectator' or an 'actor,' but even as a 'co-author' and a 'priest' by whose active participation, the cosmic rhythms are transformed."[60] The overall development of human beings goes hand in hand with the transformation of reality because of the intrinsic ontological connection between human beings and reality. Therefore, the enhancing of human beings also entails the enhancing of reality.[61] This view is certainly a guideline and incentive to all those who work for the betterment of the human society. For Panikkar, a human being is not just one of the many rings in a lifeless chain of entities, but is unique and irreplaceable because of the infinite value, namely the Divine.[62]

9.   Re-Visioning of Time

One of the prominent features of Panikkar's vision is his idea of time. For him, time originally connoted a predominantly qualitative intuition in the sense that each being has its own time.[63] It is tantamount to saying that time is the peculiar way in which each being can exist. Therefore, time and being are co-extensive. There is time as long as being exists and being exists so long as it has time to exist. This shows that time is not exterior to being. Instead, it is part and parcel of the constitution of being. It is interior to being. Temporality is an essential dimension of reality though reality is not exhausted by it.

He makes a very good blend of the ancient Greek and the Indian traditions in order to express the original meaning of time. In the Greek tradition, time originally implies the 'life' of being. This shows the intrinsic connection between time and reality in the deepest level. In the Indian tradition, time is the 'life-breath' of reality (prāṇa).[64] Life matures beings and encompasses being. Further, it is time again that makes change in being. He nicely puts together all these traditional insights in his vision to show the dynamic character of reality.

Another interesting feature in the idea of time is the significance of the 'present.' Panikkar observes that the modern human being has no time to live in the 'present' as s/he idolizes the future. The consequence is that s/he becomes a machine losing one's uniqueness.[65] Human being, like a machine, works and lives almost in an automatic manner. This implies that human values like love, friendship, beauty, inner joy, etc. hardly have a place in this world of acceleration and repetition. Human beings hardly get time for nurturing human values and fellowship. This has created a sense of estrangement from the Divine, other human beings and nature. Eternity becomes a real problem and a threat. In this dialectical opposition between temporality and eternity, he locates his inspiring notion of *tempiternity* as a solution to this problem. What he proposes is that human being does not need to look for eternity in the future. It is something already present 'here and now' in the present moment itself.[66] Therefore, he urges to live 'life in its fullness' in the 'present.'[67] The implication of this view is tremendous in the modern scenario of work, which we will deal in the coming section.

10. New Outlook on Human Work

Panikkar's understanding of work is very much connected with his understanding of time. He proposes a contemplative attitude to both, time and work. The manner, in which he mingles these ideas, is noteworthy. His idea of *tempiterntiy* has a great influence in his concept of work. The Cosmotheandric intuition is the emergence of new consciousness that is an invitation towards a contemplative mood. This mood is closely connected with Panikkar's understanding of the third moment of consciousness, namely the *trans-historical consciousness*; indeed, contemplation is the trans-temporal mode in which one lives fully in the present moment.[68]

He combines work and *tempiternity*. Work enables us to live in the 'present' and it is through working within time and space that we are able to transcend our historical predicament and thereby transform time itself.[69] It is in work where *time* and *timefulness* meet and enable the worker to enjoy the present and to consecrate his/her life authentically and fruitfully. Work becomes a contemplation and worship that helps a human being to be fully oneself; in fact, an act of worship is an act which allows and enables us to realize our being, to realize the cosmos what they really are.[70] This does not mean that any work becomes automatically contemplation or worship. Panikkar sets one condition for this: it must be a desireless action. He compares the unmotivated action of the contemplative with the understanding of *Bhagavadgīta* that the highest action is desireless action doing for the act itself. Therefore, the result of the action is renounced by the contemplative. An act is done simply for the sake of itself without asking a 'why.' The primacy is to the act itself so that work will have to yield its own meaning.[71] In this manner, "kiss will be a kiss; the dance a dance; the poem a poem."[72]

The contemplative act is creative, a new beginning not a conclusion.[73] Here, Panikkar presents with much enthusiasm a very risky and adventurous way of living without looking into the future. The examples he gives for contemplative life seem to be evocative and provocative at the same time: "If you are a contemplative, you may become a Samaritan on the way and come late to the meeting, or just remain playing with some trifle which happened to catch your fancy. Ultimately, you have no way to go, no place to reach."[74] After all, the meaning of life does not rest in its achievement. The authenticity of these words become clear when we compare these words with Panikkar's personal confession: "I remember having spontaneously avoided situations where I could have acquired honours and power. I have never regretted avoiding these, but I must admit that I thought about them in weak moments."[75]

These words seem to be genuine and exemplary; indeed, they point towards a desireless life.[76]

The contemplative expects nothing from the future and for him/her, happiness is now, not in the future or in achieving anything.[77] For Panikkar, the length of our life doesn't matter because nothing is there to achieve in the future; the contemplative has achieved it today itself: "Your life will not be unfulfilled even if you do not reach your golden age but meet with an accident along the road."[78] Though these words appear to be a kind of 'indifference' or 'disinterest' to life, they have something remarkable to convey to all who become desperate or disappointed even with small failures in life. When a worker attains this contemplative mood, according to Panikkar, his/ her work becomes worship; after all, human realization takes place not in the future but in every moment of life and the final achievement is present from the beginning until the end.[79]

A Call to Integration

To conclude, in this article I was trying to spell out the basic characteristics of Cosmotheandric vision which is yet to be better interpreted or meaningfully explored (or re-discovered). We have seen that Panikkar's vision is multi-dimensional and integral. It tries to integrate the whole reality and gives meaning to it. The three dimensions namely Divine, human and cosmic are interconnected and interrelated without losing their particularity and uniqueness. There is a mutual interpenetration (*perichoresis*): "If I climb the highest mountain, I will find God there, but likewise if I penetrate the depths of an apophatic Godhead I shall find the World there. And in neither case, will I have left the heart of Man."[80] The relationship could not be more intimate. Nothing is isolated from the whole reality and isolated being for him is an abstraction. This integral approach

makes his vision appealing and attractive and it encourages
us to lead an authentic life which is our very vocation itself.
Panikkar expresses the meaningfulness of his own life in the
articulation of his vision as he writes: "In order to be authentic,
the experiment must be also experience; it must originate in
the deepest corners of one's own personal being."[81] Also, he
observes that he has passed through the three stages: of a *scientist*
who experiments with objects, of a *philosopher* experiments with
ideas and of a *monk* who experiments with himself. The third
stage carries with it the heaviest burden of existential venture.[82]
Here the experiment becomes experience. The integrity of his
own life helps Panikkar articulate his integrated vision namely
the Cosmotheandric vision.

Panikkar's rhythmic understanding of time and the
contemplative attitude for an integration of life make his vision
evocative and inspiring. His vision challenges us to build up a
better world, which gives dignity to human values, enhances
respect for nature, and entails an ever more emphasized notion
of the Divine who is permeatingly present in cosmos. This
vision helps us understand better that we are knots in a network
of relationships in which, from electromagnetic to Divine,
and from angelic to human, are interrelated and intertwined.
Therefore, a spirituality based on the Cosmotheandric vision
would be a deeper awareness of the sacredness of creation that
would lead us to live an authentic life of harmony, communion
and love. It promotes harmony with the cosmos, communion
among all humans and confidence in the Divine. It is a vision
of symbiosis which calls us to integration.

Bibliography

Books

Panikkar, Raimon: *Worship and Secular Man*, London, Longman & Todd, 1973.

-------: *The Trinity and the Religious Experience of Man*, New York, Orbis Books, 1973.

-------: *Vedic Experience Mantramanjari: An Anthology of Vedas for Modern Man and Contemporary Celebration*, London, Longmann & Todd, 1977.

-------: *Intrareligious Dialogue*, London, Paulist Press, 1978.

-------: *Myth, Faith and Hermeneutics: Cross-Cultural Studies*, New York, Paulist Press, 1979.

-------: *Blessed Simplicity: The Monk as Universal Archetype*. New York, Seasbury Press, 1982.

-------: *The Unknown Christ of Hinduism: Towards an Ecumenical Christophany* (Revised and enlarged edition), Bangalore, Asian Trading Corporation, 1982.

-------: *The Cosmotheandric Experience: Emerging Religious Consciousness* (edited with an introduction by Scott Eastham), Maryknoll, Orbis Books, 1983.

-------: *The Silence of God The Answer of Buddha* (translated by Robert R. Barr), Maryknoll, Orbis Boks, 1989.

-------: *A Dwelling Place for Wisdom* (translated by Annemarie S. Kidder), Delhi, MotilalBanarsidass Publishers, 1993.

-------: *Cultural Disarmament: The Way to Peace*, Kentucky, Westminster John Knox Press, 1995.

-------: *Invisible Harmony: Essays on Contemplation and Responsibility*, (edited by Harry James Cargas), Minneapolis, Fortress Press, 1995.

Articles

Cousins, Ewert: "RaimundoPanikkar and the Christian Systematic Theology of the Future," *Cross Currents* (Summer 1979).

D'Sa, Francis: "Myth, History and Cosmos," *Jeevadhara*, 25 (January 1984).

PanikkarRaimon: "The Myth of Pluralism: The Tower of Babel-A Meditation on Non-violence" *Cross Currents*, 29 (Summer1979).

-------: "Indology as a Cross-Cultural Catalyst," *Numen*18 (December 1971).

-------: "Cross-Cultural Studies," *Monchanin* 50 (June-December 1975).

-------: *The Intrareligious Dialogue*, (London, Paulist Press, 1978).

-------:*A Dwelling Place for Wisdom*, tran. Annemarie S. Kidder, (Delhi:MotilalBanarsidassPublishers, 1993).

-------: "There is No Outer without Inner Space,"*Cross Currents* XXXIV (Spring 1993).

-------: "Religious Pluralism: The Metaphysical Challenge," in *Religious Pluralism*, ed., Leory S. Rouner (Notre Dame: University of Notre Dame Press, 1984).

-------: "A Self-Critical Dialogue," *The Intercultural Challenge of R. Panikkar*, ed., Joseph Prabhu, (Mary knoll, New York: Orbis Books, 1996).

-------: "Towards a Dialogical Dialogue," *Interculture*, 20 (1987).

-------: "A New Society for a New Millennium," *Journal of Dharma*, 27, 1 (January-March 2002).

-------: "Mysticism of Jesus the Christ," *Mysticism in Śaivism and Christianity*, ed., Bettina Baümer(New Delhi:D.K. Printworld, 1997).

-------: "Toward a Typology of Time and Temporality," *Philosophy East and West*, XXIV (April 1974).

-------: "The Law of *Karman* and the Historical Dimension of Man,"*Philosophy East and West*, XXII, no.1 (January 1972).

-------: "The Contemplative Mood: A Challenge to Modernity," *Cross Currents*, XXXIV (Fall 1981).

-------: "Time and Sacrifice:The Sacrifice of Time and the Ritual of Modernity," *The Study of Time III: Proceedings of the Third Conference of the International Society for the Study of Time, Alpbach-Austria*, ed., J.T.Fraser (New York: Springer-Verlag, 1978).

-------: "Samdhya, The Vedic Prayer" *Indian Theological Studies*, 14, no.1 (March 1977).

-------: "The Contemplative Mood," A Challenge to Modernity," *Cross Currents*, XXXIV (Fall 1981).

Endnotes

[1] Cf., R. Panikkar, *The Cosmotheandric Experience: Emerging Religious Consciousness,* ed., Scott Eastham, (Maryknoll, Orbis Books, 1983), 72.

[2] Cf., R. Panikkar, "The Myth of Pluralism: The Tower of Babel-A Meditation on Non-violence" *Cross Currents*, 29 (Summer1979), 202.

[3] Cf., R. Panikkar, "Indology as a Cross-Cultural Catalyst," *Numen*18 (December 1971), 175. "Geographical boundaries are rapidly losing their importance as barriers to the spread of cultural values: not only are

gadgets diffused all over the globe within a few years of their invention; popularized ideas from all the continents are now travelling at the speed of light to the furthest corners not only of the world but also of the human psyche."

4 Cf., R. Panikkar, "Cross-Cultural Studies," *Monchanin* 50 (June-December 1975), 13.

5 R. Panikkar, *TheIntrareligious Dialogue*, (London, Paulist Press, 1978), 99.

6 Cf., R. Panikkar, *A Dwelling Place for Wisdom*, trans. Annemarie S. Kidder, (Delhi:MotilalBanarsidass Publishers, 1993), 90: "As long as I can remember, I have felt a great need to encompass reality, or better, to become reality—to live."

7 Cf., R. Panikkar, *A Dwelling Place for Wisdom*, 90: "Thus all my life I have been dealing with ultimate questions—not in a purely theoretical manner but by fully participating in them as person."

8 Cf., R. Panikkar, *The Cosmotheandric Experience*, 4-5: "For well over fifty years I have been thematically concerned with the problem spelled out in this book...my lifelong fondness for synthesis, theandrism, myth and apophatism, all vouch for this attitude which I now formulate as a hypothesis..."

9 R. Panikkar, *A Dwelling Place for Wisdom*, 91.

10 R. Panikkar, *A Dwelling Place for Wisdom*, 93. Cf., 92: "Personal circumstances (of biological, historical and biographical nature) prompted me to *accept* the venture of a conversion without alienation, of appropriation without repudiation, of synthesis without syncretism, of symbiosis without eclecticism."

11 Cf., R. Panikkar, *A Dwelling Place for Wisdom*, 93.

12 Cf., R. Panikkar, *The Unknown Christ of Hinduism: Towards an Ecumenical Christophany* (Bangalore: Asian Trading Corporation, 1982), x:"If one writes a book with one's life and pays for it with one's blood, if intellectual activity consists of life lived and experience suffered, rather than being a mere secretion of the brain, then what I have written is part of I was; and what I was cannot be blotted out."

13 Cf., R. Panikkar, *A Dwelling Place for Wisdom*, 77.

14 Cf., R. Panikkar, *A Dwelling Place for Wisdom*, 79: "Writing, to me, is meditation—that is medicine—and also moderation, order for this world...writing allows and almost forces me to ponder deeply the mystery of reality. It certainly involves thinking, contemplation. But at the same

time, writing means that I have to add form, shape, beauty, expression, revelation to this mystery of reality…Writing presupposes thinking but also shaping and carving our thoughts; cleaning them, clothing them with colours, smells and forms, even strengthening and putting them to action. It is an incarnation process where the "word becomes flesh."

[15] R. Panikkar,"There is No Outer without Inner Space,"*Cross Currents* XXXIV (Spring 1993), 69.

[16] Cf. R. Panikkar, *Invisible Harmony: Essays on Contemplation and Responsibility*, ed. Harry James Cargas (Minneapolis: Fortress Press, 1995), 59-60; cf.,R. Panikkar, *The Cosmotheandric Experience*, 144, footnote 17.

[17] Cf., R. Panikkar, *Invisible Harmony*, 169. This passage points to this fact.

[18] R. Panikkar, *Blessed Simplicity: The Monk as Universal Archetype*(New York:Seasbury Press, 1982), 17. Also see his *Invisible Harmony*, 145.

[19] Cf., R. Panikkar, "Religious Pluralism: The Metaphysical Challenge," in *Religious Pluralism*, ed., Leory S. Rouner (Norte Dame: Universty of Norte Dame Press, 1984), 113.

[20] Cf., F. D'Sa, "Myth, History and Cosmos," *Jeevadhara*, 25 (January 1984), 18.

[21] Cf., R. Panikkar, *A Dwelling Place for Wisdom*, 142.

[22] Cf., R. Panikkar, *Invisible Harmony*, 180. Here Panikkar observes the beauty of pluralism as a symphony—the inexplicable concord out of so many dissenting voices. Pluralism tells us that one should not assume for oneself the role of being a conductor of the cosmic orchestra.

[23] Cf., R. Panikkar,*The Cosmotheandric Experience*, 13: "We need a horizon in order to see and to understand, but we are aware that other people have other horizons; we aspire to embrace them, but we are aware of the ever-elusive character of any horizon and its constitutive openness." See also R. Panikkar, "Philosophy as Life-Style," *A Dwelling Place for Wisdom*, trans. Annemarie S. Kidder, Delhi, Motilal Banarsidass Publishers,1993, 93-94.He views the *advaidic* approach as a conjoining substitute. According to Panikkar, *advaida* is the basic intuition that opens up a worldview in which the diversities are neither absolutized (dualism) nor ignored (monism), nor idolized (pantheism), nor reduced to mere shadows (monotheism).Cf.R. Panikkar, "The Myth of Pluralism," 226: "And this advaidic approach has the confidence that what appears to be in conflicts (when viewed dialectically) can be transformed into creative polarities."

[24] Cf., R. Panikkar, "A Self-Critical Dialogue," *The Intercultural Challenge of R. Panikkar*, ed., Joseph Prabhu, (Maryknoll, New York: Orbis Books,

1996), 247: "In short, my criticism on universalism is not a universal affirmation...it tallies with my defence of pluralism, which is not a pluralisitic statement...it is simply my opinion, which I am striving to defend in a convincing manner." See also R.Panikkar "A Self-Critical Dialogue," 254.

[25] Cf., R. Panikkar, "A Self-Critical Dialogue," 257.

[26] Cf., R. Panikkar, *The Cosmotheandric Experience*, 17.

[27] Cf., R. Panikkar, *The Cosmotheandric Experience*, 77.

[28] Cf. R. Panikkar, *A Dwelling place for Wisdom*, 72.

[29] Cf., R. Panikkar, "Towards a Dialogical Dialogue," *Interculture*, 20 (1987), 14-15.

[30] Panikkar has shared the same view during my meeting with him in Barcelona on 19th November 2005. The manner in which he spoke itself is a testimony to this. If we examine his earlier writings before 1970, we can understand that the term "cosmotheandrism" itself has been modified and changed in the light of his new studies and experiences. Previously he used "Theandrism." He took the decisive step from his earlier positions to add the dimension of "cosmos."

[31] On April 29, 2006, he sent me a letter congratualting on the completion of my work and commenting on the criticism that I made.

[32] Cf., R. Panikkar, *The Cosmotheandric Experience*, 105.

[33] Cf., R. Panikkar, *Blessed Simplicity*, 52-53.

[34] Cf., R. Panikkar, *Blessed Simplicity*, 52-53.

[35] R. Panikkar, "A Self-Critical Dialogue," 288. Italics mine.

[36] Cf., R. Panikkar, "A New Society for a New Millennium," *Journal of Dharma*, 27, 1 (January-March 2002), 14.

[37] Cf., R. Panikkar, *The Cosmotheandric Experience*, 138.

[38] Panikkar shows the dual dimensionality of the Earth using the Indian traditional terms: *bhūmi* and *pṛthvi*. The term *bhūmi* implies that which exists here before us and that which nurtures all creatures. *Pṛthvi* means that which stretches out before us in an ever-expanding horizon and that which receives all steps we make, all the growth that may occur in us. The Christian scholastics considered the world to be the primary source of knowledge.

[39] Hermetic philosophy is a philosophical view which has a religious approach to the cosmos involving a regenerative experience.

[40] In the Jaina philosophy, all the living beings have an*ātman*, principle of consciousness, of life. For more cf. R. Panikkar, *Vedic Experience, Mantramnajari: An Anthology of Vedas for Modern Man and Contemporary Celebration* (London:Longmann& Todd, 1977), 123.

[41] Cf., R. Panikkar, "A Self-Critical Dialogue," 288-89.

[42] Panikkarhas coined many terms like *Cosmothenadric,Tempiternity* etc.

[43] Cf. Ewert Cousins, "RaimundoPanikkar and the Christian Systematic Theology of the Future," *Cross Currents* (Summer 1979), 152. Here, Cousins compares Panikkar with Francis of Assisi.

[44] The title of one of the Italian books of Panikkar is *Ecosofia: la nuovasaggeza-per unaspiritualità della terra* published from Assisi in 1993. For a detailed discussion of this theme, cf. D'Sa Francis, "*Sacramendum Mundi*: Preface to a "Cross-Cultural Re-Vision of Sacraments," *The World as Sacrament: Interdisciplinary Bridge-Building of the Sacred and Secular*, eds., Francis X. D'Sa, Isaac Padinjarekuttu and Jacob Parapally(Pune:Jnana-DeepaVidyapeeth Theology Series, I, 1998), 263-64.

[45] Panikkar argues that even the extra-mundane things have their reference necessary to the world (*saeculum*) though these might also be somehow negative. For more, see R. Panikkar, *The Cosmotheandric Experience*, 64.

[46] R. Panikkar, *The Cosmotheandric Experience*, 66.

[47] The humans, for example cannot survive without breathing, food, etc.

[48] Panikkar shared me this idea during my meeting with him in Barcelona on 19th November 2005.

[49] Panikkar, *Myth, Faith and Hermeneutics:Cross-Cultural Studies*, (New York, Paulist Press, 1979), 6.

[50] This idea is shared by Panikkarduring my meeting with him with a caution that every example can be misleading.

[51] Cf., R. Panikkar, *Blessed Simplicity*, 83: "It (contemporary monkhood) cannot renounce the secular world because *it does not believe it to be secondary*; it cannot renounce activity in the world because it believes this to be *indispensable*." Brackets and italics are mine.

[52] R. Panikkar, *Blessed Simplicity*, 84.

[53] Cf. R. Panikkar, *A Dwelling Place for Wisdom*, 90. Here, Panikkar acknowledges that the Christian doctrine of the resurrection of the body has become a symbol to him.

[54] R. Panikkar, *Blessed Simplicity*, 84.

[55] R. Panikkar, *Blessed Simplicity*, 84.

[56] R. Panikkar, "A Self-Critical Dialogue," 276.

[57] Cf., R. Panikkar, *A Dwelling Place for Wisdom*, 62.

[58] Cf., R. Panikkar, *The Cosmotheandric Experience*, 131.

[59] Cf., R. Panikkar, *The Cosmotheandric Experience*, 131.

[60] Cf., R. Panikkar, *A Dwelling Place for Wisdom*, 62.

[61] R. Panikkar, *TheCosmotheandric Experience*, 65.

[62] Cf. R. Panikkar, "Mysticism of Jesus the Christ," *Mysticism in aivism and Christianity*, ed., Bettina Ba mer (New Delhi:D.K. Printworld, 1997), 128-30.

[63] R. Panikkar, "Toward a Typology of Time and Temporality," *Philosophy East and West*, XXIV (April 1974), 161-64.

[64] R. Panikkar, *The Cosmotheandric Experience*, 142. Another term for time in the Vedic tradition is *āyus*, which means the vital force of being, the existential span or duration of every being.

[65] Cf., R. Panikkar, "The Law of *Karman* and the Historical Dimension of Man,"*Philosophy East and West*, XXII, no.1 (January 1972), 38.

[66] It seems to be similar to the Christian theology which says, "already,but not yet."

[67] Cf., R. Panikkar, "The Contemplative Mood: A Challenge to Modernity," *Cross Currents*, XXXIV (Fall 1981), 265. Panikkar's view encourages us to live reality in its fullness without desperation. Panikkar's view corresponds to the modern slogans like: "The best day is today," "The best moment is the present moment" etc.

[68] R. Panikkar, *Invisible Harmony*, 18.

[69] R. Panikkar, "Time and Sacrifice: The Sacrifice of Time and the Ritual of Modernity," *The Study of Time III: Proceedings of the Third Conference of the International Society for the Study of Time, Alpbach-Austria*, ed., J.T.Fraser (New York: Springer-Verlag, 1978), 702.

[70] R. Panikkar, *Worship and Secular Man* (London:Darton, Longman & Todd), 48.

[71] It seems that Panikkar also advocates for actions that will be useful for others instead of personal gain. For more, see Panikkar, "Samdhya, The Vedic Prayer" *Indian Theological Studies*, 14, no.1 (March 1977), 27-28.

[72] R. Panikkar, *Invisible Harmony*, 12.

[73] R. Panikkar, "The Contemplative Mood, A Challenge to Modernity," *Cross Currents*, XXXIV (1981), 264.

[74] R. Panikkar, *Invisible Harmony*, 8.

[75] R. Panikkar, "Philosophy as Life-Style," 93.The authenticity of Panikkar reveals more in the coming sentences: "The idea of becoming a political figure, a bishop, a general director, or something like that is not always unpleasant. It took years before I could even mention this. And I still suppress here a page of my original manuscript."

[76] Panikkar points out that in order to be authentic, it must originate from the deepest corners of *one's personal being*." For more see R. Panikkar, "Philosophy as Life-Style," 93.

[77] In this way, time has been redeemed, overcome or denied.

[78] R. Panikkar, *Invisible Harmony*, 8.

[79] R. Panikkar, "The Contemplative Mood", 267. As we have seen earlier, the idea of Panikkar has great affinity with existentialism and the philosophy of life.

[80] R. Panikkar, *The Cosmotheandric Experience*, 151.

[81] R. Panikkar, *A Dwelling Place for Wisdom*, 93.

[82] Cf. R. Panikkar, *A Dwelling Place for Wisdom*, 93.

Response

Prof Isaac Parakkal OIC in his article "Holistic and Advaitic Visionof Panikkar," brings out succinctly the cosmotheandric vision of Panikkar towards a new vision of being human.

Cosmotheandric Vision is a harmonious relationship that unites the Divine, human and cosmic reality. Raimundo Panikkar has developed this vision of reality with reference to the Christian Trinity, the non-dualism Vedanta Hindu *advaita*; and *radical relativity* of the Buddhist *pratītyasamutpāda*. Within human awareness, the *cosmotheandric* intuition is the undivided consciousness of the totality where the differences between them are affirmed and transcended. This awareness is an intimate and constitutive collaboration to construct Reality, to make history advance, to continue the process of creation.

The mystery of reality is never fully understood. if something of it can be understood, that understanding is incomplete. It is not just an epistemological problem but an ontological fact. 'Consciousness' relates not only to humans but to everything that is actually or potentially known. Within human experiences, Panikkar recognises aesthetic, intellectual and mystical dimensions. He says that the technocratic culture of today has forgotten the mystical realm. Being genuinely human involves the triad of all above three in correlation with matter, thought and freedom.

He identifies the integration of cosmotheandric reality to Christ. To understand Him and identify with Him we need a shift from the Book to the Word. Liberated by the Word we can have the human, cosmic, and divine dimensions of life being affirmed, reverenced, and brought into a deep harmony. The way in which the divine and conscious dimensions of reality are rooted in the world and its cosmic processes is called by Panikkar as 'sacred secularity.' As we see the relatedness and the united form of reality, it impels to present Dialogue as the Way of Life which alone can lead us to an integrating and all-inclusive Life.

Some relevant questions that may be raised are: How can one initiate this cosmotheandric vision within the (limited) frames of one's religion? How does this vision enable one as human being to have a dialogue within oneself? - **Joby Tharamangalam OP**

From Ecology to Ecosophy in the Context of Raimon Panikkar's Cosomotheandric Vision

Mathew E. P. SJ

Abstract

This essay highlights the ecological predicament and indicates certain aspects of ecosophy that Raimon Panikkar visualized within the wider horizon of Cosmotheandric vision. Panikkar was not very fond of the term ecology. Rather he introduced the term ecosophy. Panikkar believed that *eco-logy*, the science of ecology, will only affirm the attitude of exploitation of nature as a resource and strengthens the scientific and technocratic paradigm. The underlying belief is that ecology (oikos) will be controlled by human logos (rationality). The need of the hour is a vision that highlights the *Sophia* of the *Oike*. Panikkar's sense of ecosophy helps us to avoid 'monocultures of mind' and become truly intercultural.

Key Words

Ecosophy, planetary boundaries, age of ecology, cosmotheandric experience, humanum, organism, environment

The image of the planet earth from space is reproduced as a marvellous photo of a blue marble swirled around with white clouds. This marvellous image evokes a profound sense of the earth as a community of life. Astronauts who have seen this view in reality speak of its transforming power. Saudi Arabian astronaut Sultan bin Salman al-Saud, part of an international crew, recollected: "The first day we all pointed to our own countries. The third day we were pointing to our continents. By the fifth day, we were all aware of only one Earth." This wonderful narration echoes the required transformation of our vision that is badly needed more than ever.

This essay attempts to highlight the ecological predicament and to indicate certain aspects of ecosophy that Raimon Panikkar visualized within the wider horizon of Cosmotheandric vision.

The Age of Ecology

It is common knowledge that Ernst Haeckel coined the term in 1866. He defined it as the science of relations between organisms and their environment. Ecology examines how organisms interact with each other and their nonliving environment including factors such as sunlight, temperature, moisture, and the vital nutrients. Ecology views organisms in their context, life cycle, environment and their place in the cycle of energy use. The key word is interaction. Ecologists try to understand the interactions among organisms, populations, communities, ecosystems, and the ecosphere.

The present era is rightly christened as the age of ecology. In this new millennium a new consciousness of the earth is taking hold among people around the globe. Contemporary science has discovered new knowledge of earth's intricate working. Today, more than ever, we are aware of the age, the vast size and the complexity of the universe, the cosmic process that shape the universe, the astonishing complexity of the biological evolution, and the interconnectedness of all life-forms. Compared to the past, there is greater awareness of the natural world and the many different delicate and intricately interconnected cycles that have nurtured and sustained life for millions of years, giving fertile soil, clean water and a pure atmosphere. At the same time we are becoming aware of the fragility of the environment. The human practice of unchecked consumption, exploitative use of resources, and the increasing pollution all around are affecting the life support system of land, sea and air while leading host of other species to extreme distress and extinction. The life-sustaining mechanisms are breaking down day by day. In many places fresh water once teeming with life is dead, beautiful coasts have been turned into sewers; fertile soil lies barren or has turned into desert. Forests, often described as the lungs of the earth, are reduced to wasteland, and cities are choked with smog. Emissions of 'greenhouse gases' continue to affect the atmosphere in ways that threaten the balance of life on the planet. The climate change could severely disrupt the lives of all of humankind.

The ecological crisis that affects all of us goes beyond caste and creed, the sovereignties and national boundaries, the rich and the poor. Whether we like it or not, the human induced destruction of this blue planet is unprecedented in history. There have been very serious warning signs. We are bombarded with statistics. The Earth is warming faster than at any time in the past one thousand years. The level of carbon dioxide in the atmosphere has increased to such an extent that it is affecting the climatic patterns. The existing man made emissions of greenhouse gases leads to global warming. Warning signals of ecological crisis are experienced in terms of acid rain, pollutions of air and water, depletion of forests, vanishing of species and the consequent loss of biological diversity. We have the crossed planetary boundaries.[1]

Today, more than ever, there is a broad consensus that ecological issues cannot be treated simply as scientific, technological and political problems. On deeper analysis they raise fundamental questions about our values, the kind of beings we are, and the way our lives should be organized. Hence any response to ecological crisis has to be holistic indeed.

From Ecology to Ecosophy

Raimon Panikkar was not very fond of the term ecology. Rather he introduced the term ecosophy.[2] Panikkar's contention was that eco-logy, the science of ecology, reflects the attitude of exploitation of nature as a resource and strengthens the scientific and technocratic paradigm. The ecological consciousness arises from the realization that this planet earth is limited in many ways. Resources are running out or will run out in the future. So if a benign attitude of care for the earth is adopted it will continue to be shallow and not deep enough. The underlying idea remains the same, namely, one of control of nature. In other words, ecology (*oikos*) will be controlled by human logos (rationality).It affirms the triumph of a logic-dominated rationality. The need of the hour is a vision that highlights the *Sophia* of the *Oike* that will further the integrity and harmony of the one cosmic home that promotes an enlightened sense of interconnectedness. A vision based on ecosophy believes that a purely rational approach is not conducive to integral well-being.

As we attempt to further the understanding of Panikkar's thoughts, it is imperative that to highlight some aspects of his analysis of what he calls, "the Ecological Interlude."[3] According to him three main experiences seems to question the foundations of human self-understanding. The first, in his own words, "is the experience that the *humanum* seems to exclude the Earth."[4] The resources are not there forever and ever. The petro-dollar crisis of the seventies is a stark reminder. What is available is appropriated by a tiny minority. The gruesome exploitation and the imbalance have come to the level of unacceptable proportions. The second experience is the humanistic crisis which may be best expressed as the "myth of human progress." The fact is that in spite of all the advancements in technology and progress of rationality, irrationality seems to thrive. The human induced ecological crisis is simply not acceptable. The twentieth century has suffered two world wars. And may be one for the twenty-first century? Hence the humanistic crisis exposes the "myth of human progress." The following quote sums up the third crisis. "The God of history remains idle, the God of the philosophers is indifferent, and the God of Religion no longer seems very much concerned about the human condition."[5] The three-fold crisis "cannot be solved by partial reforms or half-measures." A new vision is needed which would go beyond fragmentation. According to Panikkar this new vision is embedded in Cosmotheandric experience. It is "the equally irreducible character of the divine, the human and the cosmic (freedom, consciousness and matter), so that reality--being one--cannot be reduced to a single principle."[6]

In what way can we identify the parameters of an ecosophy that emerges from cosmotheandric experience? In practical terms it may not lead us to any action-projects. It is obvious that its great value lies in identifying the crisis, best described in the section on Crisis of History.[7] It helps us to avoid the 'Monocultures of the Mind' and truly be intercultural. It is not calling us to go back to primitivism or to an idyllic society. The alternatives are between radical transformation and a catastrophe of cosmic proportion.

Conclusion

The age of ecology makes us aware of the environmental crisis. Deeper reflection reveals the dominant one-sided rationality, driven by techno-science. Quite often the solutions proposed reinforce the dominant worldview. Apparent reforms within the same paradigm tend to be tinkering with the system. Hence the need to move towards an ecosophy that accepts and respects the wisdom of the *oike*. Obviously this has to happen within cosomotheandric experience.

I began with the image of the astronaut. Let me close with the story of the Titanic. The Titanic is a story of technological hubris and decision-making disaster in the face of risk. It presents a parallel to our contemporary ecological situation. We have reached a stage where the iceberg warning has already happened! We have made the decision to double the speed to a Full Speed Ahead! A change of course would have been the ideal for the Titanic, but it did not happen. A change of course might be bad for us too. It will be bad business. We might have to slow down and in the process loose time. Nothing, not even the ultimate risk of the death of nature, can be allowed to hold back the triumphant progress of the ship of 'rational animals!'

Endnotes

[1] Planetary boundaries refer to the nine Earth System Processes which have boundaries. It deals with atmospheric ozone depletion, loss of biosphere integrity and many other similar facets of the environmental crisis that have crossed the boundaries. It was proposed in 2009 by a group of Earth system and environmental scientists from the Stockholm Resilience Centre. The group wanted to define a safe operating space for humanity. For further elaboration of the concept see the following web source: http://www.stockholmresilience.org/research/planetary-boundaries/planetary-boundaries/about-the-research/the-nine-planetary-boundaries.html

[2] Joseph Prabhu, *The Intercultural Challenge of Raimon Panikkar*, Maryknoll NY: Orbis Books, 1996, pp. 286-287.

[3] Raimon Panikkar, *The Cosmotheandric Experience*, Motilal Banarsidas, Delhi: pp. 38ff).

[4] *The Cosmotheandric Experience*, p. 38.

[5] *The Cosmotheandric Experience*, p. 38.

[6] The *Cosmotheandric Experience*, p. 121.

[7] The *Cosmotheandric Experience*, p. 118.

Response

First of all, we would like to thank Dr EP Mathew for the excellent presentation of the paper. Author could keep his claim that this essay is a modest attempt to highlight the ecological predicament and to indicate certain aspects of ecosophy that Raimon Panikkar visualized within wide horizon of Cosmotheandric vision. The presentation done by Dr Mathew can by perceived better through three parts:

In the first introductory part he establishes the singularity of the earth as a community of life. There is also a lament that Knowledge has not helped us to coordinate but to subordinate the universe which has done more harm to the world than good. At present these ecological issues have become not just an existential issue but an Extinction(al) issue.

Second part deals with the features of Ecology as a science. Ecology examines how organisms interact with each other and their non-living environment including factors such as sunlight, temperature, moisture and the vital nutrients. Ecologists try to understand the interactions among organisms, populations, communities, ecosystems and the ecosphere. The author argues for a holistic vision for ecological crisis.

In the third part Dr EP Mathew introduces Raimon Panikkar's Ecosophy as a new vision. According to Panikkar, Ecology as a science only affirm the attitude of exploitation of nature as a resource and strengthens the scientific and technocratic paradigm. Ecosophy is a vision that highlights the *sophia* of the *Oike* that will further the integrity and harmony of the one cosmic home that promotes and enlightened sense of interconnectedness. And this New vision is embedded in the Cosmotheandric experience.

Some pointers for discussion

1. It is true that there are human=made calamities in the nature that amplifies the ecological crisis. At the same time there are also occurrences where natural calamities are purely natural calamities (such as Okhi). How shall we respond to this dichotomy? Does Panikkar's perspective give any vibrations to those who seek a solution.

2. Panikkar's Ecosophy is a vision that highlights the '*sophia*' of the '*Oike*' that will further the integrity and harmony of the one cosmic home that promotes and enlightened sense of interconnectedness. How can we build a bridge between Panikkar's *Ecosophy* and the Catholic position of *Authentic Human Ecology* which can help restore "the original balance of creation between the human person and the entire universe."? -**Andrew Francis & Jiju Paul**

Ecology, a real life concern, tries to understand the interactions among organisms, populations, communities, ecosystems, and the ecosphere. Mathew E.P. summarily explains the main challenges faced by our ecosystem and attempt to present Raimon Panikkar's views on ecosophy which is embedded in the Cosmotheandric experience.

Contrary to the popular scientific approaches to ecological crisis, Raimon Panikkar preferred the term 'ecosophy' and believes that a purely rational approach is not conducive to integral well-being. He contends that eco-logy reflects an "attitude of exploitation of nature" and was "controlled by human logos (rationality)."

Panikkar's thoughts are elaborated in the idea called "the Ecological Interlude" which can be summarized into three main experiences of understanding human self. First, human greed culminating in gruesome and unacceptable exploitation of the cosmos; the second a perverted understanding of progress and unrecognized spread of irrationality; and the last is the arbitration of the idea of 'historical God,' 'philosophical God,' and the 'religious God.' He proposes a new vision to solve the ecological problems which is embed in Cosmotheandric experience.

The present day proposals for ecological solutions are dominantly one-sided, rational and driven by techno-science. We need a holistic response to ecological crisis rather than scientific, technological and political problems. Ecosophical perspectives that accepts and respects the wisdom of the *oike* would offer better ecological views if not the solutions per se.

Dr Mathew's presentation is suggestive as it calls for a change of course in dealing with the crisis challenging our common home, as Pope Francis would like to call our cosmos. -**Ivan Muthanatt MST**

Part - III
Cosmotheandric Experience:
Journeying Beyond

Cosmotheandrism and the Concept of Tempiternity: A Phenomenological Critique

Sebastian Velassery

Abstract

There are two opposing points of view with regard to time, which pertains to Parmenides and Heraclitus respectively. Parmenides maintained that ultimate physical reality is timeless; whereas the central doctrine of Heraclitus was that the world is the totality of events and not of things. The Stoics, who regarded the universe as a dynamic continuum, understand by the cosmic cycle that 'the Cosmos,' although subject to continual metabolism, never dies and that its immortality is only another expression of the infinite extension of time, so to say, the never ceasing succession of events.

Following Panikkar's understanding of time consciousness, the author invites to go beyond time understood mythically as in ideal pictures, nor religiously as a child of God, nor rationally as a meaning whole, nor programmatically from the results of his work; rather he is understood to be a product of time and history. Contemporary man, therefore, considers his existence as what remains wholly within the spheres of time and history. If we profess a radical, 'pure' finiteness and temporality, then all irrefutable truths as well as values and all ever-valid forms of life and absolute orders are lost. But despite their denial of such supra-temporal demands, existentialists nevertheless speak of eternal moments in the now of temporality. If we pursue the idea of the 'complete finiteness,' temporality and historicity of human existence to its limits, then the result is that we no longer have access to the absolute. But the fact that we have such accessibility with God, whatever form or way, radically emphasizes the idea that Cosmotheandric experience is an implicit reality of human life.

Keywords

Time-consciousness, Tempiternity, Eternity, Holistic Time, Heidegger and time.

There are two opposing points of view with regard to time, which pertains to Parmenides and Heraclitus respectively. Parmenides maintained that ultimate physical reality is timeless; whereas the central doctrine of Heraclitus was that the world is the totality of events and not of things. The Stoics, who regarded the universe as a dynamic continuum, understand by the cosmic cycle that 'the Cosmos,' although subject to continual metabolism, never dies and that its immortality is only another expression of the infinite extension of time, so to say, the never ceasing succession of events. Similarly, the ancient Atomists, notably the Epicureans, believed that worlds composed of the same indestructible elementary particles were continually being destroyed and re-created, seem to have regarded time in much the same way also. Thus, "throughout Greek thought (and likewise in other ancient Cosmologies for example Hindu Cosmology) time was regarded as essentially periodic, because the Universe was thought to be cyclic".[1] It makes sense to believe as, F. M. Cornford points out that the origin of the circular image of time is borrowed from the revolving year *'annus'*, which means 'the ring.' "The idea of a cyclic universe did not imply a truly cyclic view of time, but only the periodic repetition of the various states of the universe."[2] Then how do we consider time as linear rather than cyclic? The historians would say that it is because of 'the rise of Christianity with its central doctrine of crucifixion as a unique event in time was the cardinal factor causing man to think of time as linear progression rather than cyclic repetition.'

Time: Measure of Human Consciousness

The first philosophical theory of time inspired by Christian revelation was that of St. Augustine who rejected the traditional concept of a cyclic universe and maintained that time is the measure of human consciousness of the irreversible and unrepeatable rectilinear movement of history. As St. Augustine says: What, then, is time? If no one asks me, I know; but, if I want to explain it to a questioner, I do not know. Yet, I say with confidence I know that, if nothing passed away, there would be no past time; if nothing were coming, there would be no future time; and if nothing were existing, there would be no present time."[3] As St. Augustine confesses: "what is now plain and clear is that neither future nor past things are in existence, and that it is not correct to say that there are three periods of time: past present and future. Perhaps, it would be proper to say that there are three periods of time: the present of things past the present of things present, the present of things future. For, these three are in the soul and I do not see them elsewhere: the present of things past is memory; the present of things present is immediate vision; the present of future things is expectation. If we are permitted to say this, I see three periods of time and I admit there are three.[4]

Kant was essentially concerned with the question of the finitude or otherwise of the Universe in time and not of time itself. He assumed that different times as parts, or delimitation, of a single underlying time and that this single underlying time is unlimited. On the other hand, Henri Bergson, with the exception of Heraclitus, is perhaps the most outstanding philosopher defending the reality of time. According to him, time is the fundamental principle and the essence of the process. For him, reality is a continuous flow like a stream. It is a process through which runs a vital impulse (*Élan Vital*). What Bergson means by *durée* may be summed up as an "indivisible, irreversible continuity, heterogeneous qualitative multiplicity and a product of mental synthesis."[5] The successive parts of time interpenetrate and permeate one another. He writes "States of consciousness, even when successive, permeate one another in the simples, of them the whole soul can be reflected."[6] In this sense, it is true that everything requires time; nothing can be without a temporal reference and it is more especially so when we are talking of the evolutionary processes. Bergson under girds this idea when he says that: "the evolution of living being, like that of the embryo implies a continual reduction of duration, a persistence of the past in the present, and so an appearance, at least of organic memory."[7] According to him, time is a form obtained by a synthesis of conscious state of the self.

Reality as Non-Temporal

F. H. Bradley, on the other hand, represents a section of philosophers who deny reality to time, which has directly derived from his metaphysics. Time according to Bradley is one such appearance. Reality, according to him, is non-temporal. If reality is non-temporal, it does not reveal its nature of time, for time, ceases to be in the Absolute. Time is unreal according to McTaggart. To him, past, present and future are the properties of events and movements but these are characteristic features that we ascribe to events.

These considerations on time in the western philosophy imply that there have been predominantly three views with regard to the conception of time. According to the Idealists, time is wholly a figment of imagination. Pythagorean School and members of Eleatic school expounded the idealist view of time. The idealistic conception of time was rejected primarily because of the reason that if all change and becoming is only apparent, then the whole world around us must be only apparent as well. It was Plato who brought out a compromise on the idealist view by positing a true reality behind ordinary apparent reality. It is mainly in this moderate form that the idealist view on time existed. Spinoza and Kant upheld a view of this kind and in our present time, such a view is held by phenomenology, analytical philosophy and philosophy of science.

While the temporal idealist is by and large mathematically inclined, the temporal realist has more often shown a leaning towards physics and other natural sciences. Without change and movement, there would be nothing for the scientists to study; thus it is a wonder that he considers time as one of the prime realities. In this way we arrive at a third view of time i.e. the rational view. Leibnitz was the first to formulate explicitly such a view. He defines time as 'an order of successions'. According to him, time is nothing but the order of succession. Succession implies that one thing occurs after the other, which again implies that there is a relationship between phenomena (from which the concept of time is developed) and the relation of before – and –after or earlier – and – later. The essential differences among these conceptions of time may be further summarised as follows: According to the idealist view, time is nothing but a concept and, therefore, dependent on (human) consciousness. According to the realist view, time is a self-sufficing entity, which is not dependent on anything else. With regard to the relational view, time is a concept and is therefore dependent on consciousness, but at the same time it is a function of the events happening in nature. The Realists emphasize the idea that, there is no time without consciousness, but neither would there be time without events.

Time: Life Breath of Reality

If Greeks conceived of time as the life of being, classical India perceived time as the life breath of reality. Hence, Classical Indian philosophers contended that it is time that 'matures beings and encompasses things.' According to them, time is the

'Lord who works change in beings; time created earth; in time is consciousness' and in a more explicit way, 'in time is life' (prana).[8] In the earliest experience of the Vedic Indians, time was described as the actual existence of beings. Resultantly, the word *Kaala* which designates time appears (only once) in the Rig Veda that speaks of *ayu* or *ayus* which means the vital force, the time of life, the long life, the existential span or duration of every being.[9] Moreover, according to the Vedic Seers, time is born with sacrifice and it is by sacrifice that it is once again destroyed. This concept is rooted but on the intimate relation between worship and time and provide us with a key to the understandings of the central place of sacrifice and man's participation in the unfolding of time.[10] This is to suggest that time and reality belong together and the experience of time amounts to the experience of reality.

Moreover, the Indian world has had its own diverse approaches to time. The most important two works on time that emerged from the religio-philosophical matrices of Indian tradition is one version of Vedanta known as the Grammar philosophy stemming from Bhartrhari's *Vakyapadiya* and the other, Madhyamika branch of Buddhist philosophy, in Nagarjuna's *Mulamadhyamika-karika*. Bhartrhari's treatment of time is rather elaborate compared to Nagarjuna's. His treatment of time is found mostly in the first Kanda and in the topical section. He lists a number of views, which he rejects. Most important of all is *Vaisesika* view according to which time is a substance *(dravya)*. The Vijanavada understanding of time as the construct of the mind and the *Samkhya* understanding of it as a potentiality of the *gunas* are also described and rejected. According to Bhartrhari, time is the most important powers of Brahman, *Kaalasakti* or power of time is a creative power of *Kartrsakti*. Accordingly, *Bhartrhari* argues that time is a cooperative cause *(Sahakari-Karanam)* of everything. It is further stated that it is the operation of the machine called cosmos.

Time implies a certain persistence of the past and duration of the subject. We may call it memory or the mere awareness that the human subject is temporal in character in order to have the awareness of time. "Time is neither merely objective (time does not belong to objects only) nor purely subjective (time does not belong to subjects exclusively). Time 'in itself' is meaningless."[11] In other words, man lives time, as time is all pervading. There is no human subject without time consciousness. Everything is in its grips; not only humans, but also matter, sentient and non-sentient alike. Thus *Bhartrhari* says: Time is the matrix of all differentiation and everything suffers the bite of time.[12] On the other hand, salvation, liberation, enlightenment, divinisation, glorification, *nirvana, mukti,* etc. consist in escaping and passing beyond time, realizing that it brings to its fullness, so to say, transcending or annihilating it.

Summing up, it can be said that time cannot be abstracted from anything because everything, including consciousness, is temporal. "Time is an aspect of the real rather than an abstraction. It is a perspective under which we envision all things."[13] Under which aspect do we envisage things when we speak their temporal dimensions? This is a startling issue, which needs thorough exploration. In order to detect the temporality of objects, we have to detect as well the temporality of the human subject, for we do not know anything non-temporal. Time seems to stick to everything. Time and Being, philosophers say, belong together. That is to say that every being is temporal. If time is abstracted from being then can we say that we would abstract the being from the whole of

Being? Many traditions argue that the sublation of time is a passage to reach the Divine. Thus, it obviates the necessity to consider that the path to realization and the way to Reality consist in overcoming time. This is called *'Tempiternity'* by Raimundo Panikkar against temporality on the one hand and timelessness (eternity) on the other.

Panikkar and Tempiternal Experience of Time

According to Panikkar, our thinking about time necessarily presupposes a 'present' as we are incapable of perceiving the 'now' without the point of reference to the present. We may remember the past and even foresee the future only from the platform of a 'present'. Hence, Panikkar would say that this 'now' seems to reveal something more than what we anticipate. There is a novelty in all that we say as the 'present' that does not come from the past and which does not determine the future exhaustively. This is an aspect of freedom that we experience in the 'now' which may be called eternity or divinity by Panikkar. We may even say that such an eternity reveals itself temporally in the now. In other words, every temporal moment is sweating out eternity. Panikkar introduces a different term here as 'sacred secularity.'[14]

Sacred secularity is an expression used by Panikkar meaning thereby that reality is temporal, yet more than temporality. Now this 'more' is not a mere juxtaposition-as if eternity, for instance, would arrive 'after' time, or as if a supra-temporal being were temporal 'plus' something else- but eternity is built into the core of temporality.[15] In this sense, every temporal moment is a sacred moment. Every secular reality is a sacred reality. This is to imply that every divinity has to be measured within materiality. In other words, divinity is to be measured and discovered in the midst of matter. In a word, eternity and temporality, sacrality and secularity belong together. One is not without the other. This profound state of reality in the words of Panikkar is read thus: "modern man has killed an isolated and insular God, contemporary earth is killing a merciless and rapacious man and the gods seem to have deserted both man and cosmos. But having touched the bottom, we perceive signs of resurrection. At the root of the ecological sensibility, there is a mystical strain: at the bottom of man's self-understanding is a need for the infinite and non-understandable. And at the very heart of the divine is an urge for time, space and man."[16] The point is that sacred secularity is an expression that reality cannot be reduced just in temporality. This is to suggest that secular dimension of reality is more than this; every reality is sacredly secular but in a tempiternal fashion and also in Cosmotheandric mode. This Cosmotheandric mode is the transcendence of the divine which is to be discerned in terms of the transparenc of the world. In other words, divinity is to be sought in the core of the matter.

In order to prove the togetherness of eternity and temporality or sacrality and secularity, Panikkar takes recourse to the *Advaitic* intuition. When Panikkar says *Advaita*, he means that the subject and the object are not two, without being one, that the Divine and Cosmos and/ or the Human are not two, without being the same.[17] It is not falling into a contradiction because the nature of reality is polar, each being constitutive of the whole. *Tempiternity*, for Panikkar, then is the non-dualistic intuition of non-dual character of reality, which is temporal yet more than temporal. It is eternal and yet temporal. Temporality and eternity are two sides of the same coin. Panikkar says: I have created the word *tempiternity* to express that, which overcomes the scheme of time here and eternity later. I think that the entire reality is *tempiternal*, that is, temporal and eternal in one and the same time in a non-dualistic relation.[18]

Holistic Experience of Time

Whereas all animals live entirely in the here and now, man has gradually learned to transcend the limitation of the 'external present.' He becomes conscious of the future state through becoming aware of his own mortality. "Our conscious awareness of temporal phenomena involves psychological and sociological factors that overshadow the physiological. It depends on processes of mental organisation uniting thought and action. It is dominated by the tempo of our attention and are acquired by the process of learning."[19] If fragmented experiences of the human subject leads to the 'externalisation' of time where acceleration, repetition and thrust towards the future are predominant categories, then a holistic experience of time would imply the 'exteriorisation' of time which would make us cherish our temporality and live the present moment in all its intensity. As we have stated earlier, temporality is an essential dimension of man and reality. Yet, man or reality is not fully exhausted by temporality. It is in this sense that interiorization of time is not just a mere acceptance of our temporality; it consists in transcending time. Transcending time does not amount to its negation, rather, it points to the discovery of the other dimension of the temporal aspect of reality. It is through this discovery that we enter into interconnection and interrelation with the divine or eternal experience. That is why, Yajna (sacrifice) and similar things are performed in order to reach the fullness of ourselves, which consist in being temporal, but not exclusively temporal.[20] Panikkar has termed it as *"tempiternity"* to express the same holistic intuition, which basically attempts to overcome the dualistic scheme 'time now, eternity later.' *Tempiternity*, then, is the non-dualistic intuition of the non-dual character of reality, which is temporal and at the same time more than temporal, so to say, eternal. Temporality and eternity are two sides of the same coin. Panikkar's submission is that we can combine temporality and eternity in a non-dualistic experience that in every temporal kernel, there is at the same time an eternal kernel, not as something that lies beyond but as something, which is constitutive of human experience.

Paradox of Time and Eternity

The concept of eternity makes a significant difference in the consideration of a variety of issues in the philosophical literature and especially in philosophy of religion. Boethius coherently defines this concept and his definition runs as follows: "Eternity is the complete possession all at once of illimitable life."[21] There are four ingredients in this definition, which calls forth attention: (i) that anything that is eternal has life. (ii) The life of an eternal being cannot be limited. (iii) The concept of duration that emerges in the interpretation of illimitable life is the third ingredient and (iv) He conceives of an eternal entity as *atemporal*.

With the possible exception of Parmenides, none of the ancients or medieval philosophers who accepted eternity as a real, *atemporal* mode of existence denied the reality of time or suggested that all temporal experiences are illusory. In proposing the concept of eternity, such philosophers and Boethius in particular, had introduced two separate modes of real existence. Eternity is a mode of existence, which on Boethius' view, is neither reducible to time nor incompatible with the reality of time. Boethius introduced and developed the concept of eternity primarily to argue that divine omniscience is compatible with human freedom and he did so by demonstrating that omniscience on the part of an eternal entity need not involve knowledge.

The ancient Greek philosophers who developed the concept of eternity were using the word 'aeon' which corresponds to its original sense of the word 'duration'. It would not be out of keeping with the tradition that runs through Parmenides, Plato, Plotinus, St. Augustine, Boethius and St. Thomas Aquinas to claim that it is only the discovery of eternity that enables us to make use of words for duration, words such as permanence and persistence. The thought that originally stimulated the Greek development of the concept of eternity was apparently something like this: our experience of temporal duration gives an impression of permanence and persistence, whose analyses of time convinces an illusion or a distortion. But the concept of eternity finds its first detailed formation in Plato who makes use of it by working out the distinction between the realms of being and becoming and received in turn its fullest exposition in pagan antiquity of the works of Plotinus.

Coming back to the Cosmotheandrism of Panikkar, we would admit that the notion 'Cosmotheandric' is the irreducible dimensions of reality into three, so to say, cosmos, theos and anthropos., thereby means, earthly, divine and human. According to Panikkar, these three dimensions are not only interrelated but are interdependent. None of these dimensions can subsist without the other two. Panikkar explains thus: "The Cosmotheandric principle could be stated by saying that the divine, the human and the earthly-however we may prefer to call them-are the three irreducible dimensions which constitute the real, ie; any reality in as much as it is real. What this intuition emphasizes is that the three dimensions of reality are neither three modes of a monolithic undifferentiated reality, nor are they three modes of a monolithic undifferentiated reality, nor are they three elements of a pluralistic system. There is rather one, though intrinsically threefold, relation which expresses the ultimate constitution of reality. ..I am also stressing that this relationship is not only constitutive of the whole, but that it flashes forth, ever new and vital, in every spark of the real."[22] Panikkar's vision is that there is no reality without these three dimensions. That is to say that reality is reducible to three dimensions. This is again to state that there is no God without man and the world. And it implies also the idea that there is no man without his Gods and his subjective world.

The paradox of time and eternity exist for the destiny of both the world and of the human subject. Man is said to enter into the eternal life after death. But eternal and immortal life regarded from within and not objectified is essentially different in quality from the natural and even the supernatural existence. It is a spiritual life in which eternity is attained while still in time. If man's existence were wholly taken up into the spirit and transmuted into spiritual life so that the spiritual principle gained final possession of the natural elements of the body and the soul, then death as a natural fact would not take place at all. The transition to eternity would be accomplished without the event, which externally appears as death. Eternal life is revealed in time, it may unfold itself in every instant as an eternal present. Eternal life is not a future life, but life in the present. Therefore, it is a mistake to expect eternity in the future. Eternity and eternal life are a deliverance from time. In Heidegger's terminology, it means the cessation of 'anxiety,' which gives temporal form of existence.

For Heidegger, time and temporality are qualified and not conceived mechanically; they are, indeed the 'ground of being' so that 'transcendence is rooted in the essence of time'. Therefore, as Heidegger says in his preface to *Sein und Zeit*, time is to be defined as the possible horizon of the very understanding of being. 'Being finds its sense in temporality.' Time and decay govern all things. Through temporality, what he means is that we are not concerned with something that is simply there, but which cannot be eliminated. The most important point, however, is Heidegger's view that 'Dasein' can be accomplished only in temporality in so far as existence is always fulfilled in it. According to him, the present moment is capable of acquiring a timeless temporality and thus transcending itself in its full presence. Jaspers makes such a point thus: eternity and transitoriness meet in such a moment of time. In view of the fact of transitoriness that conditions human life, our most intimate concern should be to show forth the human his most precious moment. 'Never again' becomes the real value in life, and this is the reason that death, which denies permanency, cannot affect us. Man is supposed to be completely finite, and yet in this finiteness there is something transcending it as super-finite, yet remaining finite. Thus an attempt is made to introduce a temporal eternity into what is not eternal.

The term eternity is obviously ambiguous and vague. Originally, it was used to express the idea of eternal continuance as superiority to time, e.g. of the spiritual person, which, being a real person of intrinsic value,' does not perish. In this case it outlasts time and remains superior to time in its living consistency. Even Heidegger expresses a similar conception of infinity, when he poses the question whether finiteness is at all possible without the notion of infinity. If, as he says, we are prepared 'philosophically to construe' God's eternity – and

Heidegger is not prepared to do this- it would be suitable to use the term 'infinite temporality.' Thus Kierkegaard's religious-metaphysical attitude of encountering the eternal in the moment of time may mean the condensation of time in eternity, whereas Heidegger and Sartre admit that inner human existence can be freed from time only in the sense of oblivion of time. If human experience cannot transcend the framework of relative finiteness in the present situation and temporal dimension, then freedom from time remains subjective in character. Jaspers ascribes that the 'temporal is seized as the appearance of eternal being'. Thus eternity is felt in the sense of existential subjectivity and does not carry us into a sphere possessing a content, which would truly free us from the transitoriness of finite existence.

Conclusion

On a closer examination, it is understood that there is more than mere oblivion of time in the above sense of eternity. Panikkar, I am afraid, prefers to understand eternity in the sense of not merely oblivion of time but freedom from time and as the expression of timelessness. Time is set aside wherein we may fully realize a profound moment, without being able to affirm a supra-temporal content. In such an experience, man remains in temporality, but is bound to go beyond his temporal dimension. As distinct from such an understanding, eternity may also be described as a never-ending duration of an ever-finite world. Times goes on and on. Against this notion is the 'independence from time' in the notion of 'eternity' and its supra-sensual contents, which determine man's existence and action. This includes the idea of the achievement of the eternal values that are grounded in time but eternal and hence tempiternal. Temporality as such annihilates the promise of

Eternity, which time carries. But, tempiternity that Panikkar conceives is an eternity of constant passage, the stream of moments. It is a mixture of Heidegger and Jaspers governed and conditioned by Advaita. The real eternity of which time is the promise (in the language of *Samkhya and Vedanta, it is kutastanityata*) which is undelivered, while what is delivered is the mere eternity of passage. The failure of time to be what it promises to be and thus *Nagarjuna* asserts thus: "therefore, time does not exist."[23]

Man is no longer understood mythically as in ideal pictures, nor religiously as a child of God, nor rationally as a meaning whole, nor programmatically from the results of his work; rather he is understood to be a product of time and history. Contemporary man, therefore, considers his existence as what remains wholly within the spheres of time and history. If we profess a radical, 'pure' finiteness and temporality, then all irrefutable truths as well as values and all ever-valid forms of life and absolute orders are lost. But despite their denial of such supra-temporal demands, existentialists nevertheless speak of eternal moments in the now of temporality. If we pursue the idea of the 'complete finiteness,' temporality and historicity of human existence to its limits, then the result is that we no longer have access to the absolute. But the fact that we have such accessibility with God, whatever form or way, radically emphasizes the idea that Cosmotheandrism or Cosmotheandric experience is an implicit reality of human life.

Endnotes

[1] Whitrow, G.J. *The Natural Philosophy of Time*, Clarendon Press, Oxford, London 1984, p.26, footnotes.

[2] Ibid, 26. Footnote.

[3] Bourke, Vernon, J, (ed) *The Essential Augustine*, A Mentor Omega Book, Published by The New American Library, 1964, p.229.

[4] Ibid, 29.

[5] Bergson, Henri, *Time and Freewill*, Trans. F.L.Pogson, George Aeon and Unwin, London, 1950, p. 98.

[6] Ibid, 98.

[7] Bergson, Henri, *Creative Evolution* Trans. Arthur Mitchett, George Allese, Unwin London, 1954, p. 11.

[8] Cf. Panikkar, *Time and History in the Tradition of India: Kala and Karma*, Cultures and Time (Paris: The UNESCO Press, 1976), pp. 63-68.

[9] Rig Veda, X.42.9. Also cf. Panikkar, *The Vedic Experience: Mantramanjari. An Anthology of the Vedas for Modern Man and Contemporary Celebration*, Indian Edition. (Pondicherry: All India Books), pp. 216-24.

[10] Panikkar, Raymundo, "Time and Sacrifice- the sacrifice of time and the Ritual Modernity," *The Study of Time III*, eds. J.T.Fraser, N.Lawrence, D.Park, (Berlin 1978), pp. 683-725.

[11] Vatsyayan, Kapila (Edited), *Concept of time: Ancient & Modern*, Essay "Kaalasakti: The Power of time" by R. Panikkar, Sterling Publishers Pvt. Ltd., New Delhi, 1996, p. 24.

[12] Ibid, 21.

[13] Ibid, 24.

[14] Savari Raj, Anthony, "Towards A Trans-Historical Existence: Cross-cultural Reflections on Human Time-Consciousness" a paper read in the national seminar in Goa University, February 2004.

[15] Panikkar, Raimundo, "The End of History: The Three-fold Structure of Human Time-Consciousness". *Teilhard and the Unity of Knowledge*, (eds), King T.M. and James F. Salmon, (New York: Paulist Press, 1983) p.112.

[16] Panikkar, Raimundo, *Cosmotheandric Experience: Emerging Religious Consciousness*, Scott Eastham, edited with Introduction, New York: Orbis Books, p. 77.

[17] Savari Raj, Anthony, "The Radical Trinity" in *Crossing the Borders: Essays in Honour of Francis X. D'Sa*, Eds. Anand Amaladas, Rosario Rocha, (Chennai: Satya Nilayam Publications, 2001), pp. 179-92.

[18] Panikker, Raimundo, "Alternative a la Culture Moderne" Interculture 15 (October-December 1982), p. 25.

[19] Whitrow, G.J., *The Natural Philosophy of Time*, Clarendon Press, Oxford, London 1984, p. 373.

[20] Panikkar, Raimundo, *The Vedic Experience*, op.cit; pp.346-55.

[21] E. K. Rand, (Ed.) in H.F. Stewart, E. K. Rand and S.J. Tester, Boethius: *The Theological Tractates and the Consolation of Philosophy*, London, Heinemann, Cambridge, Mass: Harvard 1973.

[22] Panikkar, Raymundo, *The Cosmotheandric Experience: Emerging Religious Consciousness*, Scott Eastham, edited with Introduction, New York; Orbis books, 1993.

[23] Madhyamika' Sastram, p. 163.

Response

Human beings seem to have been gripped and strangled between the inalienable realties of 'here and now' and 'eternity'. The temporal and timeless, transient and permanent, ephemeral and eternal, are the conscious duel entities that humans experience in their mundane life which for philosophical genius is a serious problem to be reflected and resolved. 'Time' is a highly complex phenomenon without which no measurement of life-events could be possible. 'Tempiternity' is a philosophical fusion of 'time-eternity continuum' centred on which the author of this article, Sebastian Velassery, profoundly explains the Cosmotheandric vision of Panikkar. The future in the 'present' and the ever in the 'now' is to be the fundamental unit of existential experience of human beings.

Eternity reveals itself temporally in the now and every temporal moment is sweating out eternity. This is an aspect of freedom that we experience in the 'now' which may be called eternity or divinity by Panikkar. He calls this with a different term as 'Sacred secularity'. *Tempiternity*, for Panikkar, then is the non-dualistic intuition of non-dual character of reality. He believes that the entire reality is *tempiternal*, that is, temporal and eternal in one and the same time in a non-dualistic relation. The conscious and holistic intuition and experience of human beings can and will overcome the dualistic scheme 'time now, eternity later'.

'Cosmotheandric' concept of Panikkar is the irreducible dimensions of reality into three; cosmos, theos and anthropos. It is a blend of the earthly, divine and human. According to Panikkar, these three dimensions are not only interrelated but are interdependent and constitute the real. Although, humans are subject to the paradox of time and eternity, they are understood to be a product of time and history. Human beings remain in temporality, but are bound to go beyond his temporal dimension. In line with Heidegger's perception, i.e.

'transcendence is rooted in the essence of time', Panikkar accentuates that Eternal life is revealed in time, it may unfold itself in every instant as an eternal present. Eternal life is not a future life, but life in the present. And God cannot be without man and world. Thus the author vindicates, referring west and eastern philosophers cum Vedic reference in succinct manner that in Panikkar's 'Cosmotheandrism', there is an implicit reality of human life with a ray of Tempiternity. -**John Michael**

Violence and Peace: Construction and De-construction of Borders by Journeying with and beyond Raimon Panikkar

Johnson J. Puthenpurackal, OFM Cap

Abstract

The present study, based on Raimon Panikkar and some of the contemporary western thinkers, is a look at the phenomenon of 'violence' and 'peace' in terms of 'construction' and 'de-construction' of borders respectively. The first part of the study sheds light on human violence in terms of 'construction of borders' considered both ontologically and ontically; ontologically as creation of borders around one's being and one's having; and ontically as construction of divisions and rejection of pluralism. The second part clarifies peace in terms of cultural disarmament as the de-construction of borders. The study is concluded by making a note that violence is the result of human *decision and activity*, whereas peace is the result of human *disposition of receptivity*; violence is created, peace is received.

Keywords

Violence, peace, borders, construction, de-construction, pluralism, being, having, activity, receptivity.

1.   Introduction

In the context of a Seminar on Raimundo Panikkar, I am trying to give thought to two related notions, violence and peace, by thinking along with and beyond the thought of Panikkar. As the person and thought of Panikkar is widely characterized in terms such as: being beyond borders, widening the borders, breaking down the boundaries, cosmic thinking, etc.,[1]we look at the phenomena of 'violence' and 'peace' in terms of 'construction' and 'de-construction' of borders respectively. Basing ourselves on and thinking beyond Panikkar's thought-pattern, and taking inspiration from some of the contemporary western thinkers, we try to develop these notions. We consider these two notions together as they are closely related, although we do not believe that mere absence of 'violence' is tantamount to the presence of 'peace'; but we relate these notions in our reflective search through the medium of 'border' by referring to its presence and absence, in the sense of construction and deconstruction. We begin with the phenomenon of violence, and then proceed to that of peace; we shall wind up our study with some concluding reflections.

2.   The Phenomenon of Human Violence

'The human is a mystery, an enigma, a riddle!' This has been the general conception about the human. Despite the fact that the human has been subjected to scrutinizing analysis and thorough investigation from the perspectives of the various disciplines of knowledge, s/he continues to be a *mystery*! The 'human as a mystery' entrenches itself when we try to predicate *violence* with the humans. "Humans as violent..!!" Can the humans be considered as *violent*, just as they are considered as rational, ethical, relational, linguistic, sexual, temporal, etc.? Is *violence* one of the ontological characterizations of humans?

The phenomenon of violence among humans is as old as the humans themselves.[2] In spite of the fact that humans are gifted with reason and moral sense,[3] they have been involved in mortal combat and conflict down through the centuries. This *irrational* behaviour of the humans is again beyond the *rational* comprehension of the humans. Violence among the rational humans makes the humans still more mysterious! We make an attempt to take a philosophical look into this mysterious phenomenon of humans being violent.

2.1   Human- Vs. Animal-Violence

Does not violence exist among the non-human creatures? Are only the humans violent? Although violent actions exist among the non-humans, we are of the opinion that only humans are violent,sinceonly humans consciously and calculatively choose to be violent; the non-humans are violent not by choice but by instinct necessitated by situation. Among the non-human animals there is the tendency of 'holding the territory'–an area under the control of a pair or a group. Those who trespass into this territory are sure to be chased away, attacked, or even killed. The boundary of this controlled area is rather 'elastic'; the area becomes bigger or smaller according to the 'need' of those in control of the area. Thus 'holding the territory' is need-linked.[4] The 'need' is related to *breeding* and *feeding*–the two basic needs.[5] A protected area under one's control is needed for 'breeding'–for self-perpetuation by mating and protecting the mates and the young ones;it is also required for 'feeding'–for self-preservation and food.[6]

From what is presented above with regard to the violence among the non-humans we note that they enter into violence and fights, either when their basic needs are under threat or in view of meeting their basic needs. When it comes to the question of the humans, we have a different picture! Violence and wars among the humans are not very often need-related. But among the so called 'undeveloped *primitives*'[7] and the tribals too, violence is mostly need-linked, just as in the case of the animals. Such 'original' people too have an area under their control, and the 'size' of the area is related to the 'need' they have; and they too do not go out into another's area, unless threatened by the other, or necessitated by the growing 'needs' brought about by unforeseen natural calamities. But as the humans became more sophisticated and 'civilized,'[8] violence has not been any more *need*-linked, rather *greed*-linked.

Although our main focus of attention is on human violence, even in the violence of the non-humans we notice the presence of 'border': a border around the group (of animals, of birds, and even of the so-called primitives) is created according to the 'need,' and it is not kept enlarged without any sufficient need. The intruders are driven away, and they are not chased after beyond the borders, as the 'civilized' humans do.

Thus there is a great difference between the animal violence and human violence; we are baffled at the phenomenon of human violence, and ask ourselves as to how the humans have landed in such a situation. We take a philosophical look at this question, considering it in terms of 'borders.'

2.2 'Construction of Borders': Ontologically Considered

We look at 'Construction of Borders,' taking indirect inspiration[9] from Panikkar's thought. Insofar as 'construction of borders' is based on the very nature of human being, it is ontological; insofar as it is the result of human choice, it is ontical.[10] We carry out the ontological consideration by referring to the human tendency *of* being someone and of having *something*: human *pride* and *greed* respectively.

2.2.1 'Construction of Borders' around One's *Being*: Human Pride

The most important reason for human violence is to be found in human pride, which we characterize as the 'building up of a fortress or border around oneself, one's being, one's self.' We can find a philosophical reason behind this human tendency to create borders around one's self.

Western philosophy and culture, according to Heidegger, has been very much subject-centred. The process of 'objectifying' manifests itself even in the forms of manipulating and subjugating the object—the cosmos, the humans, the Divine. The powerful subject has control over the object. The apparently innocently begun intellectual domination grew in its intensity in the crude forms of control, manipulation and exploitation. Hence the ultimate 'reason' for human violence and fights can be traced back to the domineering character of human subjectivity with unbridled 'freedom.'[11] The attitude of domination began to show itself gradually in more and more crude and sophisticated forms of violence and wars.

According to Emmanuel Levinas, Western philosophy has been considering everything under the encompassing notion of Being, in its various guises, such as the One, the *Same* (*le Même*), the Totality, the there-is (*il y a*), etc., as a result of which the other-than-Being [Transcendence, exteriority, Infinity, the Other, alterity (*l'Autre*), etc.] was excluded. Such a philosophy of the *Same* is a celebration of the narcissism[12] of the ego, with over-emphasis on *autonomy* and individual freedom. The 'I' or the ego, in its totalizing tendency, looks at the other in terms of an economical relation of 'utility' and 'profit.'[13] Thus Levinas, through his characterization of Western philosophy as *totalizing* and *auto-nomous*, interprets the self as *desiring to be itself* by consolidating and expanding itself into the world of things and persons.

In this struggle to totalize everything into oneself, the 'things' may submit themselves; but difficulties arise with persons who too demonstrate the same totalizing tendencies. The ego-centrism of one subject collides with that of other subjects. The result is inevitable conflict![14] Everyone sees the others not as 'persons,' but as 'powers' to be conquered, giving rise to violence and wars. Thus the source of human violence consists in the totalizing tendency of the narcissistic subjectivity (Levinas), and/or in the domineering tendency of the metaphysical subjectivity (Heidegger). One's self (being, subjectivity, ego) becomes the most protected *sanctuary* of the human; one keeps it protected by creating, increasing and strengthening 'borders' around it.

But it is not only humans' never-ending desire *to be someone* (above everyone else) but also *to have something* (more than everybody else) that constantly provokes the humans to enter into violence and wars.

2.2.2 'Creation of Borders' around One's *Having*: Human Greed

The ego-centric subjectivity in its narcissistic drive tries to expand its circle of domination and totalization by appropriating as much as possible—by giving free vent to one's greed for possession. In the world of today, possession is valued in terms of money. The power of money has become today almost the only criterion of one's 'status' in the society.

Money[15] can be looked at in terms of Marcel's distinction between 'being' (être) and 'having' (*avoir*). 'Having' stands for the most fundamental relation that a human being has towards material things.[16] Although I can relate myself to other things various ways—using, admiring, consuming, destroying, etc.—I need first to *have* them for other uses, and money is a 'having' that is most commonly present; money is thus a having that is both *foundational* and *universal*. Although in principle the *having* externalizes the object of having, it does not succeed in that. "The self becomes incorporated in the thing possessed."[17] As a person increases his possessions, his being becomes more and more bound up with these possessions. Rightly does Marcel hold that "our possessions swallow us up."[18] The desire to possess is kept on constantly kindled that there seems to be no end to it! As the desire to have possessions has no limit, humans tend to acquire as much wealth as possible even by violence and bloodshed. Today's culture of globalization is a culture of 'having.' The 'reason' behind most of the violence and wars is nothing other than the craze to build up one's economic power.[19] Thus the desire of *having something* or the greed for amassing wealth is yet another 'why' of human violence.

It is to be specially noted that violence is necessitated not necessarily by genuinely 'objective' needs, but 'constructed'[20] needs, as it is evident from most of the wars. In the contemporary culture the meaning of 'need' is so redefined as to include what has been ordinarily understood as 'greed.' The 'boundary' around the meaning of *need* is not merely pushed wider today so as to include many more so-called 'needs' in the notion of *need*, but rather it is almost totally eliminated so as to interpret anything that one wants as one's need! The humans are kept ever unsatisfied by the creation of new needs,[21] and by converting greed into need. In other words, by presenting *greed* as *need*, a 'reason' is created for violence.

Thus after one's 'being' (self, ego, subjectivity), one's 'having' (money, possessions) becomes the most protected *sanctuary*, around which one builds up 'borders'—borders around 'me' and 'mine.' Insofar as one wants *to be higher* than and *to have more* than everyone else, one keeps on strengthening and widening these 'borders.'

2.3 'Construction of Borders': Ontically Considered

What has been clarified as the ontological 'why' of human violence—creation of borders around one's being and around one's having—becomes clear when we give thought to it in itsontic concreteness. The ontological tendency of creation of borders becomes a reality when it is ontically appropriated by one's *decision*, as a result of which violence is born. Our ontical consideration has two aspects that are related in a strange manner:on the one hand, humans keep on constructing and multiplying divisions among the humans based on borders of human construct; on the other hand, the very same humans are unprepared to accept the differences or pluralism, caused by borders.

2.3.1 Divisions of Human Construct

It is an undeniable fact that humanity consists of numerous groups and sub-groups with precise boundaries around them. Here we are forced to ask: 'were these various human groups already existing from the beginning, or did the human family get divided in the course of time? Are the various groups and divisions human-construct? If so, is there any philosophical *reason* as to why the humans keep on constructing divisions?

We can find some 'reason' in Western philosophy, which was born as *logology* with the great masters of Greek thought—Socrates, Plato and Aristotle—in response to the pre-Socratics' *mythological* way of philosophizing. According to them, philosophy has to be a science of logic (*logology*) with its accompanying characteristics of conceptual clarity and precision.[22] Thus for the last two millennia, Western metaphysical philosophy has been a triumphant march towards greater conceptual precision and clarity, which has its negative consequences. One of such consequences is the creation of borders. Conceptual philosophy, in giving precise definitions for a notion, has been entrenching the boundary around it. To define something means to place something within precise boundary. Thus every precision that is added to a notion, for instance the Christian notion of God, is an addition to the 'wall' that separates the Christian 'God' from other 'gods.' The distance between various religions is widened. Our contention here is only this: when the 'identity' of a group—be it political, linguistic, cultural, religious, economical, racial, or caste, etc—is clarified in legal and conceptual terms, a boundary is created around it.

How does the creation of boundaries contribute towards violence and conflicts? A strong affinity is created among those within the boundary, as a result of which those outside the boundary are looked at with suspicion. The situation becomes emotionally charged and the relation between 'our people' and 'other people' is prone to be very fragile; and conflicts and violence can easily break out without any provocation. The only 'reason' for most of the conflicts between ethnic, linguistic, political, cultural, religious, or caste groups is that 'they' do not belong to 'us'; 'they' are outside the boundary of ours!

The 'otherness' of the other is due to the fact that the other happens to be on the other side of the border, mostly constructed by the humans. Just because some happen to be born on the other side of our political territory, our caste-group, our religion, our race, …and finally around our individual selves and possessions, they become the 'others' for 'us' to be distanced from, and an unwarranted 'sacredness' is attached to such 'borders' of human construct: violence is the outcome![23]

2.3.2 Rejection of Pluralism

Humans create pluralism and divisions by multiplying borders, and they are also unwilling to accept and live with pluralism by their conscious choice, giving rise to violence. "Despite the culture of globalization trying to swallow up every *difference* under the 'umbrella' of the same—same culture, same economic system, same morality, etc....—the 'differents' have become more *different* today, and pluralism is more evidently manifest."[24] Thanks to the powerful and widespread media, everybody today is in the know of the reality of pluralism,[25] and postmodernism celebrates it.

Pluralism is not just an academic question about the One and the Many; it is an existential question as to how we have to live in the midst of variety of options. Although we can no longer live cut off from one another in our geographical boxes, economical capsules, cultural areas, racial ghettoes, religious sanctuaries, political castles, etc., many are not prepared to accept this reality; they reject pluralism! The rejection of pluralism is nothing but one's unwillingness to accept *the other as different*. Although pluralism has to be lived, in the words of Raimon Panikkar, by a 'dialogical tension' with the variety, the various human groups have been entering into 'dialectical conflict' with one another.[26] This gives rise to violence and conflicts. As humans become more 'civilized' with the culture of globalization, the dividing 'walls' between individuals and groups have in the least disappeared; rather they are made stronger and higher. The essence of civilization seems to consist in the exercise of power[27] over others in the form of violence. The 'global village' has brought about only 'uniformity,' and not a unity that accepts and respects the otherness of the other. Hence individuals and institutions, groups and nations look at one another with suspicion and distrust. In the words of Panikkar, "Our civilization is a civilization of armed reason. Our reason is no longer...wisdom or experience. It is experiment and power. Our reason makes conquerors of us...,"[28] convincing,[29] conquering every other who think and act 'otherwise.'

Thus, as humans, moved by their leaning to create borders around their 'persons' and 'possessions,' decide to create divisions and/or reject all divisions (pluralism), violence and conflict come about. In one's *proud* and *greedy* march forward, the human finds everyone else as a *rival*, as a hindrance to one's narcissistic existence. As the craze for power and possession is present in all spheres of life, individuals, institutions and nations enter into violent and inhuman means to realize this craze. Thus wars and conflicts among the humans are not a rare possibility, but a frequent factuality.

3.   The Phenomenon of Peace

Although violence is rampantly present among the humans, there have been attempts to create peace. Thus *war* and *peace* seem to have been coexisting in human history; but we find that as humans progress, they seem to keep on promoting both war and peace—more sophisticated war and more artificial peace! Raimon Panikkar makes a loud reflection on this question.[30] Taking inspiration from him we try to give expression to the phenomenon of peace.

3.1   The Philosophy of Peace in Panikkar's Vision

Panikkar presents an existential situation, in the background of which he thinks aloud on the philosophy of peace. When a war or a quarrel breaks out, everyone asks the question as to how it began; none asks as to how it can be ended. The *rational* animals look for the *reasons* for the occurrence of violence, and then try to restore peace by eliminating the causes—of course, by violence! Panikkar's *philosophy of peace* is unfolded in his reflective questioning of the above-given approach that has been prevalent in the civilized world. The genitive in 'philosophy *of* peace' can be taken as objective and as subjective, depending on whether 'peace' is taken as object or subject of philosophy. Peace as the subject, giving rise to philosophy, is very alien to Western thought which is regarded as "the hunt for truth with the rifle of reason."[31] From one's inner disposition of peace, philosophy has to emerge. When our soul is duly cultivated, and our spirit is harmoniously formed, then *philosophia pacis* arises. It is a philosophy that reflects the harmony of reality, and contributes towards it. Thus philosophy is the cause and the effect, the subject and object of peace—effect, as it arises from a calmed spirit; cause, since it increases the harmony of the universe. But Panikkar holds that peace has to be taken primarily as the *subject*. Hence he says that peace is not anything that the humans create or work out, but something that they receive. It is a matter of common experience that the struggle for peace has been generally a violent struggle—*creation* of peace by violence! Hence Panikkar finds that peace is neither given nor created, it is *received*.[32] Receptivity implies a 'feminine' attitude. But our civilization has relegated the feminine approach to a position of inferiority. In a culture that exalts the masculine attitude of giving, imposing, creating, etc., the feminine attitude of receiving has hardly any place.[33] Peace can come about only insofar as humans move along with the rhythm of being with openness and receptivity, qualified by sincerity; when the receptivity is diplomatic and hypocritical, one can have only a simulated peace.

After having proposed his basic approach to peace, Panikkar gives nine *Sūtras* on peace.[34] We present here only the important ones in a flow of thought. Peace is not the exclusive prerogative of the humans, and hence it consists in our participation in the rhythm of being. We are responsible for the rhythm of the universe. In cooperating with the universe, we enhance and transform it. Outer peace and inner peace are advaitically related; though they are different, they cannot be separated. Only persons of inner peace–like Christ and Gandhi–can work towards the outer peace. Peace is neither conquered for oneself, nor imposed on others; it is rather received and discovered. Peace is both *Gabe* and *Aufgabe*, gift and responsibility. As we receive the *gift* of peace, we have the *responsibility* to maintain and to enhance it. As popularly believed, victory never leads to peace. Victory is always victory over people, and not over evil. The conquered cannot enjoy the peace of the conquerors. Peace is possible only with *cultural disarmament*; we need to disarm ourselves of our cultural superiority. No one culture can claim to be the ideal for others to look up to, and to learn from. We need a cooperative venture, as "everybody has something, and nobody has everything."[35] The meaning of peace cannot be narrowed down to just one meaning with precise and definite boundary; the meaning of peace is ever emerging and growing. Hence rightly has Panikkar said that peace pertains to the order of *mythos*, and not of *logos*. As peace does not have a single meaning, we cannot impose our concept of peace on others. When a powerful group makes the powerless abide by one's terms and conditions, one is imposing one's limited notion of peace on the other. Here 'peace' that belongs to the open horizon of *mythos* is strangled into the confines of *logos*. Giving a religious tinge to the *sūtras* of peace, Panikkar says that genuine peace can be had, not by restitution and punishment, but by forgiveness and reconciliation supported by dialogue. Lost innocence calls for a new innocence;peace is not restoration of what was lost. Hence the only way to peace is a way 'ahead,' and not a way 'back'; and the way ahead is the way of reconciliation.

After having proposed the above-given thought as his philosophy of peace, Panikkar reaffirms that the problem of peace is not solved merely by having an efficient administration; it has to be received with one's whole being. Peace is not the mere absence of war, but an opportunity to devote ourselves to the cosmic order that includes the human order as well.

3.2 Peace through Cultural Disarmament: De-Construction of Borders

Panikkar proposes *cultural disarmament* as the fundamental condition for peace. He has coined the expression 'cultural disarmament' with the meaning 'depriving of the arm of culture.' Culture is taken here in the wider meaning that involves every aspect of human existence—religious, political, social, ethnic, moral, linguistic, etc. Culture in this wide sense can be used as a weapon against the other. By cultural disarmament we defuse the weapon of culture, which is used to be imposed on others. Preparedness to rid ourselves of the presumption of 'superiority'–which is same as cultural disarmament–is the condition for all other types of disarmaments. Such disarmament is necessary for the establishment of dialogue on an equal footing with other cultures of the earth. Cultural disarmament alludes to a radical change in the predominant myth of contemporary humanity–the powerful and vociferous humanity. The feeling of 'superiority' and cultural colonialism are to be done away with. In order to have peace, one needs to consider every other at least as equals, if not higher than oneself.

What is referred to by cultural disarmament is nothing other than deconstruction of borders. We prefer to use the term 'deconstruction'—a term coined by Derrida—rather than destruction or elimination of borders; the reason will gradually be clarified. When one is armed with one's culture—religion, caste, nation, ethnic group, etc—one builds up and strengthens a wall of border around it. The desire and arrogance of *being someone* (with one's cultural specificities) above everyone else makes one look down upon others with contempt and hatred. It is nothing but human pride that makes one presume that one's culture, religion, morality, outlook, understanding and knowledge is superior to that of others. In order to keep oneself superior, one tries to keep others 'inferior' even by inhuman and violent means. This is the reason why Panikkar proposes cultural disarmament as the fundamental condition for peace; and he reiterates this thought more clearly—a thought that respects unity and uniqueness of the varieties—through notions such as cosmotheandrism, interculturality, religious pluralism, sacred secularity, cosmic confidence, rhythm of being, inter-independence, mutual fecundation, ontonomy, tempiternity, etc. Here we have the 'reason' for our preference of the term 'de-construction.' As this term is coined with the help of the negative prefix, it does not have the logically opposite meaning of 'destruction,' but rather it points to the supra-logical situation of construction and destruction.[36] In deconstructing the borders around oneself, one is united with others without ceasing to be oneself: unity and uniqueness.

It is in incorporating the whole cosmos by breaking open the various concentric circles of borders—borders of caste and creed, nation and language, human and nature—that we become cosmic persons in the cosmic home. In this cosmic situation of borderlessness, we experience peace with everybody and everything—the paradise-situation of perfect peace and reconciliation. The situation of cosmic home is a situation of harmony[37] and freedom in humans' open disposition of receptivity, and it is brought about as a result of the de-construction of borders of various kinds—'cultural disarmament,' in the language of Panikkar. Peace is nothing but such a situation of harmony and freedom.

Harmony is 'balance'—everything has its place, and thus everything should be integrated; nothing can be discarded, as everything has its place. Harmony implies harmony between the inner and the outer, the bodily and the spiritual, the natural and the cultural, the masculine and the feminine—an *advaitic* relation[38] of unity and uniqueness. Harmony is so encompassing that it embraces all dimensions of reality, even the so-called good and evil.[39] Harmony implies not only a *coincidentia oppositorum* but also a space in which there is room for all, without unitary reductionism. Without such a harmony there cannot be any peace. Harmony embraces the subject and the object, the knower and the known. Harmony by its very nature belongs to the ultimate structure of the universe; the whole cosmos is harmonious. Peace has to be found in the harmony of reality, in which humans too find peace. When 'harmony'—of individuals and societies, of nature and cosmos—is disturbed, peace too disappears! Aurobindo has rightly said: "All problems of existence are essentially problems of harmony."[40]

Freedom, insofar as it includes the freedom of nature, of the individuals, of the society, of the state, of the non-human animals, and of the cosmos, is closely related to harmony, and thus to peace. Ordinarily freedom is taken as the 'freedom of choice'—a choice made by the human subject. To be able to choose this or that thing from the supermarket or to vote for this or that candidate, is a very relative freedom, since the spectrum of choice is limited to what the supply offers. Human freedom consists in one's ability to be what one is, along with every other person and thing in the cosmos. In such an approach there cannot be 'conflict of freedoms,' as everyone and everything has its uniqueness and harmonious unity. Such a situation of harmony and freedom is peace. Where *ontonomy*—unity and uniqueness—of everything is accepted, where freedom of everyone and everything is respected, there exists peace. Hence an imposed peace that cares little for freedom is no peace.

Conclusion

We have made a reflective journey through the phenomena of violence and of peace; violence was philosophically considered, contrasting it to peace through the medium of 'borders': construction and de-construction. Although both violence and peace are not negative phenomena, there exists a difference between them: violence is the result of human *decision and activity*, whereas peace is the result of human *disposition of receptivity*; violence is created, peace is received. Although the approaches that we take to violence and peace are different, it is not without reason that we have considered them together in this study. Violence and peace cannot go together; at the same time, absence of one does not imply the presence of the other. Peace is not a negative phenomenon that comes about wherever there is the absence of violence. Only outer peace, and not the inner peace, can be destroyed by violence.

Thus, although violence and peace are closely related, there is no necessary relation between them.

As we are living in the technocratic world of today, we are condemned to live with more sophisticated violence and more artificial peace. As everything is calculable and within human control, we live and move and have our being in an artificial world, where peace too comes out as prefabricated and fake. The powerful impose *order* and determine what peace is. Modern science, armed with reason, is violent, making us conquerors by con-vincing (*cum+vincere*) others rationally.[41] With this conquering approach peace can hardly be reached. Einstein has said: "With the splitting of the atom, everything has been changed except the way we think."[42] The *culture of certitude* started by Descartes has led to the *civilization of security*.[43] To live in insecurity and uncertainty is intolerable for rationality. It is better to place our trust in reality than in our powerful 'betters' that we claim to be. We need, hence, to disarm ourselves from the wishful thinking that the *civilization of security* is capable of establishing peace, which is not reached by a treaty, just as love with a decree. Only reconciliation leads to peace. In true reconciliation there are neither victors nor vanquished. All come out winners because the whole, of which we are parts, is respected. Reconciliation is achieved through dialogical dialogue. The problem is not with the enemy, but with one's not being able to deal with them. We need to have the wisdom for such dialogue that transforms destructive tensions into creative polarities.

Endnotes

[1] The title for the Commemorative Volume on Panikkar is thoughtfully given, *Raimon Panikkar, Being Beyond Borders: A Commemorative Volume* (Bangalore: Asian Trading Corporation, 2012). This edited volume

contains several studies, most of which refer to the 'cosmic' dimension of his thinking.

[2] Almost all the religions teach that from the beginning of human creation they turned out to be persons in conflict with one another. According to the Bible the killing of Abel by Cain was the beginning of a long stretch of violence and wars among the humans.

[3] According to the Greek myth of creation, the human creation took place in three stages, and only at the last stage humans were endowed with the gift of 'moral sense.' This was intended to make the humans live in peace and harmony. But, in spite of all these, are the humans better adjustable and peaceful, than the animals that do not have the 'moral sense'?

[4] Cf. W.H. Thorpe, *Animal Nature and Human Nature* (London: Methuen & Co. Ltd., 1974), 250ff.

[5] We do not find animals killing other creatures just for the 'fun' of it; once their need is met, they are not interested in hunting after creatures and in killing them. But the humans are in this respect totally different.

[6] Cf. Johnson Puthenpurackal, "Humans as Violent: A Philosophical Look," in *Violence and Its Victims: A Challenge to Philosophizing in the Indian Context*, ed., Ivo Coelho, (Bangalore: Asian Trading Corporation, 2010), 22. It is generally observed that the animals do not go out of their 'area' either in search of food or in search of mates. So the 'fights' occur ordinarily within their assumed area of control.

[7] We do not use the expression 'primitives' not in the pejorative sense of 'uncivilized and crude' people, but rather in the positive sense of 'those people uncontaminated by the modern sophistication and impersonality.' It is our conviction that such persons are more 'genuinely human' than the so called 'civilized' people.

[8] We are using the term 'civilized' here in the pejorative sense of 'being contaminated by non-human characteristics.' For a study on civilization as different from culture, cf., Johnson Puthenpurackal, "Culture and Civilization: A Philosophical Probe into Their Relation," in *Religion and Culture: A Multicultural Discussion* (Festschrift in Honour of Francis X. D'Sa, SJ), ed., Clemens Mendonca & Berd Jochen Hilberath (Pune: Institute for the Study of Religion, 2011), 5-16.

[9] We use the expression 'indirect inspiration' for the following reason: Panikkar refers in his writings to 'eliminating the borders' and 'bringing down the borders' while speaking of peace, harmony, etc. If peace is

the result of elimination of borders, then violence must be the result of the creation of borders.

¹⁰ The distinction between 'ontological' and 'ontical' is of importance. *Ontological* refers to the Being (*Sein*) of something, whereas *ontical* refers to something as an entity (*Seiendes*). Thus the ontological 'why' of human violence is to be found in the very Being of the humans. But the ontical 'why' may be found in the individual persons.

¹¹ Freedom as understood in such a tradition is a freedom of choice, which does not respect others' freedom. One is concerned only about one's own *freedom* even at the neglect of that of others. When the powerful enter into mortal combat with the powerless, the freedom of the *one* is protected, of the *other* is destroyed!

¹² The term 'narcissism' is coined by Freud, basing himself on the Greek myth of Narcissus (or Narkisos), according to which the attractive young man became so enamoured with his reflection in water, that he fell in love with himself. Thus narcissism stands for self-love.

¹³ Heidegger has made a masterly interpretation of the modern technology in terms of Western metaphysical tendency of 'intellectual domination' becoming 'physical manipulation' of reality. For a more detailed study of Heidegger's critique of Western thought and technology, cf., Johnson Puthenpurackal, *Heidegger Through Authentic Totality to Total Authenticity: A Unitary Approach to His Thought in Its Two Phases* (Louvain: Leuven University Press, 1987), 112-16, 120-31; Idem, "Technology to Ecology: Provocation to Evocation: A Probe into Heidegger's Thought," in *Call to Evangelization: The Franciscan Response in the Socio-Ecological Context of India*, ed., J.J.Puthenpurackal (Janampet: ICRF, 1997), 108-27.

¹⁴ In his explanation of conflict, Levinas must have been influenced by Sartre, according to whom every subject tries to reduce the other to an object by his hateful stare. The result is mutual enslavement and conflict.

¹⁵ For a philosophical consideration of the phenomenon of money, cf., Georg Simmel, *The Philosophy of Money*, trans., T. Bottomore & D. Frisby (London: Routledge, 1990); Johnson Puthenpurackal, "The Phenomenon of Money: A Philosophical Look," in *Truth, Power, Money: A Postmodern Reading*, ed., Stanislaus Swamikannu (Bangalore: Asian Trading Corp., 2004), 77-91.

¹⁶ It must be noted that one can have a relation of 'having' even to other humans, in which case they are seen and used as any other material object.

[17] G. Marcel, *Being and Having* (Dacre Press, 1949), 148.

[18] Ibid.

[19] The attack by the U.S. on Iraq is purely motivated by the desire to have control over the oil-wealth in Iraq. But, since this reason is not 'presentable' in the civilized world, some other reasons are cooked up and presented for public consumption.

[20] In the phenomenological sense, objectivity is constituted in and by the experiencing subject. But we use the expression 'constructed' not in the phenomenological sense, but in the sense of 'creating, cooking up, etc.'

[21] It is the need of the market economy to keep the people in need of satisfaction, or unsatisfied; and they promise to sell satisfaction; but in fact, we buy from the market, not satisfaction, but dissatisfaction, since new needs are created and we are kept 'unsatisfied,' as we apparently satisfy the present needs.

[22] We base ourselves here on Heidegger's critique of Western metaphysics. For a detailed presentation of it, cf., J.J. Puthenpurackal, *Heidegger: Through Authentic Totality to Total Authenticity*, 120-31.

[23] The present study is partly based on another study carried out by the present author. Cf., Johnson Puthenpurackal, "Humans as Violent: A Philosophical Look," in *Violence and Its Victims: A Challenge to Philosophizing in the Indian Context*, 19-38.

[24] Johnson Puthenpurackal, ed., *Pluralism of Pluralism: A Pluralistic Probe into Philosophizing* (Bangalore: Asian Trading Corporation, 2006), 7.

[25] The different ways of thinking and acting in different parts of the world are made public by the powerful media of today. But it must be noted that the differences are presented as something to be looked down upon and overcome.

[26] Raimon Panikkar, *Invisible Harmony: Essays on Contemplation and Responsibility* (Minneapolis: Fortress Press, 1995), 77.

[27] R. Panikkar quotes Lewis Mumford in his *Cultural Disarmament: The Way to Peace* (Kentucky: John Knox Press, 1995), 82.

[28] R. Panikkar, *Cultural Disarmament*, 88.

[29] 'Vincere' in Latin means 'to conquer.' Panikkar exploits this root-meaning in the English term: to con-vince.

[30] Although his reflections on peace are scattered in the different books of his, they receive some shape in his *Cultural Disarmament: The way to Peace;* our study is largely based on this book.

[31] Ibid., 13.

[32] The expressions, 'creation of peace' and 'giving of peace' have a masculine tone of subject, carrying out activity on the object. The philosophy and/or culture of the West has been one of subject asserting itself; and this assertion grew in its intensity, making it a violent one. Cf. Johnson Puthenpurackal, "Humans as Violent: A Philosophical look," in *Violence and Its Victims: A Challenge to Philosophizing in the Indian Context*," ed., Ivo Coelho(Bangalore: Asian Trading Corporation, 2010), 24-28.

[33] The Western gesture of greeting with a handshake has replaced the more Eastern gestures of embrace, kiss, deep bow, *añjali*, etc. Both the gestures are totally different in their inner meaning. Although they are used to greet a person, shaking hand has a meaning of 'giving,' and embracing has a meaning of 'receiving.' It is a small indication as to how the 'feminine' is replaced by the 'masculine' in every aspect of the contemporary humans.

[34] Panikkar, *Cultural Disarmament: The Way to Peace*, 15- 23.

[35] Johnson Puthenpurackal, "Complementarity," in *ACPI Encyclopedia of Philosophy* (Bangalore: Asian Trading Corporation, 2010), 306.

[36] The present author has made a study on the special meaning that the terms with negative prefix can have. Cf., Johnson Puthenpurackal, "Advaita and Aletheia: An East-West Parallel." In *Studies in Vedanta: Essays in Honour of Professor S.S. Rama Rao Pappu* (15th International Congress of Vedanta; Andhra University, Visakhapatnam), 199-211 (New Delhi: D. K. Printworld, 2006).

[37] The notion of *rta* in Indian thought is almost equivalent to that of 'harmony.' Cf., Antony Mookenthottam, *"rta,"* in *ACPI Encyclopedia of Philosophy* (Bangalore: Asian Trading Corporation, 2010), 1203-06.

[38] Panikkar uses this expression very frequently in his thought to refer to a non-metaphysical relation that transcends identity and difference, unity and uniqueness.

[39] Contemporary Western philosophy has begun to transcend the either/or dichotomy of good and evil, sacred and profane, beautiful and ugly, true and false, etc.

[40] Aurobindo, *The Life Divine* (Pondicherry: Aurobindo Ashram Press, 1955), 1:2.

[41] Panikkar exploits the etymological meaning of 'convince' (*cum* + *vincere* = to conquer with) to suit the meaning he wants to convey. Panikkar, *Cultural Disarmament*, 88.

[42] As quoted by Panikkar, *Cultural Disarmament*, 95.

[43] Ibid., 96.

Responses

The construction and deconstruction of the phenomenon of violence and peace by Johnson Puthenpurackal is deep, highly philosophical, thought provoking, logical and unique. It can appeal both to intellectuals and ordinary people both in content and style.

The author begins the analysis from the enigma of human existence. Humans, in spite of being gifted with rationality and morality, have been involved in irrational behavior and violence. For the non-humans, their instinctual violence is to protect their basic needs: breeding and feeding; therefore, they demark their boundaries. But for the civilized humans, demarcation is greed-based. Panikkar speaks about 'eliminating borders' and 'bringing down the borders,' while responding to establish peace and harmony. Taking this as a point of departure, the author constructs the border of violence from ontology. This tendency of violence is borne of human greed and pride: from 'having something,' and 'being someone.' Further, he says pride enlarges borders. Domineering culture leads to narcissistic tendency of ego and looks at the other as utility and profit resulting in treating the other to be conquered or possessed. Today, possession is valued in terms of money and status in the society.

Violence is necessitated by constructed needs and not by genuine needs, and needs are redefined in terms of greed. On the one hand humans keep on constructing and multiplying division, and not ready to accept pluralism on the other hand, leading to a 'dialogical tension.' Further, the emphasis on precision and clarity due to the shift from mythology to logology leads to the creation of boundary. Within the group there is a strong affinity, but same group looks at the other with suspicion. This leads to violence.

The phenomenon of peace is a subjective enterprise, one's inner disposition, harmony of self with other or participation in the rhythm of being. Peace is not created but received. It is a gift. As a gift it entails responsibility. Peace is achieved by 'cultural disarmament,' i.e., by discarding one's cultural superiority or by treating every culture as complementary. Genuine peace can be experienced through forgiveness and reconciliation. Accepting the other makes the culture borderless; the human a cosmic person; and the world a cosmic home.

The wealth and resources accumulated by some of the Indians are enough to cater to the basic needs of the country, and even more. But the greed of 'having more,' of these select few, keeps the overall citizens underprivileged. This is true of certain multinational companies eating up small-scale industries, agricultural, and natural resources. Leaders are becoming more power-crazy and thus are unable to see, listen and sense the plight of the primitives, minorities and marginalized.

Religions and their custodians who are meant to bind (*re-ligare*) are becoming instruments of commerce and trade. Sacred scriptures, traditions and history are tampered to contain vested interests. The need of the hour is 'disarmament,' of that which enslaves. Our journey of mythology to logology needs to be reversed. Yet, peace and harmony is possible!? Should we accept peace and violence as an enigma, and try to live as is encountered or continue forgiving seventy times seven? How far a victim can suffer violence or how far is the suffering justified?
--Raju Felix Crasta

Privileged am I to stand here filled with admiration for the product of your philosophizing Rev. Dr. Johnson Puthenpurackal, to give a response to this thoughtful and well-studied work of yours and to seek for some clarification.

Violence and peace

These are not only the puzzles of the minds of philosophers and other scholars but also are the major concerns of every ordinary human person in today's sophisticated modern world. Your study has indeed given us a glimpse into the cause and nature of these two common yet complicated realities.

Violence: why is it there at all in spite of the fact that none loves it? Certainly, you have given us the truth as you presented that it is due to the desire of man **to be something** and **to have something** representing his pride and greed respectively.

Well, it is true that man's desire has grown to include in the term 'need' what was earlier considered greed.

Creating borders for oneself is one of the most contributing enhancers for human violence. Humans cannot but consider the otherness of the other as outside one's own boundary.

Peace

We all want to have it but none has it. Where is it? Hardly anyone knows it. But your presentation has nurtured our minds to analyze it.

When 'harmony' of individuals and societies, of nature and cosmos is disturbed, peace too disappears! Because, peace is where harmony is.

In order to have peace, one needs to consider every other at least as equals, if not higher than oneself. This calls us to respect the otherness of the other in spite of the fact that he is outside my boundary. Where unity and uniqueness of everything is accepted, where freedom of everyone and everything is respected, **there exists peace.**

The thought of Panikkar which says that genuine peace can be had by **forgiveness and reconciliation** supported by dialogue, is something that exalts the uniqueness of human person – **a concept worthy of us-humans alone.**

Some questions may be helpful

1. Is violence of humans a property of his rationality or why can't we explain it in terms of his own instinctual response to his surrounding?

2. Humans construct borders and consider those outside of it to be others. Is it not a commonality in nature among animals as already you mentioned, and are we also not rational **animals**?

3. If my rationality is what causes me to be more violent than animals then is my rationality a blessing or a curse to the humanity?

4. Is it not true that our tendency to have something and to be something has helped us to progress? Certainly, we would not have been what we are today if things were different. Would have we been?

5. Is disarmament possible at all in today's world? Of course, I have no difficulty in accepting that disarmament leads to peace. You said violence and wars are part of nature and we are not outside this nature. Therefore, I feel your call for disarming is a call to move out of our nature itself. --**George Bush**

Cosmotheandric Vision: Critique of Modernity and Some Prejudices

M. George Joseph

Abstract

It is an urgent and inevitable call to the members of the modern society to rethink of and restrain from their eccentric intervention in the normal functioning of the universe that has fragmented, displaced, disoriented and destabilized the *cosmotheandric* relations. In the midst of our desperation with the present world, Panikkar reminds us of our past glory of living together in the nature which we were not aware of then, but now re-buildable with the conscious attitudinal change "to gather the scattered fragments, even if they are only crumbs."[1] The tripartite division of the book *The Cosmotheandric Experience*, twice, describes the three human attitudes in relation to three time-consciousnesses. The ecumenic, primitive, archaic, mythic, nonhistiorical and pre-historical are of one kind. The economic, historical, rational, scientific, modern, futuristic, utopian and ideologies are of the second type. *Cosmotheandric*, catholic, transhistorical, present, kairological, new innocence, new cosmology, mystical, etc are the third type, which Panikkar advocates. In the search for such a spirituality, Panikkar could have modelled his philosophy after pluralistic realism of Buddhism instead of non dualistic idealism of Advaita.

Keywords

Lost innocence, New Innocence, Ecological metabolism, Sthithaprajna, Trans-rational, Cosmotheandric spirituality, Advaita.

Raimon Panikkar, through his classic *The Cosmotheandric Experience,* invites
the contemporary Man to experience "the totally integrated intuition of the
seamless fabric of the entire reality: *the cosmotheandric vision.*"[2]It is an urgent
and inevitable call to the members of the modern society to rethink of and
restrain from their eccentric intervention in the normal functioning of the
universe that has fragmented, displaced, disoriented and destabilized the
cosmotheandric relations. In the midst of desperation, Panikkar reminds us
of our past glory of living together in the nature which we were not aware
of then, but now re-buildable with the conscious attitudinal change "to
gather the scattered fragments, even if they are only crumbs."[3] The tripartite
division of the book *The Cosmotheandric Experience,* twice, describes the three
human attitudes in relation to three time-consciousnesses. The ecumenic,
primitive, archaic, mythic, nonhistiorical, pre-historical etc are of one kind.
The economic, historical, rational, scientific, **modern**, futuristic, utopian and
ideologies are of the second type.*Cosmotheandric*, Catholic, transhistorical,
present, kairological, new innocence, new cosmology, mystical, etc are the
third type. The first type was simply a living of *cosmotheandric*, harmonious
life without articulating or judging the condition of their experience. It
is a life that millions of people still live and enjoy. For many who have
passed through the first or live in the second stage of experience, it is a
nostalgic invitation: a call to the mythical tradition. The second type is a
dominant mode of life, defining meaning and dictating relations. Panikkar
is uncomfortable with the destructive greatness of the modern and criticizes
the insensitivity of the modern man.The third type is a critical rethinking
on the second, inspired by the first, and a visualization of the *cosmotheandric*
experience of integral coexistence of plural individual units without losing
their uniqueness.

Future Shock

Human is the only being that spoils the present for the sake
of future. And the same recurs when the future becomes the
present. Alvin Toffler described future shock as the disease of
change. Its symptoms are already here. It is no longer a distantly
potential danger.[4] It began with rapid industrial development
and overproduction. "… until now (the period of modernity)
not a single historical regime has pervaded the four corners of
the world… But science and technology are on the brink of

penetrating everywhere, and the pan economic ideology is more and more becoming the only system of "communication." ... We are fast heading toward one single System,"[5] Modernism is the most influential philosophical, socio-cultural, political and economic tradition in the history. It pervaded globally, penetrated deeply into all cultures and societies, altered social, cultural, political and economic laws and practices and made the world totally new in every respect. Modernism was critical of the European medieval traditions and overcame them with new thinking and life style. No other period of history has ever witnessed the influence of thought on the daily life of people so much; similarly, no thought has ever influenced politics and economics as that of the modern period. With modernity we gained a lot, mostly new, but we paid heavy price for the same. We were not aware that we came out of paradise in search of it. Raimundo Panikkar's renowned work, *The Cosmotheandric Experience*, though focusing on the integrating human attitudes, spends much of its space in detailing the author's anguish over the failures of modernity and in criticizing them with his mythical and mystical perspectives especially by showing the failures of logos/ reason, the arrogant tower of Babel (Babylon)[6] challenging the uniqueness of nature and God.

Scientific Humanism was the greatest challenge against the *Cosmotheandric Experience*. Anthropos, though part of cosmos, stood apart and encountered with it in the process of anthropomorphizing it. Science which had been provoked by wonder and grown out of curiosity unravelled the mysteries of the universe. Copernican revolution changed the world view and the human attitude to knowledge and culture. People began to question the mythical foundations of knowledge. Modern thinkers who had been enlightened by science and technology questioned irrationalism and superstitions and believed that science and technology would liberate humanity from hardship and misery. But they failed to realize the cosmic revelation that was implied in the Copernican discovery. The shift from geocentrism to heliocentrism, new revelations on the planetary motion, studies on the laws of gravitation and so on were proper invitations to view the essential relation existing in the cosmos. But revolution in knowledge and technology empowered anthropocentric outlook and dominance over the universe. "The center of gravity shifts from the cosmos to Man and when, after Copernicus, the Earth ceases to be the cosmological center of the universe, the loss is recouped because Man then steps into the vacuum and becomes the center. This is the period of all sorts of humanisms. We have here an *anthropocentric* vision of reality."[7] Humans of historical consciousness lost humility and wisdom, boasted on the cosmic revelations as human achievement. It was considered as an opportunity to domineer over and exploit the world. Natural relation of cohesion was substituted with subjugation. Knowledge and technology was not revelatory, unravelling the mysteries of the universe, but instrumental in competitively conquering and exploiting nature. Knowledge was not holistic but compartmentalizing and discriminating. We stopped dialoguing with our cosmos and happily engaged in monologue. "Man is the "king" of creation, the lord of the universe…"[8] He was crowned as the modern creator who had killed the old creator and buried on the mountain top.[9] He makes himself, history[10] and future by mercilessly encountering with nature and remodelling everything to his taste and pleasure with no concern over his cosmos. Thus, "Historical time is that particular (human) time-consciousness which believes in the autonomy of the "human" race vis-à-vis the time of terrestrial and supraterrestrial entities. And this historical time, called "human" time, is mainly understood as the thrust toward the *future*- in which the fullness of existence … will be achieved. This human time implies the conviction that we are in bondage, not yet completed, and for that reason we must struggle against Nature, against fate, against the Earth or matter. It is a struggle for freedom against anything supposedly antagonistic to MAN. Our destiny is (in) the Future."[11] Political Economists justified liberal economy as the most suitable economic system for building human destiny, because it is founded on such human traits as pursuit of happiness, enjoyment of freedom, fulfilment of greed and preservation of life and security. The vices that had been most despised in the old moral code were accepted by the capitalist value system as the most beneficial. Bernard Mandeville, in his book *The Fable of the Bees: or Private Vices, Public Benefits,* observed that "Selfishness, greed, and acquisitive behaviour, he maintained, all tended to contribute to industriousness and a thriving economy. The answer to the paradox was, of course, that what had been vices in the eyes of the medieval moralists were the very motive forces that propelled the new capitalist system. And in the view of new religious, moral, and economic philosophies of the capitalist period, these motives were no longer vices."[12] One is entitled to earn by doing anything that is legally acceptable and satisfies the taste and interest of the other. The economic system that is intended to fulfil the needs of all fails, instead helps a few to flourish by rewarding the meritorious for their service to the rich only. "Self-sufficiency is destroyed in favour of profit... And profit is only for the successful ones. Success here means to be *better off* than your neighbour. The medieval western theologians who argued against usury as an anti-natural device, i.e., against the idea that money generates money, were not so wrong, ...*and* ...the principle of exploitation of Man by Man

inherent in the modern economy. It is very system that calls
for human exploitation. It is abuse as a system."[13] The birth of
super technologies accilerated the exploitaiton of nature, the
emergence of supermen subjugated men. Human exploitation
over humans is successful if the exploitation over nature is
maximized.

Liberty, equal opportunity and human dignity eliminated
traditional distinctions and hierarchies but in their place
instituted naked, shameless exploitation.[14] "Once all hierarchical
distinctions are levelled down- no castes, no guilds, no
aristocracies- the only differentiating factor becomes money,
which is one's way of distinguishing oneself from others."[15]
The pan-economic ideology binds all. The being of being
is determined by what the being has. The abundance in the
market fails to alleviate poverty and scarcity. During the period
of accumulation, a large number of the world population died
out of famine. "Every "human" good becomes subservient
to its monetary value. Some privileged people may prosper,
but happiness will elude them."[16] The poor are exploited
and the rich are alienated. "There is not only despair among
the poor. There is equally disenchantment among the rich...
Those who live in scientific and technological comfort have
discarded the Gods and now find that their practical Supreme
Value shows signs of radical impotence. ..It is ingrained in the
System that the rich get richer and the poor poorer. But no
solution is at hand, and we have lost innocence."[17] Socialism
and communism with ideal remedies for all maldies were
born from the womb of capitalism. Utopian thinkers and
ideal systems infused society with grand revelations and great
revolutions for liberation, but collapsed on the weight of their
own ambitions. Instead of creating a true democracy, political

utopias generated varioius forms of authoritarianisms like dictatorship, totalitarianism and fascism. "Armaments proliferate to maddening proportions- and have to, or else the present economic system would collapse tomorrow. The pan economic society is bound to explode sooner or later."[18] The spirit of internationalism was broken into pieces with two World Wars in which civilians were persecuted in the name of ideologies and people in every part of the world underwent untold misery. *"The Third World War has already come,* and the atomic phase of it will be only the predictable outcome and final act of a drama, ... a world tragedy of massive proportions and devastating implications."[19] Rational sensibility was converted into instrumental reason. "The myth of progress has practically collapsed. The *historical* situation of the world today is nothing less than desperate. There is really no issue of "development" for the famished masses which make up over half the world's population. There is no consolation for the millions who have been mentally and physically handicapped by malnutrition. It is no answer to proclaim that modern technology *can* overcome all these shortcomings when in fact it *cannot* alleviate the present predicament of those who are in the meantime victims of this situation, and it *does not* solve all the problems it could (utopically) resolve. What is worse, people have lost all hope that the lot of their children is somehow going to better."[20] Knowledge, instead of liberating humanity from ignorance, became an instrument of manipulation and exploitation. Technology that came into existence as a solution to many of our problems happened to be weapons of accumulation and of destruction. Reason, Science and Technology: the symbols of human liberation from ignorance, superstitions, scarcity, slavery; everything failed, a moment of desperation and rethinking.

The Lost Innocence

Once up on a time there was a paradise where human beings lived in nature along with animals, plants and Gods; all of them felt that they were simply there. None of them experienced that they were separate realities. "World is not a habitat or an external part of the whole or even of myself…My relationship with the World ultimately no different from my relationship with myself: the World and I differ, but are not two separate realities, for we share each other's life, existence, being, history and destiny in a unique way."[21] The nonhistorical person lived in the divinized universe. "Man shares the world with the Gods. He still drinks *Soma* with the Gods. The Gods do not yet form a clan of their own, as they will do when history is about to begin. It is the world of history that views the pre-historical world as "full of Gods". This is a vision from the outside. In the nonhistorical consciousness, it is the world itself that is divinized, or rather divine."[22] In the ecumenic age cosmos was the center. Man was not aware of himself independent of others. Therefore, his thinking was passive. He was not a creator. He did not create others to his taste. "…we, human beings, who are projecting our feelings and attitudes onto the things with which we deal. We personify, we anthropomorphize the World, while in truth things are simply there, insensitive and passive. If we take this attitude seriously, we shall have to add not only that God is merely our own projection, but that all the "others" are also projections of our own egos."[23] We created gods for our comfort and destroyed them for our convenience. The egoistic man looks at everything, defines them and projects them as he wants. He becomes active and nature becomes passive. Thus he disturbs or destroys the existence of a harmonious universe. A harmonious coexistence would have been possible if humans were non-egoistic, passive and humble.

In such a world everything remains in its place, undisturbed and in the order of nature. When we lost our innocence to be in the world and to be with God, we lost our relationship with world and God.

Ecological Metabolism to Chaotic Accumulation of Waste

If the nonhistorical person was not a maker or a creator, what was his means of consumption? Was he not stealing from nature's bounty? So long as humans catch prey or collect food with hands and tear them with teeth and consume raw, things are fine and ecological. But once the humans extend their hands, sharpen their teeth, change their consumption pattern, they are bound to disturb the natural order. "The three worlds- Heaven, Earth, Man- all share in one and the same adventure. What begins at the subatomic level, the assimilation of one thing by another in order to survive, culminates in the drinking of the Soma and the eating of the Eucharist. It is all subsumed in that primordial dynamism we call sacrifice: our partaking in the universal metabolism that lets Life be (come) alive, and by which the entire reality subsists."[24] Every part in the universal metabolism is in the process of sharing, assimilating and progressing. While living and dying, we support lives. "... while pre-historical Man uses roughly 90 percent of his income for food,[25] the citizen of the so-called developed countries spends only 10 percent... Food is dynamic communion with the entire universe, food is sharing in the cosmic metabolism, it is the symbol of life, the intercourse with all that there is, the greatest bond among humans and equally the greatest sign of fellowship."[26]Modern man accumulates 90 percent to waste, to produce an unbelievable surplus for unwanted consumption in the present to the destruction of future. With 90 per cent surplus, we keep 90 per cent without food. "You cannot *enjoy* three square meals a day, but you can very well produce and accumulate unlimited foodstuffs for use as future political and military weapons."[27] The pre-historic man was not future oriented. Thus he did not disturb his present for the future. By living in the present, they preserved the future. "You are not the owner but the "enjoyer" of your time... The meaning of life does not consist in building a Great Society on Earth, a powerful organization, but rather in enjoying life in the best possible way... You begin every day anew. Each day has enough of its own weight."[28] Pre-historical man lived with all in the nature, and did not cross the domain that the nature had prescribed for him.

Towards New Innocence

We are conscious of the innocence of the ecumenic time, we experience the crises of the economic period and ardently seek the revival of innocence, though unable to go back to the past, but by approaching with a catholic attitude and responding sensibly to the revelations of nature in time. The lost innocence cannot be regained, but the broken innocence can be repaired and a new situation of innocence can be created. Following are some of the practical steps towards new innocence.

Yogic Perspective

A yogic experience may be perceived as *Cosmotheandric* vision. A yogi enjoys balance within and harmony[29] with the universe and Gods. A person is spiritual: experiencing divinity everywhere and in everything including in her/himself; rational: knowing good and willing good, discerning right and good from wrong and bad, and ensuring future; emotional: romanticizing her/his dedicated and committed service for the general welfare, and also in devoting to Gods and finally appetitive: eating, drinking, consuming and digesting for the survival sake. Everything is there and everything should be there. One should not domineer over the other or define the other. Balance within establishes balance with everything else.

Cosmotheandric person is inspired by the past and lives in the present as a responsible person for the future for the benefit of all. S/he is a yogi, conscious of three time framework, past present and future; possesses three attitudes, to be in the world, to be a human person and to be with Gods. Neither of them binds anyone else nor are they bound by anything else. S/he is a *sthithaprajna* maintaining equanimity within and with everything else. Because of the overemphasis on 'Man the maker', his creative powers domineer over the others. This attitude is instrumental that breaks all the relations and entering into conflict within and with everything else. Can we regain our lost equanimity, the innocence that we had in our relations? *Cosmotheandric* vision is a search on the possibility of discovering the lost innocence.

Reconciliation

The *cosmotheandric* vision is addressed to the anthropos who challenged the love and care of the mother, because they found broken relation advantageous to promote their interest. God the father is humiliated, and the Earth the mother is injured. Thus, *The Cosmotheandric Experience* is an invitation extended to the estranged children to enter into an unconditional dialogue with the mother, moderated by the father. The dialogue may open a chance to re-establish the lost relation. Thus *cosmotheandric* vision is a philosophy of reconciliation: the father is to be consoled, the mother is to be cured and the children should enjoy peace and happiness. If children lead a harmonious life, parents enjoy peace and happiness. It is an interaction not encounter. "*Harmony* is the supreme principle- which does not mean that it has been achieved. The meaning of life consists both in entering into harmony with nature and in enhancing it."[30] *Cosmotheandric* person volunteers to serve for the enhancement of harmonious relationship. S/he belongs to the modern period with the transhistorical time consciousness. Historical person reduces every experience into known patterns and informed parameters and leaps into the vast spheres of unknown or uninformed in the effort to transcend all the limitations and problems. On the contrary, transhistorical person realizes the predicaments of transcending and tries to rectify those damages created by the historical person. The volunteer of *cosmotheandric* vision acts with the following awareness:

1. "Modern Man has killed an isolated and insular God, contemporary Earth is killing a merciless and rapacious Man, and the Gods seem to have deserted both Man and cosmos"[31] because of the alienation and estrangement and

2. "The economic moment is not only a fact, it is also an irreversible one. Our task is not to abolish it, but to overcome its absolute grip on modern Man,"[32] because it is the only available platform to start with and therefore

3. ".... many of our modern problems have been in large part created by the very scientific civilization which now tries to solve them,..."[33]

Trans-Rational Approach

Transhistorical consciousness is trans-rational. It is an attempt to transcend the limit of reason while knowing and experiencing. Transhistorical consciousness is the search for the ways of rectification. It motivates us to dedicate for the experiencing of the *cosmotheandric* relation. Many philosophers tried to

establish rationally justifiable grounds for ethics. But no effort
was fully successful, because the thinkers failed to recognize
that the human inclinations to be moral are not simply born
out of rational command but also out of passion. It is the
passion that risks us to do more than moral imperative. Thus
transhistorical ethics is trans-rational in nature. Trans-rational
ethical principles are rationally justifiable and morally trans-
rational, ie, moral demand is appealable to every sensible
mind to commit for the welfare of others. Trans-rational may
be described as the human inclination to do more than one's
moral duty, yet appealable and acceptable to all rational minds.
In other words, one discovers such responsibilities as to do
more than one's duty. Most of our insights and inspirations
are not rationally cognizable but not irrational. Transhistorical
moral consciousness transcends the limit of reason to make
the moral life reasonable. "Love transcends reason and science.
Faith, hope and trust are human inclinations, and most of
the time functions outside the purview of pure reason and
matters of scientific facts."[34] But we are inclined to love and
serve. Without expecting anything in return we love and share
within the family. Gandhi observed that many of our families
enjoy great peace and prosperity because of the self-suffering
love of the members of a family and he exhorted us to extend
our love and commitment to all for the general welfare and
common good.[35] We know the fact that the hard toil of many
is required to keep us happy and comfort. Neither we nor they
are aware of the unknown love implied in such acts.

Reparation

Transhistorical consciousness is an emerging attitude with hope
and action, with love to preserve the cosmos. "What is needed
to solve the many problems of the world is the combined effort

of people, with a new consciousness (or a new innocence). We must overcome the age of individualism and ideologies. And we are not alone either, that's important. The new consciousness that is trying to emerge is the one which realizes that there are certain things which we don't understand but of which we are a part. Our incomprehension however does not excuse us from taking responsibility. Quite the contrary, we have to assume responsibility as we have never done before."[36] Trans-rational moral responsibilities are incomplete without practical solutions. Moral person cannot simply solve environmental damages. For example, the accumulation of waste due to developmental technologies cannot be set right merely by ethical awareness. Chemical, electronic, electromagnetic and nuclear waste can be disposed only with better technologies. "What humanity needs is not a wholesale discarding of advance technologies, but a sifting, indeed a further development of technology along ecological principles that will contribute to a new harmonization of society and the natural world"[37] Thus what is required is the science and technology with *cosmotheandric* concern and commitment. Hence we have to discuss on the trans-rational morality of the scientists. Scientists doing their duties demanded by their profession are right but insufficient. Most of the researches are market driven. The output of market oriented research fetches money and fame to the researcher. But scientists with transhistorical attitude may have to lose their temporary gain and dedicate themselves in the curative research that can correct the damages inflicted on the universe. All other transhistorical consciousnesses have to recognize such scientists and support their efforts. *Cosmotheandric* vision is a daring aspiration of a few persons with transhistorical consciousness who are still challenged by anthropocentric arrogance and greediness.

Prejudices

Panikkar sometimes shows attachment to certain philosophical traditions without proper justification and criticizes certain other philosophical positions and religious statements without considering their interpretative dimensions. In reality, those systems may have some teachings that agree with the *cosmotheandric* vision and some others that disagree with the vision.

Prejudice- I

Every sensible person is pained by the damage done against cosmos. Many of the so called achievements of modernity are to be blamed for the crisis. But Panikkar's attack upon modernity, at some point, is beyond justification. He blindly attacks all modern values including human rights that have ramification on conservation of animals, plants and the environment. "Modern political and social reforms tend to "conscientize" these people by giving them a sense of history, by inciting them to be actors in history and authors of their own destiny, instead of mere objects of exploitation. They are taught to organize themselves and struggle for their rights. It is when they enter history, however, that they discover the great deception: they have come too late, and can never be the masters of history."[38] But he fails to observe that the resistance against deception deter abuse of humans and also of nature. Panikkar's nostalgic love for the primitive culture closes him from thinking of their reformation. If they are not reformed and incorporated into the modern culture, they will be further exploited and destroyed. Human predicament and failures are inevitably present with any human effort, but they cannot prevent us from optimism and action. Panikkar himself believes in this optimism, otherwise he would not have presented *The Cosmotheandric Experience/* vision to us.

Prejudice- II

Panikkar is needlessly prejudiced against judaeo-christian-Islamic traditions. "There is no doubt that the acme of historical consciousness is tied not only to the judaeo-christian-Islamic tradition but also to western dominance of the entire planet,..."[39] He accepted primitive culture and Indian qualified and non qualified non dualisms (*Visistadvaita* and *Advaita*) as integral and holistic and criticized Judeo-Christian and Islamic religions for taking the Gods away from the world as an *absolute Other*. "Man does not become less human when he discovers his divine calling, or the Gods lose their divinity when they are humanized, or the World become less worldly when it bursts into life and consciousness."[40] Knowledge is not reduced by giving, and the reality is not reduced by extending. But theologizing is a process of ranking God with unique status and placing Him in a separate realm. Theologizing is also a process of reforming religions by removing crude rituals from religious practices. Every religion, including the primitive and Indian, speaks of God that is far away and near by. Judaeo-Christian-Islamic religions, though advocated the principle of divine intervention in the world, theorized the gap between the God and the world. Most of the religious criticisms, Abrahamic as well as Indian, against the superstitious and inhuman cults and clannish practices reformed the religions periodically. They were appreciated by the refined minds of those religions.

Prejudice- III

Panikkar holds a world view of coexistence of unique and different individual units as an integral whole of interdependent real units. While substantiating his philosophy, he is uncritically biased towards primitive tribal world view and *advaitas*. "The divine permeates the cosmos. The forces of Nature are all divine.

Nature is "supernatural", so to say. Or rather, Nature is that which is being "natured," born – from or of the divine. Pre-historical Man's home, his background, is a cosmotheological one."[41]But he does not take note of the fact that the religious sense and taboos of prehistorical communities were signs of social exclusion and egoistic aggressions. Primitive religions were clannish: open within and opaque with others. They see gods everywhere except in the neighbouring tribes. Similarly, worshiping animals as gods and goddesses paves way for the loss of our right over the choice of food and disturbs social harmony.

Prejudice- IV

Cosmotheandric spirituality brings an ontological dimension into interrelatedness of realities with no hierarchy of relations. The difference of existence of cosmos, theos and anthropos is from the fundamental unity of reality. They "are distinct, but not separable. My head is distinct from me, yet cannot be separated from me... The head is essentially the head of a body."[42] Though we know the differences among the parts, we don't treat them as the other. What is good for one part of the body is good for the whole person. Panikkar's understanding of God is similar to *Visistadvaita* pantheism in the context of all inclusive nature and Sankara non-dualism in the context of oneness[43] of reality, because "Neither duality nor plurality can ever be the ultimate solution, because by the very fact of their inherent multiplicity they allow for further questioning. This thirst for unity is not only ontological and epistemological (unity of being, unity of intellection), it is also sociological and political (unity of humankind, unity of civilizations) Societies tend to unite and agglomerate; people have a tendency toward assimilation and socialization."[44] Panikkar, by following unity as the ground for *cosmotheandric* experience, established a non-empirical ground for socio-political, cultural and economic relations among humans. If unity is required for a harmonious relation, differences can be accepted as justifiable argument for conflict and ill treatment. If belonged to the same folk, nepotism and favouritism are acceptable! Casteism can be appreciated. "When we think of a philosophy for peaceful coexistence, we have to conceive a type of philosophy that recognizes and respects all with their differences. Otherwise we are falling into the trap of dominant philosophy imposing itself on all."[45] Otherwise unity is an assertion over diversity and an inclination towards uniformity. Similarly, Panikkar describes philosophy as an active and intelligent listening to the Rhythm of Being.[46] *Rhythm of Being* with the emphasis on order and nature of reality is a usage of the dominance. The purpose is to discipline and control all to its tune. It is teleological following the definition of the dominant. Difference is intolerable and considers as a reason for segregation and unequal treatment instead of treating it as an opportunity for harmonious relation and coexistence.

Advaita of Sankara may not provide a suitable philosophical framework for upholding Panikkar's world view, because *advaita* epistemology and metaphysics maintain levels of knowledge corresponding to the gradation in the order and nature of reality, Brahman being the highest in the hierarchy. Thus, from *prathibhasika* to *paramarthika*, with the change in mental state, our experience of reality varies and in the process, many aspects of reality are concealed and selectively revealed to project dominance of one over the other. A philosophy that conceals many dimensions of realities 'even if they are only crumbs', cannot be considered as a suitable philosophical model to describe the multidimensional *cosmotheandric* coexistence.

Proximity of *Cosmotheandric* Vision to Buddhism

Considering the unique aspects of *cosmotheandric* vision, Panikkar's philosophical position, scope and methodology differ from many philosophical traditions. He expressed his philosophy as something close to assimilative traditions like that of advaita due to his love for philosophies of integration. His Trinitarian view is a non-ambiguous affirmation of all with their differences. He symbolizes it through the analogy of the circle. "There is no circle without a center and a circumference. The three are not the same and yet not separable."[47] Buddhist pluralistic, non-centric, essenceless, continuous existences of dependent originations may be considered as proximate philosophical base for comprehending the past and the future in the present: the inspiration and enthusiasm from the past, responsibility and commitment to the future, and exist in the present moment. Everything is in the present and in everything else. "A more mature spirituality discovered that the business of saving our individual souls was neither a business nor a real salvation, because such individualistic souls do not exist: we are all interconnected, and I can reach salvation only by somehow *incorporating* the entire universe in the enterprise."[48] Inspired by Panikkar, I wrote on nirvana in an article, "Movement is the nature of relationship." It is a movement of or from one to the other with a reciprocal movement. One affects the other, but the other is not for me. If the other is for me, it is a mode of making the other a useful object for me. But genuine relation is detached neither for nor against, but simply a fulfilment. The enlightened one acts but not enjoying the fruits but the effects of his/her good deeds transforms the environment. This is nirvana."[49] Nirvana is not negative as usually defined, but selfless positive existence for the liberation of all. Thus, Buddhism, though its Bodhisattva concept, exemplifies the significance of the bodily existence of the enlightened human persons in the world in relationship with the beings around, laying an altruistic and inclusive path for liberation. "Nirvana is not an absolute non-existence of reality but absolute presence of the reality in and through everything. It is like the presence of salt in the dish after being dissolved. It is not its own existence but the Existence. Nirvana is the dissolution of the self into the reality without losing its unique identity. Salt is dissolved in the dish, but salt is tasted in the dish. Emptying the self makes one selfless and the fruits of the selfless actions bear fruit in everything. This selfless behaviour in the world is the *maha-karunnyam* or great compassion that Buddhism refers about."[50] On the contrary, the philosophies of unity, knowingly or unknowingly, retain an attitude of arrogance and dominance ready to accommodate all within like an ocean swallowing all rivers into it. The philosophy of pluralistic coexistence is like the spices and other recipes in a curry: everything into everything else and makes the dish tasty. All factors or individual units have to forgo the self centric attitude or ego consciousness and relate with the other.

Bibliography

George Joseph, M, "Transhistorical Attitude and Protective Possibilities of Science and Technology", *Eubios Journal of Asian and International Bioethics,* Vol. 23 (4) July 2013.

George Joseph, M, "Pluralistic Worldview of Buddhism towards Coexistence", *Biocosmology- Neo-Aristotelism,* Vol.5, Nos. 3&4, Summer/ Autumn, 2015.

George Joseph, M, *Critique of Modern Culture: Marx and Gandhi*, Jnanam, Pune, 2005.

Hunt, E. K. and Lautzenheiser, Mark, *History of Economic Thought: A Critical Perspective,* PHI, New Delhi, 2011.

Marx, Karl and Engels, Frederick, *Selected Works,* Progress Publishers, Moscow, 1970.

Panikkar, Raimon, *Cosmotheandric Experience*, Motilal Banarsidass, Delhi, 1998.

Panikkar, Raimon, *The Rhythm of Being*, Orbis Books, New York, 2013.

Puthenpurackal, Johnson, J., (ed), *Raimon Panikkar: Being Beyond Borders*, Asian Trading Corporation, Bangalore, 2012.

Soccio, Douglas J., *Archetypes of Wisdom*, Wadsworth Publishing Company, Belmont, 1995.

Toffler, Alvin, *Future Shock*, Random House, New York, 1970.

The following website is also referred. www.shareinternational.org/archives/ religion/rl_cfnew-innocence.htm

Endnotes

[1] Raimon Panikkar, *Cosmotheandric Experience*, Motilal Banarsidass, Delhi, 1998, p. 2.

[2] Ibid., p. 1.

[3] Ibid., p. 2.

[4] Alvin Toffler, *Future Shock*, Random House, New York, 1970, p.12.

[5] Raimon Panikkar, Op.cit., p. 108.

[6] Genesis 11:1-15.

[7] Raimon Panikkar, Op.cit., p. 36.

[8] Ibid., p. 33.

[9] Nietzsche described how modern deveopments in knowledge and science empowered man to do things without God and morality in *Thus Spoke Zarathustra* and *The Gay Science*. Refr: Douglas J. Soccio, *Archetypes of Wisdom*, pp. 493-97.

[10] Marx and Sartre described the creative freedom as an important human value

[11] Raimon Panikkar, Op.cit., p. 100.

[12] E. K. Hunt and Mark Lautzenheiser, *History of Economic Thought: A Critical Perspective*, PHI, New Delhi, 2011, p. 32

[13] Raimon Panikkar, Op.cit., p. 115.

[14] Karl Marx and Frederick Engels, "Manifesto of the Communist Party", *Selected Works*, Progress Publishers, Moscow, 1970, p. 38.

[15] Raimon Panikkar, Op.cit., pp. 115-16.

[16] Ibid., p. 111.

[17] Ibid., p. 110.

[18] Ibid., p. 111.

[19] Ibid., p. 117.

[20] Ibid., p. 109.

[21] Ibid., p. 72.

[22] Ibid., pp.95-96.

[23] Ibid., pp. 144-45.

[24] Ibid., p. 137.

[25] 90% of pre-historical man is less than 10% of the historical man.

[26] Raimon Panikkar, Op.cit., p. 98.

[27] Ibid.

[28] Ibid., pp. 96-97.

[29] Harmony is also a human usage expressing the nature of reality as we love to see it. Who knows what the real nature of things is?

[30] Raimon Panikkar, Op.cit., p. 96.

[31] Ibid., p. 77.

[32] Ibid., p. 36.

[33] Ibid., p. 37.

[34] George Joseph, M, "Transhistorical Attitude and Protective Possibilities of Science and Technology", *Eubios Journal of Asian and International Bioethics,* Vol. 23 (4) July 2013, p. 144.

[35] George Joseph, M., *Critique of Modern Culture: Marx and Gandhi,* Jnanam, Pune, 2005, p. 215.

[36] "The New Innocence- Interview with Raimon Panikkar by Carmen Font", *Share International,* October 1996, www.shareinternational.org/ archives/religion/rl_cfnew-innocence.htm, referred on November13, 2017.

[37] Raimon Panikkar, *Cosmotheandric Experience,* footnote- 110, p. 37.

[38] Ibid., pp. 116-17.

[39] Ibid., p. 107.

[40] Ibid., pp. 74-75.

[41] Ibid., p. 96.

[42] Ibid., pp. 150-51.

[43] In *The Rhythm of Being,* Panikkar translates Advaita as **adualism** to overcome the problems of quantification and gradation of reality and claims that "*Advaita* denies both that "reality is one" and that "reality

is two" precisely because it discovers that the real is not reducible to intelligibility.", pp. 216-17.

[44] Raimon Panikkar, *Cosmotheandric Experience*, p. 7.

[45] George Joseph, M, "Pluralistic Worldview of Buddhism towards Coexistence", *Biocosmology- Neo-Aristotelism*, Vol.5, Nos. 3&4, Summer/ Autumn, 2015, p. 455.

[46] Ivo Coelho, "Panikkar's Approach to Reality: Epistemological Foundations", in Johnson J. Puthenpurackal, (ed),*Raimon Panikkar: Being Beyond Borders*, ATC, Bangalore, 2012, p. 114.

[47] Raimon Panikkar,Op.cit., p. 75.

[48] Ibid., p. 151.

[49] *Biocosmology- Neo-Aristotelism*, Vol.5, Nos. 3&4, Summer/ Autumn, 2015, p. 460.

[50] Ibid.

Response

The paper is very systematically developed. Basically the paper is developed in three phases; cherished primitive past glorious living with nature in harmony; destruction of nature, others (humans), mystical richness by modernity where anthropocentrism has taken place with the advancement in science and reason; finally the solutions to regain the lost innocence by forgoing one's ego centrism and relating with nature (Mother Earth), Divinity (Father God/s) and the other human person in harmony.

Human being doesn't become less human when he discovers his divine calling, or the gods lose their divinity when they are humanized, or the world become less worldly when it bursts into life and consciousness.

Can we genuinely claim that the pre-historic human beingswere not future oriented?

Nirvana is not an absolute non-existence of reality but absolute presence of the reality in and through everything?

Having stated that integration of all systems would mean taking dominance of one over many, how can you propose again Buddhist philosophy could be a ground for Panikkar? Have you not fallen back to what you have just condemned? - Sateesh Kumar

Rediscovering the Sacred in Nature

Donald R. Frohlich and *Carlos Miguel Gómez*

Abstract

This paper explores the main elements of the modern, mechanistic and disenchanted image of nature, shows some of the ways in which it is defective and, in the light of Panikkar's cosmotheandric insight, suggests one way in which the contemporary understanding of nature may allow for the rediscovery of the presence of the Divine.

Keywords

Mechanistic Reductionism, Disenchantment, Extended evolutionary synthesis, Cosmotheandric insight, Spirit in nature, Panikkar.

Introduction

There appears to be a relatively extended consensus that we have entered, or are approaching, an epochal change. Both our ways of life and manners of understanding reality present all the signs of a deep crisis that demands the search for alternatives. Clearly, our relationship with "nature" is a neuralgic point in this transformation. This relationship implies a particular understanding of nature that gradually arose and consolidated during the beginning of modernity, and now is felt as problematic and in need, not so much of correction, as of replacement. (cf. Nagel 2012) In this paper, we first explore some aspects of the modern concept of nature; then show why this is problematic, and finally point to a possible direction for a new understanding.

1.   The De-Sacralization of Nature

As with all fundamental concepts, "nature" is a highly contested notion. (Evers 2011) Indeed, it is "profoundly ambivalent, reflecting the aspirations, longings and fears of those who appeal to it." (McGrath 2006, 86) In western languages, and due to the foundational Aristotelian notion of *physis*, the concept still can be used in two deeply connected senses. On the one hand, as that which distinguishes something making it what it is, that is, its essence, that which is given as opposed to what is humanly-made (*tecnè*). On the other, as the structures, processes, constituents and laws of the external world, as it may be understood, but which nonetheless opposes that which transcends it, the 'supernatural' or 'metaphysical'. Thus, in both senses, the concept of nature is built from oppositions to that which is not natural. Both senses, of course, have a long history of conflicting interpretations.

For our purposes, we will focus on an image of nature that not only still dominates in the West, but has colonized other latitudes and is basic for our current ways of living and our dealings with the world. Certainly, it is not the only image of nature that has emerged in modernity, but its influence has far exceeded that of the alternatives. This image started to emerge during the seventeenth century and gradually consolidated as a basic presupposition of modernity. The image presents nature in mechanical and impersonal terms, replacing ancient metaphors of nature as a living organism, sometimes richly imagined in poetry and painting as a nurturing mother, a womb or even a nurse. (Cf. McGrath 2006, 105ss) Although the developments of physics in the twentieth century deeply challenged this image, it has not lost dominion over western mentality to the present. Interpreted as mechanism, nature started to be seen as an inert, entirely regulated and controllable, material system of laws in which the divine need not play any role. Following R. Wesfall, Alister MacGrath points out four characteristics of the mechanistic understanding of nature (2006, 99ss):

(a) It can be described mathematically so all natural process can be measured and quantified. (b) Instead of an organic entity, directed to aims and perceived as sharing certain characteristics with human beings (life, intention, meaning), it is "a world of passive matter, made up of individual particles or atoms, whose behavior was governed by mechanical laws." (McGrath 2006, 99) (c) It was the "other," a neutral and passive object in front of the epistemic subject, with which it has no essential affinity. The human observer, thus, not only was considered as entirely independent from nature, as a pure mind representing the world from the pieces of information it gets from the senses; but knowledge itself was seen as an enterprise that does not require the previous commitments and the engaged participation of the knower in the world. (Cf. Dreyfus and Taylor 2015, 5ss) Finally, (d) nature became an autonomous secular system, which not only could be explained in its own terms, without appealing to God or any other supernatural entity, but which also was not to be felt as inhabited by the spiritual beings of the enchanted world.

Even if the development and social reception of Newtonian mechanics played an important role in this process of disenchantment of nature, as Charles Taylor (2007) has thoroughly shown, this was not the only or main cause. Indeed, the theory of universal gravitation, "encouraged the view that the universe was a single uniform mechanism, governed at all times and in all places by the same fundamental laws of motion." (McGrath 2006, 107) But this was, however, not enough on its own to empty nature of the feeling of a divine presence. A whole change in the horizon of self-understanding was necessary. This change involved, on the one hand, a transformation of what was conceived as the meaning and ends of human life. This is, a shift in the understanding of human fullness: "... between a condition in which our highest spiritual and moral aspirations point us inescapably to God, one might say, make no sense without God, to one in which they can be related to a host of different sources, and frequently are referred to sources which deny God." (Taylor 2007, 26).

On the other hand, the disenchantment process implied the emergence of a new sense of the self, different from the selves living in an enchanted world. While the latter are open to all sorts of external spiritual influences that directly affect their lives as sources of sacred power and meaning, our modern secular selves are closed in themselves, as the exclusive sources of meaning in the world and the only intentional will that can be found. Taylor denominates as "porous" the first type of self and "buffered" the second. (2007, 35ss) For modern "selves" there is only meaning in the world as a result of its own operations. This is a fundamental shift, central for desacralizing nature, which now can be understood as a universe, a system of mechanical laws regulating the interaction of material particles, and not any longer as a cosmos, a hierarchical and purposive order in which humans are meaningfully connected with the rest of creation through a divine ordering principle. (Taylor, 2007, 59ss).

Interestingly, while the idea of nature as cosmos allows us to think of its creator as simultaneously distinct from the creation but deeply related to it (Evers 2011, 331), the understanding of nature as universe expels the divine from the world and reduces it to the maker of the mechanism. As we have pointed out, the mechanical image of nature seriously challenged the possibility of divine action in the world and gravely narrowed the understanding of the Creator. How could God interrupt the strict system of natural laws he created for the sake of benevolently intervening in his creation? Would not the belief in Providence contradict the idea of the perfection of physical order? In a universe that was interpreted as a perfect and self-sustaining machine, the only role left for God was that of an enteral watchmaker, who once having completed his work, can completely take distance from it. This, according to Taylor, lead to a fourfold reduction of the role of the divine in nature and the human world.

Firstly, we found an "eclipse of further purpose" beyond human good. (Taylor 2007, 222) In opposition to the idea of nature as a cosmos, in which everything has a purpose and is ordered for the benefice of creatures, mechanical laws and purposes lack direction and meaning. Only within human society and action can we find meaning and purpose, and these gradually began to be seen as something to be created more than discovered. Certainly, the exclusion of final causation and teleological explanations from science is commonly credited as one of the main features of modern science. While for Aristotelian physics knowing the nature of something implied discovering its fourfold cause, (i.e. its origin, its finality, its material composition and its form) with Galileo's causality, ceased being understood ontologically: physics should now focus not in the cause of being, but on the measurement of variations. (Zubiri 1974, 288) With this transformation, only efficient causes count as a proper explanation. Thus, nature is no longer understood as the substance of a thing, but as the necessary order of laws and causal relations that can be mathematically described. In Boyle's words: "Nature is not here to be looked on as a distinct or separate agent, but as a rule or rather a system of rules according to which those agents and the bodies they work on are, by the great author of things, determined to act and suffer." (1996, 106)

Accordingly, measurement, as we pointed out earlier, becomes a fundamental feature of the natural order. To be, is to be measurable. However, measurement cannot tell us anything about being, but only about the variation of material entities in a closed system that no longer points to a transcendental purpose.

Second, we find an "eclipse of Grace." (Taylor 2007, 222) Since the only place in which meaning and purpose can be found is in human subjectivity and society, it is reason that can discern or produce the appropriate moral and political orders. Modern subjects have to assume the responsibility of constructing and realizing a rational way of living, which gradually starts to be seen as autonomous and independent with respect to all particular religious worldviews. Thirdly, there is an eclipse of mystery. In a desacralized nature, with no further purpose, there is nothing hidden that eventually cannot be explained according to the natural sciences. God's providence "consists simply in his plan for us, which we understand." (Taylor 2007, 223) There is no place for particular divine interventions into the natural order, no more room for miracles.

Finally, there occurred an eclipse in the belief that human life was directed towards a different, transcendent state, beyond its currents limitations, for which God had created it. (Taylor 2007, 224) Not only was the belief in the after-life a frequent target of innumerable attacks, but also exclusively immanent goals came to be regarded as the only reals.

One important consequence of the mechanistic understanding of nature is that it opened up the possibility for a naturalistic understanding of the universe, which continues to be a fundamental principle of science: reality is a closed system which has to be explained exclusively in its own terms, avoiding any reference to something "beyond." (Cf. Trigg 30ss) Certainly, this approach has been very effective for the development of our scientific understanding of nature. But naturalism as a methodological principle is not always easy to differentiate from naturalism as a metaphysical position, which reduces reality to the physical world. Indeed, as it has been repeatedly suggested, this is no longer a scientific position, but a philosophical one. To claim the contrary implies transposing the limits of empirical knowledge.

2.   Problems with the Reductionist Paradigm and the Theory of Evolution by Natural Selection

One way to see the limits and complications with this image of nature is to focus on the current developments in life sciences. In a more balanced, but still highly reductive and materialistic framework, eminent evolutionary biologist Ernst Mayer summarizes what he refers to as the *Autonomy of Biology* in several lectures. In his oft cited Walter Arndt Lecture, Mayer states:

> One can assign ... [the instantiation of modern biology] ... to three different sets: (A) the refutation of certain erroneous principles, (B) the demonstration that certain basic principles of physics cannot be applied to biology, and (C) the realization of

the uniqueness of certain basic principles of biology that are not found in the inanimate world. (2002)

Under "erroneous assumptions", Mayr includes vitalism and teleology, while under "non-applicable physical laws" he lists Essentialism, Reductionism, and Determinism, as well as "Laws" of Physics (versus "Concepts" of biology). Finally, Mayr goes on to comment on evolution, the reality of bio-populations and variability, natural selection, and dual causality as phenomena not found in the inanimate world.

Mayr also intimates that biology, *sensu lato,* can be divided into sets of both "how" and "why" questions, concluding that the field consists of two sciences: one committed to the study of function (explained by chemistry and physics), and the second dedicated to the study of history (as known by experimental and paleontological evidence). To be sure, Mayr's divisions are problematic (especially considering the roles of reduction and determinism in the study of function). From our perspective in the early 21st century, they seem both somewhat arbitrary, and ambitious; perhaps in the extreme. His lecture concludes with a call for necessary and specific consideration of interrelation and holism. Leaving the great biologist's attempts aside, the life sciences have decidedly defaulted to a position of overly influential reductionism, within a framework of questionable deterministic models.

In his famous treatise, *On the Origin of Species by Means of Natural Selection, or the Preservation of Favoured Races in the Struggle for Life,* Charles Darwin (1859) made five poignant observations in proposing a theory of evolution by natural selection:

1. Some forms (individuals) are better adapted to current conditions than others (*Variability*).

2. Some of that variability is passed to the next generation (*Heritability*).

3. Organisms produce more offspring than their environments can support, and than actually survive to mature and reproduce.

4. Those forms that are better adapted will leave more offspring and thus increase in frequency in a population (*Adaptation* and *Reproductive Fitness*).

5. As environments change over time, new forms may become better adapted and increase in frequency (*Natural Selection*); thus, new species may ultimately form (*Descent with Modification*).

Darwin's eminently testable hypotheses aside, evolutionary theory has matured and come far. During the early twentieth century Darwin's theory was provided a credible mechanism of inheritance by the late discovery of Gregor Mendel's experiments and the elucidation of its' cellular and structural parts. The theory was made robust over thirty to forty years when R. A. Fisher, J. B. S. Haldane, Sewall Wright, and others, empirically showed natural selection to operate in a Mendelian framework in what is now referred to as the Modern Synthesis or Neo-Darwinism. Non-Mendelian forms of inheritance are well known and biologists today function in a Neo-Darwinist framework. Evolutionary theory has been modified over the past 150+ years and much of that modification is based not only in new discovery (DNA, genome structure, etc.), but in synthesis of those discoveries into a coherent body of explanation.

Biologists do not find Darwin's predictions or the Modern Synthesis generally questionable. However, a growing number of voices in the life sciences advocate for a broader and more inclusive theoretical structure that takes into account findings from numerous fields. In advocating for a research program called the Extended Evolutionary Synthesis, Oxford biologist Denis Noble argues in an abstract from *The Journal of Experimental Biology*:

Experimental results in epigenetics and related fields of biological research show that the Modern Synthesis (Neo-Darwinist) theory of evolution requires either extension or replacement. This article examines the conceptual framework of Neo-Darwinism, including the concepts of 'gene', 'selfish', 'code', 'program', 'blueprint', 'book of life', 'replicator' and 'vehicle'. This form of representation is a barrier to extending or replacing existing theory as it confuses conceptual and empirical matters. These need to be clearly distinguished. In the case of the central concept of 'gene', the definition has moved all the way from describing a necessary cause (defined in terms of the inheritable phenotype itself) to an empirically testable hypothesis (in terms of causation by DNA sequences). Neo-Darwinism also privileges 'genes' in causation, whereas in multi-way networks of interactions there can be no privileged cause. An alternative conceptual framework is proposed that avoids these problems, and which is more favourable to an integrated-systems view of evolution. (2015, 7)

Of course, this work is not alone in its critique of either the reductionist or determinist paradigms. In his contentious 2012 NYT Best Seller, *Mind and Cosmos*, philosopher Thomas Nagel writes that the life sciences, and molecular biology in particular, have failed to answer a number of important questions. It is not because the data are inaccurate or somehow lacking, but because the nature of reductive data, and limited or non-existent theoretical frameworks, does not allow them to be reassembled into reasonable, or even identifiable, wholes. Molecular biologists simply do not have the tools to address poignant questions of emergence, and those tools may not ultimately be found in a strictly empirical philosophy or practice of science.

What of the nature of deterministic models? Serious, but limited (to a very few scientists and perhaps philosophers), attention has been paid to the inadequacy of deterministic thinking to address questions of complexity, symmetry and symmetry breaks, boundary limits, and emergent phenomena. A notable exception in philosophy is a reconstruction of the ontology of Gilles Deleuze by Manuel DeLanda (2013). Here, Deleuze uses differential geometry and group theory as a gateway to an understanding of self-organization in the universe in decidedly non-deterministic frameworks. Indeed, Ilya Prigogine, Mariano Artigas and others have emphasized not only the dynamism of nature, but the apparently spontaneous emergence of new levels of organization in natural systems. Certainly, the one common characteristic of emergent phenomena is novelty, not unexpected in stochastic systems. In "Two Dogmas of Biology," Lenore Fleming aptly writes:

> The problem with reductionism in biology is not the reduction, but the implicit attitude of determinism that usually accompanies it. Methodological reductionism is supported by deterministic beliefs, but making such a connection is problematic when it is based on an idea of determinism as fixed predictability. Conflating determinism with predictability gives rise to inaccurate models that overlook the dynamic complexity of our world, as well as ignore our epistemic limitations when we try to model it. Furthermore, the assumption of a strictly deterministic framework is unnecessarily hindering to biology. By removing the dogma of determinism, biological methods, including reductive methods, can be expanded to include stochastic models and probabilistic interpretations. Thus, the dogma of reductionism can be saved once its ties with determinism are severed. (2017, 1)

In our opinion, the most significant limitations in science are deterministic approaches. These make the experience of awe and wonder especially difficult for students and young scientists alike.

Would it be accurate to say that there is more mysticism among scientists than popular press would have us think? Carlo Rovelli, an Italian theoretical physicist, anti-religionist, and who clearly does not see himself as a mystic, writes in his book, *Reality Is Not What It Seems:*

> A scientist is someone who (...) accepts the substantial uncertainty of our knowledge (...) accepts living immersed in ignorance and, therefore, in mystery (...) accepts living with questions to which we do not know the answers. Perhaps we don't know them yet or – who knows – we never will. To live with uncertainty may be difficult ... To accept uncertainty doesn't detract from our sense of mystery. On the contrary: we are immersed in the mystery and the beauty of the world. (2017, 234)

3.   The Search for an Alternative Vision: The Spirit in the Physical World

The growing awareness that a reductionist materialistic understanding of nature and reality is problematic, and that it has played a role in our contemporary social and ecological crisis, demands us to look for alternatives. Many voices have risen to offer proposals. Here we want to point out what for us, is one of the main characteristics that should be included in a new vision of reality.

Panikkar's summarizes his cosmotheandric insight in the affirmation that the divine, the human and the earthly are the three irreducible dimensions of reality (Panikkar 1999, 81). Materialism has focused exclusively on one dimension, excluding the other two. Contemporary philosophers have fought materialism, with the intention to show that subjective experience, consciousness and even rationality and value cannot be reduced to the physical. A prominent example of this quest is Thomas Nagel's recent book *Mind and Cosmos.* He claims that our contemporary materialistic world-picture, that heavily relies on new-Darwinism, is incapable of offering a satisfactory explanation not only of the origin of life, but of the existence of conscious beings, able to act based on values and reasons. Within the alternatives he explores, without definitely committing to a particular one, Nagel suggests that rather than a reductionist understanding of reality that sees physical entities and laws as the fundamentally real, it would be more reasonable to think of a monist understanding of reality in which the physical and the mental are united. (2012, 57) He also presents a case in favor of reintroducing a version of teleology, which he calls non-intentional because he wants it to be consistent with his atheism, as a fundamental law in the natural order. (67, 91, 121) This would imply that the universe has a tendency to generate conscious rational and moral beings, and that an explanation of this by mere chance is simply unsatisfactory.

But Nagel, as many others do, stops there. Mind and cosmos are a fundamental unity, but the spiritual dimension continues to be unrecognized. Panikkar, on the contrary, strives to reincorporate it. This task, it is important to say, is not mere theoretical speculation. Indeed, the recognition of the spiritual dimension cannot be the product of a philosophical argument, but requires spiritual experience. Philosophy and theology can only attempt to make this experience intelligible and to show how it relates to our other realms of experience and how an integrated view of reality can be built.

In Panikkar's cosmotheandric vision the spiritual dimension of reality does not need to be identified with a particular definition of the divine, belonging to a single tradition and demanding blind acceptance. Rather, it has to do with the realization that there is something unfathomable and inexhaustible in reality; something that cannot be ever fully grasped and challenges all our theories, models and predictions. Indeed, all our epistemic efforts are always fundamentally incomplete, historically changing and open to revision. This fundamental openness of reality allows us to regain the sense of mystery and wonder lost in the mechanistic paradigm. Additionally, it permits us to see that the divine can act in the world without interrupting the natural order; this is, without conflict with physical laws, for the natural order is united to the divine. (Panikkar 1999, 82) Equally important, the human knower is also part of reality, and not a disengaged subject contemplating passive objects.

In this sense, for Panikkar the cosmotheandric insight does not only mean that there are three fundamental dimension of reality, but more importantly, that any real and valuable understanding of reality has to take them into account; that is, everything is connected. A relational system cannot be fully understood by the analysis of only one of its parts and dimensions. Likewise, reality requires an integrating approach. Can such an approach be reached integrating current scientific methods and findings?

Certainly, this would imply not only a deep transformation of science, for which it seems indeed to be preparing, but mainly of our entire culture. This sort of epochal change and growth in human awareness is consistent with Panikkar's understanding of historical development. In his *Experience of God*, Panikkar writes that human culture has approximately ascended through three horizons to an intelligibility of the presence of the Divine; these he labeled Cosmological, Anthropological, and Ontological. Respectively, the three correspond to periods of human evolution, socio-cultural or otherwise. In describing the Cosmological Horizon, Panikkar explains:

> Human beings, but especially not exclusively in antiquity, lived face to face with the world. The universe, as an animated habitat, constituted their center of interest. Their regard was directed to the objects of heaven and earth. It was in that horizon that divinity appeared, not simply as one thing among others, but as its Lord, its Cause, its Origin or Principle. Its place is at the apex of cosmology (...) Divinity appeared linked to the world; it is the divinity of the world and in turn the world is interpreted as the world of divinity. (1999, 34)

Panikkar then speaks about an Anthropological Horizon wherein man's focus turns from nature to himself, and the perfection of the human being, followed by a horizon that culminates in an awareness, or consciousness, of Transcendence. That is, Divinity understood as Being so "other" that it transcends itself: "Divinity is not; its being is beyond Being. Its place is metaontological. It is not even Non-Being. Its apophatism is absolute." (1999, 36)

None of the three levels of awareness are exclusive, and indeed examples of overlap can be identified. However, as moderns we are keenly aware of an absence of a current sense of the Cosmological, especially where coupled with a societal and cultural misunderstanding of the role and practice of science, and a concomitant confusion with advances that are loosely referred to as "technological." How our cultural awareness and form of life can rise to the Cosmological horizon is nonetheless still an open question. But without doubt the transformation and enlargement of our scientific worldview, still based on mechanistic presuppositions, will play an essential role. Certainly, answers to larger questions are rarely found in the either/or solutions of mechanistic thinking, but commonly in the both/and approaches of historical natures that build on each other – not reject and rebuild. Creativity and insight are frequent gifts that arise from tension. It would enrich scientists interested in the emergent phenomena of nature, to consider the thoughts of Panikkar.

References

Boyle, Robert (1996). *A Free Enquiry into the Vulgarly Received Notion of Nature*. Cambridge: Cambridge University Press.

Charles Darwin (1859). *On the Origin of Species by Means of Natural Selection, or the Preservation of Favoured Races in the Struggle for Life*. London: John Murray.

DeLanda, Manuel (2013). *Intensive Science and Virtual Philosophy*. London ; New York : Bloomsbury.

Dreyfus, Hubert and Charles Taylor (2015). *Retrieving Realism*. Cambridge Ma: Harvard University Press.

Evers, Dirk (2011). "Gott und Natur in Christlicher Perspective". *Theologische Zeitschrift* 1/67, 326-349.

Fleming, Lenore. (2017). Two Dogmas of Biology. Philos. Theor. Pract. Biol. 9: 1-14 (DOI: http://dx.doi.org/10.3998/ptb.6959004.0009.002

Mayr, Ernst. (2002) *The Autonomy of Biology*. Walter Arndt Lecture. Botany Online: https://s10.lite.msu.edu/res/msu/botonl/b_online/e01_2/autonomy.htm

McGrath, Alister (2006). *A Scientific Theology: Nature*. London: T&T Clark.

Nagel, Thomas (2012). *Mind and Cosmos. Why the Materialist Neo-Darwinian Conception of Nature is Almost Certainly False*. Oxford, New York: Oxford University Press.

Noble, Denis (2015). Evolution beyond neo-Darwinism: a new conceptual framework Journal of Experimental Biology 218: 7-13.

Panikkar, Raimon (1999). *La intuición cosmoteándrica*. Madrid: Trotta.

Rovelli, Carlo (2017). *Reality Is Not What It Seems: The Journey to Quantum Gravity*. New York, New York: Riverhead Books, Penguin Press.

Taylor, Charles (2007). *A Secular Age*. Cambridge Ma: Belknap Press.

Trigg, Roger (2015). *Beyond Matter. Why Science Needs Metaphysics*. West Conshohocken, PA: Templeton Press.

Zubiri, Xavier (1974). *La idea de naturaleza: La nueva física*. En: *Naturaleza, Historia, Dios*. http://www.zubiri.org/works/spanishworks/nhd/ nhdcontents.htm

Response

The authors of this article, Donald R. Frohlich and Carlos Miguel Gómez have accompanied the readers on their search for deeper understanding of nature. They have first focussed on an image of nature that not only still dominates in the West, but has colonized other latitudes and is basic for our current ways of living and our dealings with the world. Certainly, it is not the only image of nature that has emerged in modernity, but its influence has far exceeded that of the alternatives. This image started to emerge during the seventeenth century and gradually consolidated as a basic presupposition of modernity. The image presents nature in mechanical and impersonal terms, replacing ancient metaphors of nature as a living organism, sometimes richly imagined in poetry and painting as a nurturing mother, a womb or even a nurse. Although the developments of physics in the twentieth century deeply challenged this image, it has not lost dominion over western mentality to the present. Interpreted as mechanism, nature started to be seen as an inert, entirely regulated and controllable, material system of laws in which the divine need not play any role.

Then they go on to find an "eclipse of further purpose" and "eclipse of Grace." But they are convinced that there are serious problems associated with Reductionist Paradigm and the Theory of Evolution by Natural Selection

In their search for an Alternative Vision, the authors seek for the Spirit in the Physical World. Here they use Panikkar's cosmotheandric insight in the affirmation that the divine, the human and the earthly are the three irreducible dimensions of reality. They interpret Panikkar's insight not just to mean that there are three fundamental dimension of reality, but more importantly, that any real and valuable understanding of reality has to take them into account; that is, everything is connected. This leads to an "Anthropological Horizon" wherein man's focus turns from nature to himself, and the perfection of the human being, followed by a horizon that culminates in an awareness, or consciousness, of Transcendence.

While congratulating the authors for their well-developed move towards discerning the divine in the world, some of the questions that leads to further discussion are:

How do we maintain the distinctness of the three realities, while recognising the deep and interior connection between them?

How can we elaborate on "Anthropological Horizon," without reducing it to anthropocentrism?

How does the alternative vision of seeking the Spirit in the World maintain the functional (not at all ontological) autonomy of the world and spirit?

How does the discovery of the sacred in the world (secular) lead to a more authentic life? –Bibin Babu Karuthedath.

Theanthropocosmic Vision:
A Philosophical Anthropology
from a Religious Point of View
after Wittgenstein

Jose Nandhikkara CMI

Abstract

Inspired by Panikkar, the author presents a theanthropocosmic vision of Wittgenstein. He outlines a perspicuous representation of a Philosophical Anthropology from a Religious Point of View after Wittgenstein, according to which human beings are rooted in nature, formed by community and sustained by God on the one hand and on the other, they are transforming the nature, forming the community and moving toward God. This goal is achieved by a person by being fully human by living the fundamental relations to God, fellow human beings and the nature. That would also be the measure of the success of this view of life. Wittgenstein anxiously searched his soul with regard to his work: "Will the work, so to speak, lose its meaning? I hope not; but that is possible! – First one must live, – then one can also philosophise."

Keywords

Body-Soul Relationship, Community, Cross, Human, God, Picture, Religion, Subjectivity, Theanthropocosmic vision, Philosophical Anthropology, Wittgenstein.

1. Introduction

It is very remarkable, that one is inclined to think of civilization – houses, streets, cars, etc. – as separating man away from his origin, from the noble, eternal, etc. It seems then, as if the civilized environment, even the trees & plants in it, were cheap, wrapped in cellophane, & isolated from everything great & so to say from God. It is a remarkable picture that forces itself on one here (MS 131, 186: 3.9.1946).[1]

In this paper, I present a perspicuous representation of a Philosophical Anthropology from a Religious Point of View after Wittgenstein, according to which human beings are rooted in nature, formed by community and sustained by God on the one hand and on the other, they are transforming the nature, forming the community and moving toward God. I do not assume that this is the view held by Wittgenstein; but how Wittgenstein illuminated my path and stimulated thoughts of my own and how it might intelligibly illuminate that of others who attend carefully to Wittgenstein. My modest claim is that this Theanthropocosmic view after Wittgenstein provides a framework in which living human beings could find meaning in life. It is a way of living knowingly and willingly - a form of life. The method is not a sustained deductive argument; it is a method that encourages one to look and see how we live, move and have our being. Therefore this is a question of seeing and living rather than thinking and constructing arguments and theories. With such a perspective, as Wittgenstein so perceptively shown, "I go ahead in such-and-such a way, and refuse any other path. All I should further say as a final argument against someone who did not want to go that way, would be: "Why, don't you see...!" – and that is no argument" (RFM 50).[2] That we cannot provide a theoretical justification is not ignorance;

the point of view is justified in the form of life that I live in the threefold relations to nature, community and God.

Wittgenstein often labelled his later philosophical investigations as "grammatical investigations" (PR 52, PG 71, PI 90, 150).[3] According to him, "A main source of our failure to understand is that we do not command a clear view of the use of our words. – Our grammar is lacking in this sort of perspicuity" (PI 122). This is true about the words that we use for human subjectivity (body, soul, mind, self, etc.) and God. "The thing to do in such cases," according to Wittgenstein, "is always to look how the words in question are actually used in our language" (BB 56).[4] For "only in the stream of thought and life do words have meaning" (Z 173).[5] A grammatical investigation, after Wittgenstein, is undertaken here in order to bring to light the use of words that refer to human subjectivity and God, as part of sketching an album of Theanthropocosmic views.[6]

2.   Theanthropocosmic Vision: A Philosophical Anthropology

According to Wittgenstein, "The aspects of things that are most important for us are hidden because of their simplicity and familiarity. (One is unable to notice something – because it is always before one's eyes)" (PI 129). That human beings are bodily beings with non-physical dimensions and that they are not solitary individuals but belong to communities are such obvious facts that I reaffirm in the Theanthropocosmic view that I sketch after Wittgenstein.

2.1. 'Body' and 'Soul,' and Their Relation to Being Human

Descartes rightly observed that "one can perfectly well engage in first-person thinking even though one is not in a position to keep track of oneself as a physical object."[7] From the observation that 'I could suppose I had no body', 'but not that I was not', he, however, wrongly, like many others, postulated an ego that owns and controls the body. To hold that "the ego is mental" (BB 73) is to place oneself in a long tradition, starting with Plato, of isolating the spiritual from the physical. Many who held similar views admitted that the soul is not merely present in the body, but rather very closely joined and, as it were, intermingled with it, so that soul and the body form a unit. They are, however, two separate entities and it is the 'thinking thing' that owns and controls the body and their unity is contingent.

According to Wittgenstein, "the idea that the real I lives in my body is connected with the peculiar grammar of the word 'I', and the misunderstanding this grammar is liable to give rise to" (BB 66). "How the words 'I', 'self', 'body', 'mind', 'soul', etc., are used?" is the question that we should raise if we want to clarify the nature of these concepts as well as the nature of human subject. Questions like 'What is I, body, soul, etc.?' are confusing and misleading; they are the result of wrong pictures (such as all words are names referring to objects similar to physical objects) that hold us captives. The division of a human being into body and soul results from our failure to understand the actual use of these words. "Here we have two different language-games and a complicated relation between them. – If you try to reduce their relations to a simple formula you go wrong" (PI 180). A grammatical investigation, after Wittgenstein, shows the primitiveness of the concept 'human being' and its relation to human body and soul.

Wittgenstein argued that to say that "a human being is not a body," does not necessarily imply that some new entity besides body, namely, the ego, has been discovered (WL 60).[8] According to Wittgenstein, the assumption of the ego as an independent entity results from conceptual confusions. When we are forced to recognise that the word 'I' is not used, in some important occasions, to designate a body we look for an immaterial one (BB 47). "Where our language suggests a body and there is none: there, we should like to say, is a spirit" (PI 36). This is because of the bewitching power of the picture of the language in which words always seem to name objects. According to this picture, the meaning of a word is the object for which the word stands (PI 1). If body is not a proper object for self, we feel forced to posit an immaterial substance – the real ego (BB 69). In his view, "to say that the ego is mental is like saying that the number 3 is of a mental or an immaterial nature, when we recognize that the numeral '3' isn't used as a sign for a physical object" (BB 73). What we need to do is to remind ourselves of the fact that soul is not a name of an object. That is not denying its reality. "There are inner and outer concepts, inner and outer ways of looking at human beings. Indeed, there are also inner and outer facts – just as there are, for example, physical and mathematical facts. But they do not stand to each other like plants of different species" (LW 63).[9] They relate to each other in a variety of ways in the stream of our life and thought. "The inner is tied up with the outer not only empirically, but also logically" (LW 63).

Human beings are recognized generally by the appearance of their bodies. The human bodies do change, but gradually and within a recognizable range. "We are inclined to use personal names in the way we do, only as a consequence of these facts." "If facts were different," for example, "all human bodies which exist looked alike" or "the shape, size and characteristics of behaviour periodically undergo a complete change," then, the use of names would also change. The use of the words referring to human beings depends on contingent facts and behaviour (BB 61-62). Actions like walking, eating, and bringing up children are part of our natural history (PI 25, 467). Expecting, loving, and hoping arise only in certain surroundings and situations (PI 481, 583). If we did not laugh and smile at jokes, cry and weep when hurt, turn pale and shiver when in danger, then our shared concepts of joy, pain, and fear would not have their roles in our form of life. At the bottom, our language-games in which our words and concepts are interwoven are ways of acting and ways of living (OC 204).[10] The words that we use to talk about human subjectivity are interwoven with our characteristic ways of acting and living. "Our attitude to what is alive and what is dead, is not the same. All our reactions are different. – If anyone says: 'That cannot simply come from the fact that the living move about in such-and-such a way and a dead one not', then I want to intimate to him that this is a case of the transition 'from quantity to quality'" (PI 284). This is a fundamental attitude.

Human beings are not, however, identical with bodies. Though I am bodily, I am not my body. "We can't substitute for 'I' a description of a body" (BB 74). It cannot be used without a body either, as mental and spiritual properties are expressed in and through the body. Although a human body reacts to a great variety of stimuli, even when I am asleep or unconscious, it is not the bearer of the sensations, moods, thoughts, and so on. 'I' is not used here "because we recognize a particular person by his bodily characteristics" (BB 69), a feature particularly obvious in first-person experiential propositions. We don't say "Now I feel much better: the feeling in my facial muscles and round about the corners of my mouth is good" (RPP 454).[11] When I say, 'I feel much better' others understand me from the context, tone of my voice, expression in my face, and other fine shades of behaviour. "It is always presupposed that the person who smiles is human, and not just that what smiles is a human body" (LW 84). We can have smiles only on human faces and we cannot separate smiles from the faces (LW 3). We cannot separate the inner from the outer: "'I noticed that he was out of humour.' Is this a report about his behaviour or his state of mind? ('The sky looks threatening': is this about the present or the future?) Both; not side-by-side, however, but about the one via the other" (PI 179).

The body is the medium by which the presence of the soul is brought about. It is in and through our bodies that we are present to the world and to fellow human beings and relate to them and live in collaboration and conversation. It is to be remembered, not just as an empirical fact but also as a logical fact, that 'human being' does not mean the same as 'this body', although it "only has meaning with reference to a body" (WL 62). It is in this spirit we can understand his remark: "The human body is the best picture of the human soul" (PI 78). A picture of body can correspond to an idea (*Vorstellung*) of soul. We cannot have pictures of soul. A picture of body can, however, correspond to a *Vorstellung* of a soul. We look at photographs and portraits and see human beings not just bodies. We see the expression of soul in a face and in the bodily posture. We see happy, sad, serious, or fearful persons, not just pictures of bodies.

"It comes to this: only of a living human being and what resembles (behaves like) a living human being can one say: it has sensations; it sees; is blind; hears; is deaf; is conscious or unconscious" (PI 281). Human beings are neither bodies nor bodiless selves, but beings with distinctive psychophysical characteristics. Our use of "living human being," as Evans observed, "simply spans the gap between the mental and the physical, and is no more intimately connected with one aspect of our self-conception than the other."[12] Wittgenstein wrote: "It is a primitive reaction to tend, to treat, the part that hurts when someone else is in pain" (Z 540) and, "if someone has a pain in his hand, then the hand does not say so ... and one does not comfort the hand, but the sufferer: one looks into his face" (PI 286). It is human beings, not their bodily organs like eyes, ears, hearts, and brains that behave. Emotions are exhibited in human face, tone of voice, bodily responses, and in other fine shades of behaviour. It is the human being who expresses thoughts, opinions, and beliefs in utterances and manifests them in deeds. Therefore, "instead of 'attitude toward the soul' one could also say 'attitude toward a human'" (LW 38). Indeed, "The human being is the best picture of the human soul" (CV 56).[13]

A living human being is not just a bundle of perceptions or a collection of points of views or a host of relations. He/she is living, dynamic and creative, and at the same time subject to bounds and bonds. "All the peculiarities we have noticed about 'I'-thoughts are consistent with and, indeed, at points encourage, the idea that there is a living human being which those thoughts concern."[14] The human being is, indeed, the best picture of human subjectivity (RPP I, 281). If someone insists on asking 'What is self?' we can simply answer, 'a living human being.'

2.2. "We Belong to a Community"

As we have seen the intimate union of physical and non-physical aspects of human beings, there are complex forms of relations among individuals and communities. Persons are living human beings who are substantially present in the world in collaboration and conversation with fellow human beings. It is a fundamental fact that "we belong to a community" (OC 298);[15] it is not just a homely reminder of an empirical fact but an existentially fundamental fact of life (*Tatsachen des Lebens*) that is given (RPP I 630) showing who we are and how we live. Belonging to a community does not mean, however, that an individual is always surrounded by a group of people; it is rather a basic presupposition in our characteristic practices and are fundamental to being and becoming human. In Wittgenstein's early philosophy, "the world is *my* world" (TLP 5.62); his later philosophy reminds us of as an obvious fact that 'the world is our world.' By living in the world, we transform the world and make it a human world. Individuals and communities are not contraries nor do they stand at opposite poles. They are related to each other not just empirically but logically.

Human beings are substantially present in the world, as subjects, engaging both with other subjects and objects in the world. This is fundamental, meaning, "it's something to do with the way we live" (LFM 249).[16] Human subjectivity is shown in the spatio-temporal world through one's substantial and creative presence and engagement with objects in the world. One is to be reminded, however, of the obvious fact that we are not just solitary individuals; we are in collaboration and conversation with other human beings in an inter-subjective world. This is not just something additional and consequent, but something constitutive and existential of being human. A method that is suitable for matter-in-motion cannot capture things human and the language of physics is not sufficient for expressing the characteristics of being human. One has to see the fundamental similarities and differences in our engagement with things and other living human beings. Both of them constitute and shape our streams of life. This is not merely an empirical fact, but a conceptual fact that shapes the framework of a philosophical anthropology, after Wittgenstein. Living human beings are not only rooted in the world of things but also formed by and extended to the world of persons. Being human is a joint venture of nature and society.

"How could human behaviour be described?" Wittgenstein asked: "Surely only by sketching the actions of a variety of humans, as they are all mixed up together. What determines our judgment, our concepts and reactions, is not what one man is doing now, an individual action, but the whole hurly-burly of human actions, the background against which we see any action"(Z 567; RPP II, 629).[17] As an individual, a human being is complete in himself and separate from others; he is just a being-in-the world. In the process of being human we expand our horizons to being-together-with others. Our existence becomes coexistence and pro-existence. The world is made a human world, rather than a biological environment through our co-reflection, conversation and collaboration. As active and free agents living in the world, we realise ourselves not in seclusion but in a life of conversation and collaboration with fellow human beings. Belonging to a community is a fundamental way of our being human.

3.   Theanthropocosmic Vision: A Religious Point of View

G. E. Moore, at the beginning of his lectures, had told the students that he had nothing to say on the 'philosophy of religion', though he was required to lecture on the topic. M. O'Drury thought a Professor of Philosophy had no right to keep silent concerning such an important subject and told so to Wittgenstein. Wittgenstein responded quoting Augustine's

Confessions 1.4: "*Et vae tacentibus de te quoniam loquaces muti sunt.*" Not satisfied with the translation that Drury had, Wittgenstein translated it: "And woe to those who say nothing concerning thee just because the chatterboxes talk a lot of nonsense." He added "I won't refuse to talk about God or religion."[18] The passage appears also at the end of Wittgenstein's remarks to Moritz Schlick as recorded by Friedrich Waismann on the subject of Heidegger's paradoxical statements on Being and Anxiety: "*Augustine sagt: 'Was, Du Mistvieh Du willst keinen Unsinn redden. Rede nur einen Unsinn, es macht nichts!* (Augustine says: 'What, you swine! You don't want to talk nonsense. Go ahead talking nonsense, it doesn't matter'.)[19] Wittgenstein's many written thoughts and recorded remarks, from the early *Notebooks* to the final pages of *Culture and Value*, bear a religious character and he engaged himself extensively with concepts regarding religious belief and practice. The *Nachlass* shows how these themes are intertwined with his thoughts on philosophical matters. According to Malcolm, "his reflections about himself and mankind, and even about the aims of his intensive philosophical work, were penetrated by thoughts and feelings of a religious character."[20]

According to Wittgenstein, "Grammar tells what kind of object anything is. (Theology as grammar)" (PI 373). However, "How words are understood is not told by words alone. (Theology)" (Z 144). Wittgenstein's use of 'Theology' in brackets in both occasions suggests that he thought about using this method of grammatical investigation into God-talk. Theology as grammar is a description of how people actually use the word 'God' to speak about God. According to Wittgenstein, "Really what I should like to say is that here too what is important is not the words you use or what you think while saying them, so much as the difference that they make at different points in your life. How do I know that two people mean the same thing when each says he believes in God? And just the same thing goes for the Trinity" (CV 97).

In Wittgenstein's terms, we use pictures in our God-talk. However, "The picture has to be used in an entirely different way" (LC 63).[21] Wittgenstein observed, "... when we speak of God and that he sees everything and when we kneel and pray to him all our terms and actions seem to be part of a great and elaborate allegory which represents him as a human being of great power whose graces we try to win" (LE 9). There are similarities and differences in the way we speak of God and human persons. "One kneels & looks up & folds one's hands & speaks, & says one is speaking with God, one says God sees everything I do; one says God speaks to me in my *heart:* one speaks of the eyes, the hand, the mouth of God, but not of the other parts of the body: learn from this the grammar of the word "God"!' (MS 183, 202). The *Zettel* ends with Wittgenstein saying, "You cannot hear God speak to someone else, you hear him only if you are being addressed". That is a grammatical remark (Z 717). He notes another characteristic involved in God-talk: "You can say to someone for instance: 'Thank God for the good you receive but don't complain about the evil, as you would of course do if a human being were to do you good and evil by turns'" (CV 34).

According to Wittgenstein,

When someone who believes in God looks around him and asks, "Where did everything that I see come, from?" "Where did everything come from?" he is *not* asking for a (causal) explanation; and the point of his question is that it is the expression of such a request. Thus, he is expressing an attitude toward all explanations (RC 317).[22]

For believers this is to confess God's presence and power in the created world; to see the world as God's world rather than merely as a material world, 'my world' or 'our world'. The scientific point of view does not see the world as a miracle, but something that is there for exploration, experimentation and explanation. From a scientific point of view, "The world is all that is the case" (TLP 1). Scientists try to understand its workings and to control the order of events. They are not typically moved by wonder but curiosity. There is nothing 'mystical' about it. Religious believers, on the other hand, see the world in its relation to God. The world is seen as God's world; he created it and sustains it miraculously.

The feeling of absolute safety has been described as feeling safe in the "hands of God" (LE 10). According to Malcolm,

> In Vienna he [Wittgenstein] saw a play that was a mediocre drama, but in it one of the characters expressed the thought that no matter what happened in the world, nothing bad could happen to him - he was independent of fate and circumstances. Wittgenstein was struck by this stoic thought; for the first time he saw the possibility of religion.[23]

Only in the hands of God is one absolutely safe. To be safe normally means that certain unpleasant things would not happen to me and therefore, it is categorically different ('nonsense,' according to Wittgenstein in LE) to say that I am safe *whatever* happens. This is to give an absolute value, which can be seen only in relation to God, the Absolute Reality. In his personal life, however, he could not submit himself into God's hands: "Trust in God." But I am far away from trusting God. From where I am to trusting God is a *long* way," he wrote in his diary in 1946 (MS 133, 9r).[24] He clearly saw, however, that "a being that stands in contact with God is strong" (MS 183, 56).

The experience of absolute guilt is 'described by the phrase that God disapproves of our conduct' (LE 10). According to Malcolm,

> Wittgenstein did once say that he thought that he could understand the conception of God, in so far as it is involved in one's awareness of one's own sin and guilt. ... I think that the ideas of Divine judgement, forgiveness, and redemption had some intelligibility for him, as being related in his mind to feelings of disgust with himself, an intense desire for purity, and a sense of the helplessness of human beings to make themselves better.[25]

The thought that one-day he has to give an account of his life is a dominant streak in his religious remarks. The meaning of the picture of God as Judge is shown in the life of the believers; its depth and religious significance is given by the life led by those who believe it and hold it dear.

A believer is committed to the truth of his practice. Religion, though lived within the contingencies of nature, transcends them. In religion, one has to make a leap of faith, involving a personal judgement and passionate commitment. Though religious believers belong to a community, they have to make it for themselves. They make a commitment, a fundamental option in life that affects the whole life. A believer's ultimate support in this judgement is God. For a believer the sanction and confirmation from God is fundamental. God is the bedrock where all explanations come to rest in religion.

Religion and life are inseparable, for a believer; it shows the basic character and spirit of believers living. Therefore, the life of a religious person is categorically different from that of a non-religious person. This is not an empirical difference; it is a difference in the attitude of the person. The whole world looks different to him and his attitude to the world is also significantly different. The world of religious persons is

different from those who have no faith as the believers see
religious significance in the very existence of their lives in the
world. It is the religious point of view that gives them the
ultimate meaning of life. For a believer, religion is the way of
making sense of their lives.

Religious life is not merely a practice of certain techniques
to develop certain dispositions, but practices to join in and to go
on responsibly and creatively following a religion. Wittgenstein
rightly noted: "If you want to stay within the religious sphere
you must *struggle*" (CV 98). It is a spiritual combat to lead a
fundamental way of living. For this personal struggle, a believer
needs faith. Wittgenstein wrote:

> So this can only be done if you no longer support yourself on
> this earth, but hang from heaven. Then *everything* is different and it
> is 'no wonder' if you can then do what you cannot do now. (It is
> obvious that someone who is suspended looks like someone who
> is standing, but the interplay of forces within him is nevertheless
> totally different & hence he can act quite differently than one who
> stands) (MS 120, 108c).

I cannot believe and practise a religion as long as I rest my
whole weight on nature and community. I have to suspend
myself from heaven; my ultimate support is from above. In
religious circles, faith is often characterised as a grace from God;
I am supported by God in my struggle to lead a religious life.
To believe, I need understanding, though the understanding is
characterised by faith and love rather than evidence and logic.
As in other aspects of our lives, both reason and passion are
involved in making an ongoing commitment to this fundamental
way of living, i.e., being a religious person. Religions provide
fundamental human ways of living in the world in relation to
fellow human beings and God; it also shows who we are and
how we ought to live. According to Wittgenstein, "... a religious

belief could only be (something like) passionately committing oneself to a system of coordinates. Hence, although it's belief, it is really a way of living, or a way of judging life. Passionately taking up this interpretation" (CV 73). This is to be seen as a fundamental way of being human.

> To believe in a God means to understand the question about the meaning of life.
>
> To believe in a God means to see that the facts of the world are not the end of the matter.
>
> To believe in God means to see that life has a meaning (NB 74).[26]

4. Conclusion

Wittgenstein spoke in the first person both at the end of the *Tractatus* and the *Lecture on Ethics*. He held the view that it is essential to speak in the first person. 'At the end of my lecture on ethics I spoke in the first person: I think that this is something very essential. Here there is nothing to be stated anymore; all I can do is to step forth as an individual and speak in the first person' (WVC 117).[27] Here I step forth as an individual and speak in the first person, presenting a philosophical anthropology from a religious point of view. From Wittgenstein's point of view, working in philosophy is working on oneself: "On how one sees things" (CV 24). Learning from Wittgenstein, the Theanthropocosmic vision presents how I see my life and make sense of my life in relation to God, community and nature. My philosophical concerns are interwoven with my aesthetical, ethical and spiritual passions and commitments. I realise myself and find meaning in my life in my relations to God, fellow human beings and the world. I see myself as a product of nature and community sustained by God and the project of my life is to work on the world, build up the community and walk toward God freely and faithfully.[28]

Our lives are fundamental to our philosophical investigations. Our thoughts, words and actions can have meaning only in the stream of our lives. "Our problems are not abstract" and I assume with Wittgenstein that "all the propositions of our everyday language, just as they stand, are in perfect logical order" (TLP 5.5563). This is true about the language that the believers use in religion. What a philosopher can do is to clarify the concepts as they are actually used in their original language-games and show similarities, differences and inter-connections in the context of the hurly-burly of our lives. This view of life is my personal confession showing how I live, move and have my being in the world in my fundamental relations to God and fellow human beings.

It is part of my faith that Jesus Christ, fully human and fully divine, by his death on the cross, transformed the torture instrument into the source of life and now I see my threefold relationship with God, community and the world in the symbol of a cross. I see myself at the meeting point of the horizontal and vertical bars of the cross. The lower part of the vertical bar shows my rootedness in nature. I depend on the nature for my being and becoming. I live by the fruits of nature. According to one Biblical tradition the first human being is created from the earth. The name of the first man, Adam is related to the Hebrew word for ground, *adamah*. Human beings are earthlings. According to Genesis, God formed Adam from *adamah* (2.7) and placed him on *adamah* 'to work on it and take care of it' (2.15). Though I am from the nature, live by the fruits of nature and when I die, return to it, I carry within me the breath of God; that's what makes me a living human being (2.7). That indicates that I am not merely a product of nature and that I should never be a slave to the material world;

rather I should 'work and take care of it' according to God's plan. I have a certain power over my life on earth. From my religious point of view, my relationship to nature is that of creative stewardship. It is given to me to realise myself and to work on it, to maintain and to develop. I work on nature and transform it for my well-being, for the benefit of others and for the glory of God.

The upper part of the cross symbolises my dependence on and orientation to God. I totally depend on God for my being and becoming. I see myself as a creature, servant and child. Absolute obedience in faith is required of me. God decides what is good and bad; I have to follow it and live according to His commands. That's the purpose of my life: In Him I live, move and have my being. When I try to make my life independent of and against the will of God, I am moving away from the purpose of my life; I am committing a sin. Sin is, according to this view, a futile attempt at self-realisation without reference to God, fellow human beings, and nature. As I turn away from God, I distort the harmony of my relationship to nature and to fellow human beings. In the Biblical story of the first sin, Adam and Eve disobeyed God and hid from him; they turned against each other and the work on the ground became hard and the earth produced only thorns and thistles. Instead of bringing blessings on one another and on earth, they brought curses. The cross by restoring those relations brings back, once again, the blessings on humankind and on nature.

The horizontal bar of the cross shows my partnership with my fellow human beings. According to the Biblical story in the book of Genesis, the second human being, Eve is formed from the body of the first human being, Adam. When God brought Eve before Adam, he said: "This is now

bone of my bones, and flesh of my flesh; she shall be called
woman, for she was taken out of man" (2.23). God created
Eve as a suitable helper and fitting partner for Adam. They
are equal in dignity and mutually support each other to live
in harmony on earth bringing blessings on the world for the
Glory of God. This is true not only about man and woman
relationship but with all human beings, irrespective of race,
religion and nationality. Because God is the Father of all human
beings and I am one of his children, all others are my sisters
and brothers. I am formed by nurture and contribute to the
well-being of the community. The thenathropocosmic vision
is not guided by the motto of 'survival of the fittest' but well
being of all. It becomes my religious duty to love and care for
all – especially those who are in need, materially, emotionally
and spiritually. When I move away from this religious duty, I
am turning against God, fellow human beings, and nature. This
would distort God's image in me and I move away from God
bringing curses rather than blessing on myself, others and on
the world. Ideally, I receive blessings from God and become
a blessing to others on earth: Glory to God, hope to people
and peace on earth (cf. Luke 2:14).

Bach wrote on the title page of his *Orgelbuchlein*, "To the
glory of the most high God, and that my neighbour may be
benefited thereby." That is what Wittgenstein wanted to say
about his work. In presenting a theanthropocosmic vision that
is my wish and prayer. This goal is achieved by my being fully
human by living my fundamental relations to God, fellow human
beings and the nature. That would also be the measure of the
success of this view of life. Wittgenstein anxiously searched
his soul with regard to his work: "Will the work, so to speak,
lose its meaning? I hope not; but that is possible! – First one
must live, – then one can also philosophise" (MS 183, 209).[29]

This is a high ideal and great challenge for me and I see this both as a privilege and a duty to fulfil.

Endnotes

[1] MS = Manuscripts are taken from *Wittgenstein's Nachlass: The Bergen Electronic Edition*, Oxford: Oxford University Press, 2000.

[2] RFM = Wittgenstein, *Remarks on the Foundations of Mathematics*, G. H. von Wright, R. Rhees, G. E. M. Anscombe, eds., Oxford: Basil Blackwell, 1978.

[3] PR = Wittgenstein, *Philosophical Remarks*, R. Rhees, ed., Oxford: Basil Blackwell, 1975; PG = Wittgenstein, *Philosophical Grammar*, R. Rhees, ed., Oxford: Basil Blackwell, 1974; PI = Wittgenstein, *Philosophical Investigations*, G. E. M. Anscombe, trans., Oxford: Basil Blackwell, 1953. References from the Part I of *PI* are to the numbers of the sections and that of the Part II are to page numbers.

[4] BB = Wittgenstein, *The Blue and the Brown Books*, Oxford: Basil Blackwell, 1958.

[5] Z = Wittgenstein, *Zettel*, G. E. M. Anscombe and G. H. von Wright, eds., Oxford: Basil Blackwell, 1967. It is repeated many times in MS 137, 29a, 41b, 66a; 138, 24b; 232, 765; 233a, 35.

[6] Jose Nandhikkara, *Being Human after Wittgenstein: A Philosophical Anthropology*, Bangalore: Dharmaram Publications, 2011.

[7] Campbell, *Past, Space and Self*, Cambridge, MA: MIT Press, 1995, 90.

[8] WL = Wittgenstein, *Wittgenstein's Lectures, Cambridge 1932-35: From the Notes of Alice Ambrose and Margaret Macdonald*, A. Ambrose, ed., Oxford: Basil Blackwell, 1979.

[9] LW = Wittgenstein, *Last Writings on The Philosophy of Psychology*, Vol. I, (ed) G. H. Von Wright, and Heikki Nyman, (trans.) C. G. Luckhardt and Maximilian A. E. Aue, London: Basil Blackwell, 1990.

[10] OC = Wittgenstein, *On Certainty*, G. E M. Anscombe and G. H. von Wright (eds.), Oxford: Basil Blackwell, 1969.

[11] RPP I = Wittgenstein, *Remarks on the Philosophy of Psychology*, vol. I, G. E. M. Anscombe and G. H. von Wright, eds., Oxford: Blackwell, 1980.

[12] Evans, G. *The Varieties of Reference*, J. McDowell, ed., Oxford: Clarendon Press, 1982, 256.

[13] CV = Wittgenstein, *Culture and Value*, G. H. von Wright, ed., Oxford: Basil Blackwell, 1998.

[14] Evans, *The Varieties of Reference*, 256.

[15] OC = Wittgenstein, *On Certainty*, G. E. M. Anscombe and G. H. von Wright, eds., Oxford: Basil Blackwell, 1969.

[16] LFM= Wittgenstein, Wittgenstein's Lectures on the Foundations of Mathematics, Cambridge 1939, C. Diamond ed., Sussex: Harvester Press, 1976.

[17] RPP II = Wittgenstein, *Remarks on the Philosophy of Psychology*, vol. II, G. H. von Wright and H. Nyman, eds., Oxford: Blackwell, 1980.

[18] Rhees R. ed., *Ludwig Wittgenstein: Personal Recollections*, Oxford: Basil Blackwell, 1984, 104.

[19] Wittgenstein, *Schriften* 4, Frankfurt: Suhrkamp, 1937, 69.

[20] Norman Malcolm, *Ludwig Wittgenstein: A* Memoir, Oxford: Oxford University Press, 1984, 83.

[21] LC = Wittgenstein, *Lectures and Conversations on Aesthetics, Psychology and Religious Belief*, C. Barrett (ed.), Oxford: Basil Blackwell, 1966.

[22] RC = Wittgenstein, *Remarks on Colour*, G. E. M. Anscombe (ed.), Oxford: Blackwell, 1977.

[23] Malcolm, N. *Ludwig Wittgenstein: A Memoir*, Oxford: Oxford University Press, 1984, 58.

[24] *"Auf Gott vertrauen." Aber vom Gottvertrauen bin ich weit entfernt. Von da, wo ich bin, zum Gottvertrauen ist ein weiter Weg.'*

[25] Malcolm, *Ludwig Wittgenstein*, 59.

[26] NB= Wittgenstein, *Notebooks 1914-1916*, Oxford Basil Blackwell, 1961.

[27] WVC = *Wittgenstein and the Vienna Circle*, B. F. McGuinnes, ed., Oxford: Blackwell, 1979.

[28] Jose Nandhikkara, "The Person: Project of Nature, Nurture and Grace: Philosophical Investigations after Wittgenstein", *Journal of Dharma* 37, 1 (January-March 2012), 97-116.

[29] '*Wird die Arbeit sozusagen ihren Sinn verlieren? Ich wünsche es nicht; aber es ist möglich! – Denn erst muß man leben, —dann kann man auch philosophieren'.*

Response

Prof. Jose Nandhikkara in his article '*Theanthropocosmic Vision: A Philosophical Anthropology from a Religious Point of View after Wittgenstein*' presents to us an interpretation of Ludwig Wittgenstein. He based his work on Wittgenstein's thoughts on the human subjectivity and God or religious belief to form a framework with a balanced relationship between the two resulting in a theoanthropocosmic view.

The author uses Wittgensteinian 'Language Games' to clarify the understanding of human being. The traditional and modernist's thinking leads us to the dichotomy of body and soul, the priority of the thinking thing and the dependent unity of soul and body. Using Wittgenstein, the author concludes that a human being is not reduced just to an ego as suggested by previous traditions but is much more than its body. The dichotomous understanding of body and soul forms misguided notions of human beings which are due to the inadequacies of language. There is an intimate union of the physical and the non-physical, the inner and the outer concepts that are represented to the world through the body. Therefore, Human being is not just a body but a 'living human being', a being both physical and non-physical, spiritual and bodily, who is living, creative and is subject to the limits and situatedness in this world

As 'living human beings' we belong to one human community and therefore participate in the social interactions within the community. Though we all have our individuality we come together to form this community. Therefore, individuality and community are not opposites but two modes of living in the same world. Both are fundamental to 'becoming' a living human being through belonging to a community.

As per Wittgenstein, religion forms a way of living for the believing human beings. It is a way of passionate commitment to beliefs and possessing a world-view drastically different from the non-religious. It is this world-view that determines the individuality and the community expression of the believer that is rooted in their understanding of God. The author concludes by presenting his personal religious orientation after his reading of Wittgenstein and forming this Theoanthropocosmic worldview. This worldview is rooted in his belief in Jesus Christ, good will of fellow human beings and the entire cosmos.

Some inquiries that can be taken up based on this body of work are as follows:

Though the author has presented his personal religious orientation through this Theoanthropocosmic view, how can members of other religious ideologies adopt the same?

How can a non-religious human person adopt this Theoanthropocosmic view? –**Santan Fernandes**

Statement of Cosmotheandric Conference

We, the members of Philosophy Faculty, along with 10 scholars from different parts of India met at PG Block, Jnana-Deepa Vidaypeeth from 8th to 9th December, 2017 to discuss and deliberate on the theme 'Cosmotheandric Vision' as part of Richard De Smet-Jean de Marneffe Conference. There were 260 participants in attendance.

Our Context

1. We acknowledge the great contributions especially in the field of Indian philosophy that the "Two Wise Men from the West," Richard De Smet and Jean de Marneffe has made. We are proud to follow the footprints of these two great men, in evolving a creative and contextual philosophy that responds to the issues that India faces today.

2. We are proud of Professor Cyril Desbruslais SJ, "an effective counsellor, committed teacher and an accomplished playwright," the Guest of Honour of our Conference, who has been persistently pursing a philosophy of liberation.

3. We are indebted to Prof Francis D'Sa SJ, the keynote speaker, who has introduced Raimundo Panikkar's cosmotheandric vision to the Indian intellectual atmosphere, and who has

significantly contributed to inter-religious dialogue in both India and abroad. He has been a source of our inspiration.

4. We are aware of the crisis that India and the world are currently facing, which has ecological, economic, intellectual and spiritual dimensions.

Insights

1. The crisis that we currently face is due to the overemphasis of the instrumental reason which attempts to control everyone and everything. It has its origin in modernity and enlightenment, which tried to absolutise reason and technology. The problems caused by the techno-scientific progress cannot be solved merely by more advanced science and technology.

2. Panikkar's cosmotheandric experience may help us respond to the contemporary crisis effectively. Following his experience, we acknowledge that God, human and the World are not three realities; but neither is there one, whether God, human or World. The reality is cosmotheandric. It is our way of looking that makes reality appear to us at times under one aspect, at times under another. The cosmotheandric intuition expresses the all-embracing indissoluble union that constitutes all of reality—the triple dimension of reality as a whole: cosmic-divine-human

3. Panikkar's rhythmic understanding of time and the contemplative attitude for an integration of life make his vision evocative and inspiring. His vision challenges us to build up a better world, which gives dignity to human values, enhances respect for nature, and entails an ever more emphasized notion of God who is permeatingly present in cosmos.

4. We realise that *Harmony* is the supreme principle our cosmotheandric experience. The meaning of life consists both in entering into harmony with the reality and in enhancing it."

5. Diversity and plurality are not a problem, but an opportunity to be celebrated. In diversity, even those on the periphery have a place and role and allowing them to flourish becomes the real test of freedom. So we assert that difference, diversity and multiplicity can contribute to our collective well-being.

6. Along with Panikkar, we echo, "One of the mature traits of our rightly criticized epoch is the acute awareness of what I call *sacred secularity*. This world (*saeculum*) is sacred and our secular moves have transcendent repercussions."

7. In our present world of borders and divisions, giving rise to conflicts and violence, we are convinced of the relevance of Panikkar's cosmotheandric vision of borderlessness, that include everyone of all caste, religion, language and ethnicity.

8. We strongly detest the use of all forms of violence under the pretest of establishing 'peace'!

Proposals

1. We are called to lead lives of inner peace and harmony. Such a harmonious life can make our world more creative and adventurous.

2. We are committed to work towards the promotion of a free and fair society through inclusive development by giving a voice to the voiceless, thus helping them to assert themselves and find expression.

3. We resolve to celebrate the underlying unity of humans, earth and the divine, affirming and respecting the differences present among us.

4. We want to relish and teach others to relish the non-dualistic intuition of the non-dual character of the reality, which will further the integrity and harmony of the cosmic home and can help us to receive the gift of peace.

5. There is a urgent need today to take care of the ecological needs of the planet, which has economic and cultural implications. The future of our precious and vulnerable planet depend on men and women of today.

Conclusion

The members of the Conference gathered at Jnana-Deepa Vidyapeeth, Pune, believe that we have the inner strength and wisdom to respond creatively to the crucial challenges facing humanity and the planet earth today. We resolve to make our planet earth a safe place for our posterity. While recognizing the intimate connection between us, the world and God, we realise that we have a sacred responsibility to live with each other respectfully and reverentially.

Contributors

Prof. Dr. Francis X D'Sa SJ is Prof (Emeritus), Jnana-Deepa Vidyapeeth. He received the Honorary Doctorate in Theology from the University of Frankfurt/M, Germany (2007) and Honorary Doctorate in Theology from the University of Tubingen, Germany (2016). He has specialised on Panikkar. Email: francis.x.dsa@gmail.com

Dr. Donald R. Frohlich is Professor of Biology at the University of St. Thomas, Houston TX USA, where he is Fellow in Faith and Science in The Center for Faith and Culture. He has published widely in evolution, behavioral ecology, molecular population biology, and has held visiting professor appointments in the Philosophy Departments at Universidad del Rosario Bogotá CO, UPAEP Puebla MX, and JDV Pune India (current). DRF earned MS and Ph.D. in Biology at Utah State University (1989), and a BS in Biology and Human Ecology from The College of Idaho, Caldwell ID USA (1978) Email: Frohlich@stthom.edu

Rev. J. M. X. Gnanadhas Joseph, a priest from the diocese of Ooty, Tamil Nadu, completed his Licentiate studies in Philosophy at Jnana-Deepa Vidyapeeth. Currently, he is pursuing his Doctoral Studies at the University of Innsbruck, Austria. Email: jmxgnanadhas@gmail.com

Dr. M. George Joseph is Associate Professor & Head Department of Philosophy, Arul Anandar College (Autonomous), Karumathur 625 514, Madurai, Tamil Nadu. Email: jores@ rediffmail.com or george@aactni.edu.in

Dr. Carlos Miguel Gómez is Associate Professor and Director of the Center for Theology and Religious Studies-CETRE, Universidad del Rosario, Bogotá. He earned a Ph.D. in Philosophy of Religion from Goethe Universität-Frankfurt, and a B.A. in Religious Studies from Lancaster University. Among his publications are the books Ciencia y Creación. La investitación científica de la naturaleza y la vision cristiana de la realidad (2018) and ¿Ciencia o religion? Exploraciones sobre las relaciones entre fe y racionalidad en el mundo contemporaneo (2017) Email: carlos.gomezr@urosario.edu.co

Parciush Marak SJ, a Jesuit from North East Province, India, is pursuing his Licentiate in Philosophy from Jnana-Deepa Vidyapeeth, Pune. Email: parciushj@gmail.com

Dr. E. P. Mathew, SJ has been teaching Philosophy for the past two decades at Satya Nilayam Chennai. His areas of research interest are in environmental philosophy and hermeneutics. Hermeneutics: Multicultural Perspectives and Critical Thinking and Planned Writing are his previous publications. He currently serves as the Head of the Department of Philosophy of Loyola College, Chennai. Email: mathewelanji@gmail.com

Dr. Jose Nandhikkara CMI is Professor Philosophy, Dharmaram Vidya Kshetram (DVK), Bangalore, Chief Editor of the Journal of Dharma, Regional Director of Globethics. net India, and International Fellow of KAICIID, Vienna. He is a Wittgenstinian scholar who contributes in the fields of Philosophical Anthropology, Philosophical Theology and

Comparative Religion. He holds a Licentiate in Philosophy from Gregorian University, Rome, MA in Philosophy and Theology from Oxford University, and PhD in Philosophy from Warwick University, UK. Email: nandhikkara@dvk.in

Dr. Kuruvilla Pandikattu (born 1957-) is a professor of Physics, Philosophy and Religion at Jnana-Deepa Vidyapeeth, Pune, India. Currently, he is the Dean, Faculty of Philosophy. He has been actively involved in dialogue between science and religion. Email: kuru@jdv.edu.in . Site: www.kuru.in

Dr. Isaac Parackal OIC is a professor in the Faculty of philosophy at JDV, Pune holding a doctorate in Philosophy, specialized in Metaphysics and Anthropology from the University of St. Thomas Aquinas in Rome. He belongs to the Order of the Imitation of Christ (Bethany Ashram). He has been teaching Metaphysics, Ancient and Medieval Philosophy and Ecology at JDV. Email: isaacparackal13@gmail.com

Dr. Johnson Puthenpurackal OFM Cap has a Ph.D. from the University of Louvain (Belgium) in the philosophy of Heidegger. As one of the pioneers of the 'Association of Christian Philosophers of India' (ACPI), he has been in its administration for eighteen years until 2015. Under his leadership the ACPI brought out several publications, including the two-volume ACPI Encyclopedia of Philosophy, of which he was the editor-in-chief. Presently, he is Rector of the Capuchin formation house for philosophers who study in Vijnananilayam: Institute of Philosophy and Religion (Janampet, Eluru, A.P.), where he has been teaching for twenty-eight years. Email: johnsonjp@redifmail.com

Arun Philip Simon SJ is a Jesuit scholastic belonging to the Mumbai Province. He is pursuing his Licentiate in philosophy from JDV, Pune. Email: arunsimonjy@gmail.com

Prof. Sebastian Velassery, a scholar specialised in Phenomenology is a Professor at Centre for Philosophy, JNU, New Delhi and also UGC National Emeritus. With expertise in Ethics, Applied Philosophy and Indian Philosophy, he retired from Panjab University, Chandigarh. Email: velassery1953@gmail.com

Appendices

"Wise Men from the West": Remembering Frs. Richard De Smet and Jean de Marneffe

Job Kozhamthadam SJ

Jnana-Deepa Vidyapeeth (JDV), Pune, today is the largest and internationally reputed Pontifical Institute for Philosophy and Religion, not only in India, but also in the whole of the Asian continent. This hard-earned reputation and recognition has come through the hard work and selfless dedication of several highly-gifted men and women in the past. Today we are reminiscing about two such stalwarts – Fr. Richard De Smet, SJ, and Fr. Jean de Marneffe, SJ. As Christmas draws near we are wont to think of the Three Wise Men from the East (The Magi). On this special occasion I wish to think of these great men as "Wise Men from the West," because that is what they were – wise in every way, intellectually, academically, religiously and sociably. It is more than a happy coincidence that these two men are honoured and recognized together because they were closely intertwined both in their lives and in the service they rendered to JDV in particular and the Church and the nation in general. Indeed, there were differences too, but, as I will point out later, these differences were very much complementary and mutually reinforcing, and JDV has been the lucky beneficiary of this creative confluence.

To come to the commonalities, both of them were Jesuits hailing from the same country of Belgium belonging to the same South Belgian Province before coming to India and Calcutta Jesuit Province after they made India their adopted home. Their years of life and service in JDV were also almost contemporaneous: De Smet was born in 1916, and after his arrival in India served JDV from 1954 till his death in 1997, whereas de Marneffe was born in 1918, joined JDV in 1955 and died in Pune in 1998. Their scholarly and intellectual pursuit also had much in common. De Smet was a specialist in Indian Philosophy, particularly Sankara, while de Marneffe was a scholar in Western Philosophy, particularly the British philosopher Bradley. Both made sure that their erudition, expertise and scholarship did not remain confined to the four walls of JDV, and actively participated in and contributed to the developments in Philosophy and related areas both in the national and international scholarly circles. Both were life-members of the Indian Philosophical Congress and commanded great respect and recognition among scholars, leaving an indelible mark of their excellent erudition, acute intellectual acumen, balanced views on complex issues and appreciative attitude towards other cultures and religious traditions. Both were considered good role-models who could blend harmoniously serious, rigorous scholarship with genuine, loyal religious life. Indeed they were the best advertisement for JDV as an excellent temple of learning and dynamic centre of all-round formation.

At the same time, they were no identical twins, but each one brought with him his own unique identity and aptitude to enrich JDV and lead it to greater heights in a remarkably complementary confluence. For instance, De Smet was an internationally recognized Indologist who opened a new chapter in the interpretation of Sankara's advaidic philosophy. He was a prolific writer with more than 8 books and over 350 scholarly papers to his credit. On the other hand, de Marneffe was an outstanding classroom teacher whom students respected for his clarity of thought and depth of knowledge, and loved for his humane, fair and gentlemanly personality. De Smet was a solitary, rigorous researcher who enjoyed being lost in his intellectual island churning out scholarly papers, whereas de Marneffe was a genial team-player who teamed up with erudite colleagues, particularly in the long planning and publishing of the massive *Marathi Encyclopedia of Philosophy* to which he contributed almost 40 papers. In their leadership qualities also they showed welcome diversity coupled with enriching complementarity: De Smet gave leadership mostly to scholars outside the confines of JDV, being elected the first President of ACPI (Association of Christian Philosophers of India); on the other hand, de Marneffe gave a magnificent account of his leadership talents mostly in JDV Campus, having held all the major offices of JDV, including the Presidentship for 3 years. He was the chief architect of the new Philosophy Program of JDV in the mid-1970s, particularly the credit system. With regard to their concern and sensitivity to the poor and the underprivileged too their approaches were different, but focus the same. De Marneffe had a delicate, soft corner for JDV's non-teaching staff, especially laypersons, to which a lasting testimony was the housing program he started for the workers. De Smet in his own quiet, non-conspicuous manner lent a helping hand to many a needy person whenever possible.

Perhaps the best way to conclude this brief tribute to these great men is to quote their own words about each other.

Summing up his perception of Jean de Marneffe, Fr. De Smet recalls: "Ever since I became acquainted with Father Jean, I was struck by the quality of his religious life and faithful observance of the rules, the assiduity of his work, the keenness of his intellect, and the delicacy of his personal relations with all the members of the community." In Fr. de Marneffe's view, Fr. Richard De Smet was "a friend of truth, a friend of Christ, a friend of students, a friend of the poor and a friend of his colleagues."[1] Indeed, these two "Wise Men from the West" have left us a great legacy to be proud of, an admirable example to emulate and a creative challenge to respond to. May JDV continue to be blessed with more of such able and noble men and women!

A memorial lecture series is organized annually for the staff and students of The Faculty of Philosophy, Jnana-Deepa Vidyapeeth, Pune, India.

Lecture series on Richard De Smet and Jean de Marneffe

- 2005 Prof Winand Callewaert, University of Leuvein, on "New Age Literature and Upanisads."

- 2006 Prof Richard Sorabjee, University of Oxford, on "Self-Awareness and Morality."

- 2007 Prof Archana Barua, IIT, Gauhati, on "Philosophy: East-West Perspectives."

- 2008 Prof George F Mclean, Catholic University of America on "Contribution of Philosophy to the Growth of Civilizations: Eastern and Western Perspectives."

- 2009 Prof Francis Clooney, Center of World Religions, Harvard University on "Comparative Philosophy and the Future of Interreligious Learning."

- 2010 Lecture was given by Prof Dr. Ramachandra Pradhan, University of Hyderabad, on 21 January 2011. He talked on "The Contributions of Western Philosophy to the World Cultures and the Future of Philosophy."

- 2011 Lecture: "With and Beyond Plurality of Standpoints: Pluralization and the Sadhana of Multi-Valued Logic and Living" by Ananta Kumar Giri, Madras Institute of Development Studies, Chennai.

- 2012 Lecture: June 15: "Thomas Berry's Contribution to Earth Theology: His Indebtedness to Teilhard, Yoga, Buddhism and Jung" by Christopher Key Chapple, Loyola Marymount University, USA.

- 2013 This year the Memorial lecture is transformed into an international conference on "Themes and Issues in Eastern and Western Hermeneutical Traditions," held on Jan 31-Feb 1, 2014, with 16 paper presentations.

- 2014 Lecture: January 23, 2015. Prof Sebastian Velassery, Panjab University on "Transcendence and the Transcendent: A Phenomenological Re-Thinking on Otherness" and "Apophasis as Negative Theology: Upanishads and Medieval Christianity."

- 2015 Lecture: January 21–22, 2016. International Conference on "Public Philosophy" with 15 papers. Chief Guest: Dr. Deepak Tilak, VC, Tilak Maharashtra Vidyapeeth, Pune 41137, India.

- 2016 Lecture: August 19, 2016. Prof James Ponniah, University of Madras. "Religious Violence in South Asia: Exploring Convergences and Divergences Across Nations."

The book Nishant Alphonse Irudayadason (ed) "Musings and Meanings: Hermeneutical Ripples ..." based on 2013 also released.

- 2017 Lecture: December 8-9, 2017. Prof Francis X D'Sa is keynote speaker. Theme: "Cosmotheandric Vision of Raimundo Panikkar." Other speaks: Mohan Doss SVD, George Joseph, Jose Nandhikkara CMI, Isaac Parackal OIC, Kuruvilla Pandikattu SJ, Johnson Puthenpurackal OFM Cap, Donald R Frohlich, Carlos Miguel Gómez-Rincon, Sebastian Velassery, EP Mathew. Chief Guest: George Pattery SJ.

- 2018 Lecture: July 6-7, 2018. Prof Louis Caruana, SJ, Dean, Faculty of Philosophy, Gregorian University, is the keynote speaker: Theme is "Nature and Its Intrinsic Value."

Endnotes

[1] For further details see Job Kozhamthadam, SJ, ed., *Interrelations and Interpretation: Philosophical Reflections on Science, Religion and Hermeneutics in Honour of Richard De Smet, SJ, and Jean de Marneffe, SJ* (New Delhi: Intercultural Publications, 1997), pp. xiii-xx.

De Smet - De Marneffe Memorial National Conference Faculty of Philosophy, Jnana-Deepa Vidyapeeth
Theme: Cosmotheandric Vision

Venue: Joseph Neuner Auditorium, JDVP

Dates: 8-9 December, 2017

Friday, December 8, 2017
9:10 A.M.: Inaugural Session

Prayer Song:	St Paul's Students
Lighting of the Lamp:	Dignitaries
Welcoming the Participants:	Selva Rathinam SJ, President, Jnana-Deepa Vidyapeeth

Introducing the Seminar:	Kuruvilla Pandikattu SJ, Dean, Faculty of Philosophy, JDV
Remembering De Smet & de Marneffe	Henry D'Almeida SJ
Homage to Richard De Smet and Jean de Marneffe	Cyril Desbruslais SJ
Introducing the Chief Guest:	Kuruvilla Pandikattu SJ
Chief Guest's Address:	George Pattery SJ, Vice-Chancellor, JDV

Session 2:
Venue: Neuner Auditorium

9:30	Introducing Keynote Speaker: Joe Francis
Keynote Address:	Francis D'Sa SJ (Assisted by Arun Simon, Parciush Marak and Gnanadhas Joseph)
Chair:	Dinesh Braganza SJ
10:45	Tea Break

Session 3:
Venue: Neuner Auditorium

11:15	Keynote Address Continues
12:10	Mohan Doss SVD, Dean, Faculty of Theology, Jnana-Deepa Vidyapeeth

Cosmotheandric Vision: A Theological Perspective

| 12:40 | Vote of Thanks: Ravi |
| Chair: | Stephen Jayard |

Session 4:
Venue: Seminar Hall, PG Block

2:30   George Joseph, Dean of Philosophy, Arul Anandar College, Madurai

Cosmotheandric Vision: Critique of Modernity and Some Prejudices

3:10   Jose Nandhikkara CMI, Dean of Philosophy, DVK, Bengaluru

Cosmotheandric Vision: Philosophical Investigations after Wittgenstein

Chair: Shiju Joseph CSC

3:50   Tea Break

4:10   Isaac Parackal OIC, JDV, Pune

Authenticity with Authority: Relevance of the Cosmotheandric Vision

4:50   Kuruvilla Pandikattu, JDV, Pune

All-Inclusive and All-Embracing: Holistic and Advaitic Vision of Panikkar

Chair: Gnanadhas

5:30   Free Time

Saturday, December 9, 2017

Session 5:
Venue: Seminar Hall, PG Block

9:50:   Johnson Puthenpurackal, Rector and Former Dean, Vijnananilayam Elluru

Violence and Peace: Creation and Elimination of Borders – Journeying with and Beyond Panikkar's Thought

9:10:   Donald R Frohlich and Carlos Miguel Gómez-Rincon, St. Thomas College, Houston

Rediscovering the Sacred in Nature: The Cosmotheandric Vision

Chair: John Richard

10:45   Tea Break

Session 6:
Venue: Seminar Hall, PG Block

11:10   Sebastian Velassery, Panjab University, Chandigarh

Cosmotheandric Vison and Tempiternity: A Phenomenological Critique

11: 50   EP Mathew SJ, Dean, Satya Nilayam, Loyola College, Chennai

Panikkar's Cosmotheandric Vision: Creative Critique

12:30	Concluding Session
Chair:	Joe Francis
Vote of Thanks:	Arun Simon SJ

Participants' List

1. Andrew Francis
2. Nagothu Jeevan Kumar
3. Jiju Paul
4. George Bush
5. John Richard
6. Stephen Damu
7. Sandeep Jagtap
8. Sateesh Kumar
9. Doni Raja
10. Prem Kumar
11. Emman Sathish
12. John B Gannot
13. Dasari Nireekshan Raju
14. Rijo Devasia
15. Amal Tharak Easter
16. Kumar Rao

17. Ivan D'Souza

18. Joby Joseph

19. Raju Felix Crasta

20. Varan Vardhan

21. Melbin Johnson

22. Anoop Jaison

23. Jeril Sibi Nirappel

24. Bibin Babu

25. Vijay Raju

26. Sanjay Bodra

27. Rex Reuben

28. Anish Raj

29. Emmanuel Azure

30. Michael Sudharshan

31. Melfin Joseph

32. Derin Vaz

33. Nikhil Joseph

34. Ravibhushan Kumar

35. Jobin George

36. Louis lobo

37. Joby John

38. Selva Rathinam

39. Cyril Desbruslais

40. George Pattery

41. Ginish C Baby

42. Vincent Crasta

43. Joe Francis

44. Henry D'Almeida

45. Shiju Joseph

46. Dinesh Braganza

It may be noted that this list does not include the resource persons and 200 students who participated in the first day of the seminar.